The
LAST DAYS
of
DOGTOWN

❖ A NOVEL ❖

ANITA DIAMANT

MACMILLAN

First published 2005 by Scribner, New York

First published in Great Britain 2006 by Macmillan
an imprint of Pan Macmillan Ltd
Pan Macmillan, 20 New Wharf Road, London N1 9RR
Basingstoke and Oxford
Associated companies throughout the world
www.panmacmillan.com

ISBN 1 4050 4967 7

Printed and bound in Great Britain by
Mackays of Chatham plc, Chatham, Kent

To
AMY HOFFMAN
and
STEPHEN MCCAULEY

Dear friends and colleagues

A thousand thanks

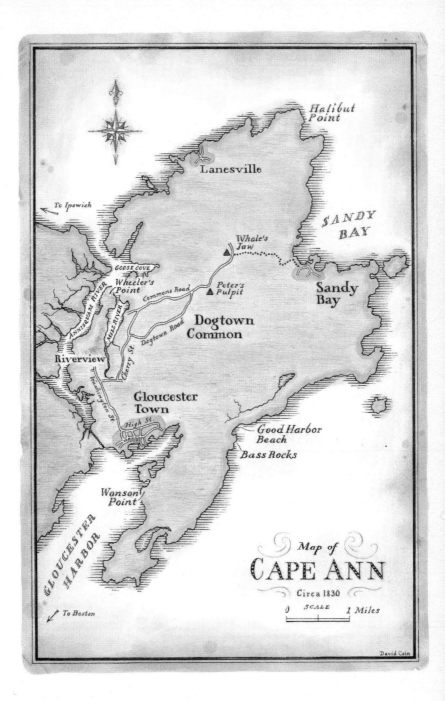

To Ipswich

Halibut Point

Lanesville

SANDY BAY

Whale's Jaw

GOOSE COVE

Wheeler's Point

Commons Road

Peter's Pulpit

Sandy Bay

ANNISQUAM RIVER

MILL RIVER

Cherry St.

Dogtown Road

Dogtown Common

Riverview

Washington St.

Gloucester Town

High St.

Good Harbor Beach

Bass Rocks

Wonson Point

GLOUCESTER HARBOR

To Boston

Map of
CAPE ANN
Circa 1830

SCALE
0   1 Miles

David Cain

WHALE'S JAW

CONTENTS

CONTENTS

AUTHOR'S NOTE

This is a work of fiction that rests lightly upon the historical record, which is spotty at best when it comes to the village of Dogtown.

There was once such a hamlet, set on the high ground at the heart of Cape Ann. You can find signs directing you to its ruins on that rocky fist of coastland, the northernmost boundary of Massachusetts Bay. A local pamphlet, *Dogtown: A Village Lost in Time,* may still be available for purchase in the bookshops of Gloucester and Rockport, which was known as Sandy Bay until 1840. This little publication contains a not wholly accurate walking map of the area and some tales about the more vivid characters said to live there long ago.

Most accounts of Dogtown's last citizens rely heavily upon a volume of thirty-one pages, published in 1906, called *In the Heart of Cape Ann or the Story of Dogtown.* Illustrated by Catherine M. Follansbee, who had a fondness for drawing witches astride their brooms, it was written by Charles E. Mann. In his prefatory note, Mr. Mann revealed that nearly all his material was gleaned from "the memories of Cape Ann's aged people . . . sweet-faced old ladies, often with sweeter voices, or men with whitened locks and time-furrowed cheeks, recalling the stories told them by the fireside by other dear old women and noble old men of a past century." In other words: ancient gossip and hearsay.

I tell you this so that you will not make the mistake of confusing my fancies for facts. And yet, the death of a village, even one as poor and small as Dogtown, is not an altogether trivial thing. Surely there was value in the quiet lives lived among those imposing boulders, under that bright sky. Why not imagine their stories as real, if not true. For the space of this entertainment, where's the harm?

The
LAST DAYS
of
DOGTOWN

The Death of
Abraham Wharf

J UDY RHINES decided to take the footpath through the pasture.
It was half the distance of walking all the way down the Commons Road and back up Dogtown Road and she wanted to get
there early enough to be of help. But the going was slow. The winter of 1814 had buckled the field with frost and there was black ice
in every hollow. If she didn't consider every step, she might end up as
bad off as Abraham Wharf, who certainly had no need of her hurry.

The cold seemed to add hours and miles to even the shortest
journey through Dogtown. Gloucester, which was barely an hour's
walk for a healthy man in good weather, could seem as remote as
Salem in February. It was a gloomy landscape even on a fine day,
with its rutted thoroughfares and ruined houses and the odd collection of souls who had washed up into the rocky hills of Cape Ann. At
least it isn't windy, Judy consoled herself.

She was the first to arrive at Easter Carter's house. "My right-hand
friend," said Easter, holding out a shawl for her. "Come by the fire."

Judy smiled at the tiny woman, hung up her cold-stiffened cloak, and took shelter in the warm wrap. After the feeling had returned to her fingertips and cheeks, she squared her shoulders and went over to take a look at the body of Abraham Wharf, which lay on the floor in the far corner of the room.

Judy lifted the faded scrap of yellow gingham that covered his face and chest. It was a shame and a sorrow. Nobody spoke of suicide much, but Judy wondered if it might be a far more common escape than anyone suspected. Then it occurred to her that there was a curious lack of blood on Wharf: if a man cuts his own throat, shouldn't his collar be soaked through? Shouldn't his hands be stained, his sleeves caked? Perhaps the cold had frozen it, she reasoned. Or maybe Easter had cleaned him up.

Before she could ask any questions, the door opened and Ruth walked in, her arms full of firewood. Judy marveled at the sight of eight real logs: the nearby hills had been stripped of trees years ago. Dogtowners burned mostly peat and dung.

Then again, she thought, Ruth brought mystery wherever she went. A stranger would be hard-pressed to see that the coffee-colored African wearing trousers and a cap was a "she" at all. Ruth had never been seen in a dress and preferred the name "John Woodman," though everyone knew her as Black Ruth. A stonemason, of all things, she lodged in Easter's attic. Judy still hoped that Easter would one day tell her more of Ruth's story. She was fascinated by everything having to do with Cape Ann's few Africans.

"Hello, Ruth," said Judy. "What a great treat you bring us." Ruth nodded, placed the logs by the fire, and retreated upstairs before the others started to trickle in.

Easter Carter's was the biggest house fit for habitation in the Commons Settlement, which was Dogtown's real name. With an eight-foot ceiling and a twenty-foot-long parlor, its fireplace was large enough for a side of beef, though it had been many years since anything so rich had sizzled there. The place was large only by comparison with everything else still standing for miles around, and it served as a tavern in everything but name and taxes. Young people and sailors tramped up the old road seeking a good time, and Easter let them have it. She loved having company, and even a corpse was welcome if it fetched in a crop of the living.

That day, the first visitors included a few ancient ladies who arrived, one by one, braving the cold to pay their respects to the deceased and hoping for a glass of ale in his honor, and perhaps even a bite to eat.

Among the early arrivals, there was but one unlined face, which also belonged to the only breathing male in the room. Taking his turn beside the body, Oliver Younger removed his hat and coughed, trying to distract attention while he nudged at the cloth with his foot to get a better look at his first corpse. But Tammy Younger saw what he was up to and smacked the back of her nephew's head with the flat of her hand.

"What in hell is wrong with you?" she said. All eyes in the dim room turned toward them. "What the hell did I ever do to be plagued with such a nit of a boy? I ask you, Judy Rhines. What merits me the village idiot here as my punishment?"

Judy placed herself between Tammy's squat form and the skinny twelve-year-old. She looked down at Abraham's body, and Oliver Younger saw the sadness in her eyes and wished he had the gumption to say something kind to her. But Tammy would shame him in front of God and the devil for showing any feeling toward Judy Rhines. He gritted his teeth and walked back toward the fire, even though that took him close to the creaking ladies gathered there, the eldest being Mary Lurvey, Abraham Wharf's bereaved sister, who stank of death herself.

Mary's red nose dripped a steady stream as she rocked herself back and forth on Easter Carter's best chair, blubbering about how he'd burn in hell for taking his own life.

"My poor, poor brother," she moaned. "I won't be seein' him in heaven, that's sure. He's going to burn, and it's on my head. It is, for I should have warned him off." She repeated this refrain every time the door opened upon another face, chapped and curious to learn if it was true that Wharf had done himself in.

Each new arrival clucked in sympathy as she settled in, thankful for the warmth and companionship in what had once been the community's great showplace. It was the only house ever to have a second story, even back in the days when the settlement was full of proud men. That was long before it had turned into a collection of broken huts and hovels inhabited mostly by spinsters and widows without children, and few with so much as an extra spoon in their cupboards. Marooned by poverty, or peculiarity, or plain mulishness, they foraged a thin livelihood selling berries and brews made of roots and twigs. For their pains, they were branded "trash-eaters" and mocked all over Cape Ann.

"No one left up there but witches and whores," said the wastrels in the taverns. "They dally with their dogs up there," said the farmers and the fishermen. And all of them traded lies about having it off with Judy or any other skirt that didn't have one foot in the grave. With a wink and a grin, they'd say, "A dog can have his day up there."

It was doubtless a barroom wit who first called the fading village a dogtown. That the slander had stuck with the force of a christening had been a bleeding thorn in Abraham Wharf's heart, and he'd never let the term pass his lips.

Defending the Commons Settlement had been his mission, and anyone who'd let him talk for more than a minute got an earful of how it used to be the finest address on the North Shore, indeed, in all the Commonwealth. According to him, the most respected families had lived there and raised the finest livestock—cattle, sheep, and oxen. Wharf had been their leader—or at least, that's how he told it. His Anne was the prettiest wife. His sheep gave the best wool. His sons had been most likely to take charge of the whole damned Cape. But that was "once't," as he put it.

"He was bitter," said Easter Carter, and she recalled Wharf's much-repeated claim that the war for independence had killed off the best of his neighbors. The ones who returned with all four limbs attached decided against the thankless work of harvesting rocks when Gloucester Harbor delivered an easier living. Buying and selling became the way to making a fortune.

"Remember how he'd say the word 'shopkeeper'?" said Judy. "Like he was speaking the worst sort of blasphemy."

"My brother didn't set a foot into church for forty years," Mary said. "Forty years he went without hearing a word of scripture." Abraham had come to sit by her fire just two nights earlier and asked if she thought that killing yourself meant sure damnation. Mary had dismissed his question with a sour warning to stop talking rubbish, and she spent the rest of their last evening together complaining about her dyspepsia and her ungrateful children.

The memory of that last conversation was a terrible shame to Mary, whose shrill sobs reminded Judy of nothing so much as a stuck pig. The unkindness of that notion caused her to hurry over to the bereaved woman with another cup of comfort. The smell of boiling cabbage, wet woolens, and cheap tobacco seemed even stronger in that corner of the room, and Judy welcomed the clean, icy blast when the door swung open again.

"Well, if it ain't Granny Day," said Easter, greeting a lady nearly as wrinkled and bald as one of last year's crab apples.

"Didn't know if I'd make it in this cold," apologized the newcomer. "But then I thought I owed it to him."

"It's all right, dear," said Easter, steering her over toward Abraham's body as she retold the story of how Cornelius Finson had found him early that morning with a long knife in his own hand.

He'd done the deed in the shadow of the Whale's Jaw, two enormous boulders that together made a perfect replica of a great fish head. Cornelius, or Black Neal as some called him, had carried the corpse to Easter, who sent him straight into town to find some able-bodied relations to carry Wharf back to Gloucester for a Christian burial.

When Granny Day opened the door, the biggest of the settlement dogs had padded in behind her. A long-haired brute, nearly six hands tall, Bear ambled directly over to Easter Carter and nuzzled at her hand. Finding nothing there to eat, he headed for the chilly lean-to, which had been tacked onto the house back in the day when there'd been food enough to require a separate pantry. A shaggy congregation was already gathered there, huddled jowl by haunch on a filthy scrap of carpet: Pinknose, Brindle, Spots, Big Brown, and Greyling. One by one, the dogs had slipped into the house behind a two-legged guest, lured out of secret burrows by the unusual commotion and the smell of cooking.

When Bear entered, the others rose so he could take the warmest spot in the center. He lowered himself in his rightful place with a sigh while the rest of them circled and scratched and settled again.

Judy Rhines smiled at the pack, watching as steam rose off the breathing heap of fur. Let them call us Dogtowners, she thought, I'm satisfied to be thought of as one of them. She felt less inclined to claim fellowship with the collection of unhappy creatures in the parlor, each one wrapped in her own dark shawl. And poor, broody Oliver, arms crossed over his narrow chest, slouched against the wall, his chin on his chest.

With his thick black hair, green eyes, and high cheekbones, he wouldn't be a bad-looking boy if he'd only pick up his head and stop scowling. Oliver caught her gaze and seemed to glare back, then took to studying the ceiling. A strange one, she thought, and wondered if he'd ever make anything of himself. It was too bad that

Oliver had nowhere else to go. Tammy was his blood-kin, but he might have been better off bound out as an apprentice: maybe some honest farmer with a softhearted wife. Of course, that was a rough gamble, too, as Judy well knew.

Oliver's great-aunt was a terror, but there was no changing Tammy Younger. Her name was often invoked by mothers wishing to keep their children from straying into the woods. They called her a witch and warned that her favorite tea included the plump fingers and toes of heedless boys and girls.

Judy thought of Tammy as a force of nature, unpleasant as a wasp's nest, but inevitable. Then again, Judy was known as a soft touch, having once been heard defending skunks and mosquitoes as having a rightful place and purpose. Abraham Wharf used to scold her about being so tenderhearted. "You take care of yourself," he'd said to her, only a month before he died. "You take good care of Judy Rhines for once't." Remembering his words, Judy Rhines drew her dark brows together and bowed her head. Oliver watched and wondered how she could grieve for such a bad-tempered old windbag.

He'd never seen her look so low. Judy usually wore a gentle half smile that drew people to her. There was a sort of natural pleasantness, an irresistible goodness to her face. Not that she was a great beauty. Her eyes were a pale brown, a shade lighter than the brown of her hair, which she parted in a sharp line over her right ear. In her homespun dress, unbleached apron, dust-colored shoes, and bare head, Judy Rhines put Oliver in mind of a hen. It was not the most flattering picture, he knew, but it was comfortable enough to let him imagine her caring for him in return.

Oliver glanced over at Tammy, making sure she hadn't caught him staring at Judy. She was at least thirty, Oliver guessed, though she could be forty.

Mary Lurvey's weeping had turned into a desperate coughing fit that fixed all attention upon her. In September, Tammy had warned that Mary wouldn't last the winter. Abraham's death would hasten that likely guess into a mystic prediction and strengthen Tammy's terrifying effect on the foolish believers who already feared her reputed powers.

After Mary quieted down, Easter served helpings of boiled cabbage and potatoes. The ladies huddled by the fire set their little china pipes on the floor and exclaimed over the plain fare like it was a wedding feast. Easter spooned more onto their plates even before they'd finished, knowing it would be their only hot meal that day and possibly the next.

Easter was one of Judy's favorites. No more than four and a half feet in her shoes, Easter had a long, beaky nose flanked by small, squinted eyes. But the face under her old-fashioned cap beamed whenever people were under her roof, especially when it was younger folks holding court and calling her "Mother."

It was Easter who'd come up with the name "Judy Rhines," and in her mouth it sounded like an endearment. Most women were called by their family name, like Granny Day or Widow Lurvey. Up in the woods, unmarried women like Easter were sometimes known by their given names, rather like naughty children. But Easter had taken a shine to the sound of "Judy Rhines" and it stuck.

It had been so long since Judy had heard "Judith Elizabeth Ryan," that if someone had addressed her so, she might not remember to answer. Judith Elizabeth Ryan sounded like a woman who owned a Sunday dress, a flowered wool carpet, and a white teapot, not someone who had often made a supper from berries and roots dug out of the woods, or who cleaned other people's houses for a length of cotton, or who kept a half-wild dog at her feet to keep from freezing on winter nights.

Just as Judy was about to take some of Easter's stew for herself, the door flew open again, hitting the wall with a bang that caused the ladies to jump and then coo at the sight of little Sammy Stanley, borne in like a scrap of driftwood on a wave of three wet skirts and a peal of laughter. Dark Molly Jacobs and fair Sally Phipps rushed for the fire, reaching their four red hands to the glow, while Mrs. Stanley closed the door with a polite flourish and walked directly to the center of the room. When she was certain that all eyes were fixed on her, she pulled a bottle from inside a ragged raccoon muff.

"What a welcome sight you are," said Tammy, addressing herself to the rum.

"In memory of Master Wharf," said Mrs. Stanley.

"Too bad the poor old fart ain't here to enjoy it," Tammy said.

Oliver laughed at the rude word, a boyish reflex he tried to swallow when he saw Judy shake her head. But Mrs. Stanley turned her famous smile in his direction as she removed her hood. Yellow curls cascaded out, unbound like a girl's, and spread out in pretty ringlets over a shirt so white it nearly glowed in the dim room.

Mrs. Stanley—no one had ever heard her Christian name—carried herself like the great beauty she'd once been. Blue-eyed and blonde, she triumphed over the wrinkles at her eyes and the slack line of her chin by batting her lashes, pursing her lips, and placing a soft hand upon the forearm of any fellow who drew near enough to catch her nearsighted gaze.

Tammy leered. "Rum, eh? What sailor got lucky?"

"Oh, goodness," Mrs. Stanley replied. "Let's not tread that path, shall we, lest your own misplaced steps come into question."

"You old whore," Tammy said. "You've got more brass than the whole of Boston sets on its tables come Election Day."

Mrs. Stanley shrugged and walked over to see the body, pulling the reluctant child behind her. She placed a hand on her bosom and bowed her head as she pulled off Sammy's cap, revealing a matching tumble of blond hair that hung down to the boy's shoulders. Oliver started to laugh at the girlish locks, but stopped when he saw Judy Rhines frowning in his direction.

Sammy, who was no more than six years old, blinked in terror and bit his lip till it bled. He'd never seen a dead man, and the sudden heat in the room made him swoony. Judy noticed the child's distress and took his hand, leading him away from the corpse and toward the back room. Sammy pulled away when he spotted the crew of dogs, who raised their heads in a single gesture and stared.

"They bite?" he asked.

"Don't fret about them," Judy said, and handed him a cold biscuit smeared with goose fat.

Sammy took the food in his hand but made no move to eat it.

"Go ahead," Judy smiled.

He looked up at her, bewildered.

"Don't tell me you're not hungry."

"Never before the ladies," he said.

"Well, that's very nice manners." Judy Rhines leaned down and said, "But right now, I think you better eat that bread before one of the dogs comes over and snaps it up."

The thought horrified Sammy, who opened his mouth as wide as he could and ate the whole thing in two bites. The salt and sheer goodness of it brought water to his blue eyes. After he swallowed, the boy wiped his mouth delicately on the inside of his cuff, took Judy's hand, and kissed it as he made a brisk little bow. She tried not to laugh and watched him cross the room to sit beside Granny Day.

Sammy had arrived two years earlier, a note pinned to his coat. No one knew what it said, or even who had brought the child. According to the gossip, when Mrs. Stanley read the message the only words out of her mouth were, "Damn me." She introduced the boy child as her daughter's son and said his name was Sam Maskey, though he was known as Sammy Stanley.

No one knew Mrs. Stanley even had a daughter till that moment. About Mr. Stanley, she placed a well-tended hand over her heart and said, "Lost at sea." No one questioned the claim though few believed it.

Sammy knew his grandmother wasn't fond of him, even though he did as he was told and kept still, which was all that grown people seemed to want of children. The first time he sat in Granny Day's grammar school, she'd had a devil of a time getting him to say his letters out loud and thought he might be deaf if not stupid. But then she spied him reading the Bible, and when she coaxed him discovered that he'd memorized all of Genesis and had started on Exodus. For that, she'd patted him on the head and given him a cracker too hard to chew.

Sammy felt Oliver Younger's eyes on him. The older boy curled a strand of his lank, greasy hair around his finger and pouted his lips. That didn't bother the boy. Mrs. Stanley had never shown him anything in the way of affection, but she'd taught him that you were more likely to get what you wanted if you were polite and smelled good, and Oliver was plainly filthy and rude.

After a moment, Oliver lost interest in the child and turned his glance away from that corner of the room. He didn't want to have to meet Granny Day's eyes; he'd quit her classroom long before Sammy arrived. He'd left the Gloucester grammar school as well, even though it had been warm and the girls would sometimes share their dinners. He just got tired of fighting for the good name of Dogtown, a place he hated yet felt required to defend.

Besides, Oliver didn't put much stock in schooling. A man could go to sea or enlist in a war without book learning. A man could come back covered in glory and with enough pay to claim Judy Rhines as his own. She'd see him in uniform and recognize him as just the fellow to take her out of the ruin of Dogtown. She'd cook for him and keep him warm and smile at him sweeter than she smiled at that pretty boy. Oliver longed to speak to her, or just to gaze in her direction without worrying about being caught.

The room grew still as Mrs. Stanley took her seat, and for a moment the only sound was the hissing of the fire. Judy fancied that the sizzles and pops were whispering about the fate of poor Abraham's soul, and she felt a sudden desire to get away from the sorrows and petty cruelties assembled in Easter's smoky drawing room. There was no telling how long it would take for Abraham's kin to make it up to Dogtown. Their cart might get stuck on the road, and February days ended fast: if an axle broke they might have to turn back altogether and try again tomorrow.

The sound of stamping feet outside gave Judy a moment's hope that they had arrived and she would be able to leave. But it turned out to be John Morgan Stanwood, who surveyed the room as if everyone had been awaiting his arrival. A cold wind blew in, while his wife and their three grown daughters shivered behind him.

"Goddamn ye, Stanwood," Tammy shouted. "Shut the goddamn door."

Stanwood took his time, kicking the frost from his boots while his wife crept past him and hurried to comfort Widow Lurvey, her mother. When the old lady caught sight of her daughter, she set up another wail that startled the dogs in the back room and set off a chorus of woofs and whines.

"You woke the hounds of hell, Mother Lurvey," scolded Stanwood. "Too bad you can't wake Father Abraham over there."

He winked at his daughters, who reddened and stared at the floor. The only one to laugh at the weak joke was Oliver, who reached for the deepest voice he could muster. With another male in the room, he held himself straighter and stood wide like Stanwood, who was bowlegged, which to Oliver looked like a proud announcement of his manhood.

Oliver scratched his chest and stole a look at the Stanwood girls, who were among the prettiest females on Cape Ann, even without benefit of fine clothes or face powder. Rachel, the oldest, was already engaged to a fellow from Annisquam; Lydia and Hannah were busy seeking husbands to get them out of Dogtown, too, attending church on Sunday only to smile at everything in pants. Oliver overheard that bit of gossip from Tammy. But the Stanwood sisters were known to him in another way.

Oliver ducked his head, remembering the August night last summer when the air stayed steamy even after sunset and the only relief from the heat and the bugs was the creek. He had been taking off his trousers when Hannah's giggle gave them away. He waded silently to near where they were bathing, and from behind the bushes watched Lydia Stanwood's plump breasts float on the water. The other sisters joined her, and four more breasts winked at him. Oliver's member was instantly hard as stone, and as the girls splashed and whispered, he put his hand there and answered the urgent, unspoken questions his body had been putting to him the past year.

After that, Oliver felt a profound respect for John Stanwood as the sire of so many breasts. Indeed, Oliver was so smitten with his swaggering presence, he didn't notice how Judy Rhines's lip curled when Stanwood asked where that damned nigger had got to anyway.

Stanwood pinched Easter Carter's leg as she brought him a cup of beer. "You got something nice for me, old girl?" he asked.

"I got the cabbage for you," she said. "I got the cabbage and beer for everyone in honor of Abraham Wharf. But don't you have a word for your poor mother-in-law over there?"

Stanwood shrugged and walked over to Mary, who hadn't let go of his wife's hand. He whispered something in her ear and then stood behind her chair, where he winked at Molly and Sally and blew a kiss to Mrs. Stanley, who clucked and wagged a finger in his direction. Stanwood tried to catch Judy Rhines's eye, too. He was a black-haired, dark-eyed rake accustomed to having women flutter at his attentions, but Judy would not even look his way.

By then, Mrs. Stanley's rum had made its way around the room and the grannies were chewing over their stories about Abraham Wharf: how he used to brag about a cousin who was a judge in Boston. How his sheep had been the living envy of every farmer up and down the Cape.

"Didn't I hear about Wharf killing an Indian for touching one of his animals?" said Granny Day. Her friends pshawed that tale to nothing: no one could recall seeing an Indian anywhere near Dogtown. But they outdid one another in recalling how loud and long he'd wept at Anne's grave, twenty years ago. Heartbroken, he was, and angry.

After she died, the four Wharf boys had moved down to the city one after the other, but the old man wouldn't budge. "As I recollect, none of them pressed their father to join them," said Easter.

Tammy snorted. "That reeking know-it-all son-of-a-bitch? Where's the wonder in that?"

Judy was still puzzling over Abraham's death. In his last year, he'd taken to spending more and more time near Whale's Jaw. "It's like God Himself put them there" was how he described the rocks to Judy Rhines. "Like a statue that God Himself had a hand in."

He also told her that, as far as he was concerned, the Whale's Jaw was the only proof of God that ever made sense to him. The fact that Cornelius had found Wharf dead beneath those giant stones made Judy wonder if he had lost even that little shred of faith.

Why had he sharpened the blade and killed himself? Did he suffer from some hidden illness or awful pain? Was there something she might have done to lessen his despair? She wasn't sure why Wharf's death had unsettled her so. He was neither a relation nor really a friend: a neighbor, an acquaintance at most. Perhaps it was just the fact of his suicide that gnawed at her. To choose death seemed a terrible insult to everyone who carried on with the lonely business of living.

As Judy pondered, the conversation ebbed to a quiet mutter and mumble. The voices lapped against Easter's walls like water against a wooden hull. Sammy Stanley dozed, his shining curls against Granny Day's knee.

The lull came to an abrupt end with an argument between Easter and Stanwood about money he'd borrowed from her. It wasn't easy to provoke Easter Carter, but there was no stopping her once she got riled. Between Stanwood's cussing and Easter's hollering, no one heard the wagon pull up, and everyone gasped as the door opened on two of Abraham's grown grandsons, their faces wearing matching expressions of annoyance and disdain.

"We're come for our grandfather," said the shorter of the two.

Easter invited them to warm up and take a drop in his memory. "Nah," said the elder, who favored Abraham in the shape of his eyes and the way he held his shoulders, one slightly ahead of the other. "We aim to be home before dark, and our only chance is to leave now. These damned roads."

"You'll be taking me, too," said Mary Lurvey, rising stiffly.

The Wharf boys stared at her.

Stanwood smiled at their confusion and explained. "This is your great-aunt Mary. Your grandpa was her brother."

"We don't have room for no old lady," said the shorter Wharf, as though she wasn't standing right there.

"Two real gentlemen," Tammy smirked.

"Witch," he muttered.

"Now, now," said Mrs. Stanley. "If a person saws a barrel in two and makes two tubs, they call her a witch."

Hannah Stanwood giggled at the proximity of two potential grooms.

Stanwood hiked his pants up and announced, "Don't worry, Mother Lurvey. We'll get you down in plenty of time for the funeral. The ground is harder'n Tammy Younger's heart, so they can't plant him too quick. Family has to stick together in times like these."

Judy Rhines waited for Tammy to turn her tongue on Stanwood for that, but she only threw her head back and laughed, blowing contempt all over the room. Stanwood's face was a map of murder, but he held his tongue and led the Wharf boys to the corpse. The two of them hoisted their grandfather with so little effort, Judy thought she might weep. In that moment, it seemed as though the whole of Abraham's life amounted to nothing more weighty or lasting than a sack of turnips.

This new commotion roused the dogs, who gathered to watch. Bear let out a sneeze and then commenced a howl that raised hairs on the back of every neck in the house. The women got to their feet—slowly and stiffly—as the body passed from the room with the dogs following after, padding out in single file like mourners leaving a church.

It was over. An unfamiliar look of misery stole over Easter's face. There would be no going to Abraham Wharf's funeral. The winter roads were too hard to make it there and back in one short winter's day, and no one but the Wharfs had any relations to stay with in Gloucester. A gloomy silence settled over the room as they all listened to the receding chorus of barking and howling that followed the wagon as it bumped down the road all the way to Fox Hill, past Tammy Younger's house, and into the world.

It was time for them to return to their crumbling houses, to sleep off the effects of the drink and revisit the taste of Easter's cabbage, to mull over the bitter day that Abraham Wharf turned up dead, and Dogtown turned out to tell him a sorry farewell.

An Unexpected Visit

JUDY STAYED to help Easter collect the assortment of chipped crockery and battered tankards that littered the room. It didn't take long to tidy up in a parlor that held but three chairs, some rough benches, and a table too small for the old man's bier. But the empty room was no shame to Easter. "You don't need a sideboard to hoist a glass" was how Easter greeted newcomers who, finding their way to her house, were disappointed by the absence of physical comforts.

After the last cup was rinsed and set aside, Easter yawned. "Why don't you stay the night with me, Judy Rhines?" she said. "We'll both sleep warmer, and it's dark out there."

But Judy was already putting on her cloak. "I'll be fine."

"You're getting to be a hermit," Easter grumbled.

"No more than Granny Day."

"I suppose," Easter laughed and kissed her cheek. "Keep safe," she called as Judy walked into the freezing night, where Greyling had been waiting.

"You coming home with me, girl?"

The dog set out, trotting a few paces ahead of her, stopping when they reached the path that cut across the field to see which way the woman would go.

Judy decided against the short cut, not that her other choice was much better. On a night as cold as this, a broken ankle could be just as fatal on a main road: no one would find her until morning, if then.

The wind sliced through Judy's clothes and burned her cheeks. She tightened the strips of homespun wrapped around her fingers and dug her hands into her armpits for warmth. Head down against the wind, she kept her eyes trained before her feet and stepped slowly. Had a traveler been abroad, he might have carried back a tale of a twisted ghoul crawling along the Dogtown road, with a fiendish familiar in the shape of a dog at its side.

Judy's thoughts turned back to Abraham. Something about his hands had bothered her: clutched, almost birdlike, as though he'd been trying to grasp at something. The last time she'd seen Abraham alive, not even a month earlier, he had been sour and complaining, but no more so than any other time. What had turned inside him? And why had there been so little blood?

The tip of her nose started to burn. Drawing the folds of her cloak tight to her face, she caught the lingering smell of tobacco from the old ladies' pipes. Soon enough, those women would be following the path into everlasting darkness or everlasting life—or wherever it was that Abraham had gone. She smiled at herself and decided that she was getting peculiar. Down in the harbor, "peculiar" was probably the kindest word they used. Crazy, fantastical, foolish. Witches and whores. Well, damn 'em to hell, she thought, and let out a short bark of a laugh.

Greyling startled at the sound, stopped, and looked back at her.

"Don't mind me, Grey," Judy said softly. "And here we are."

Her house was as old as any in Dogtown but by no means the

worst off. The pitched shake roof did not leak, nor did the windows rattle. Reaching for the latch she whispered, "God bless Cornelius Finson." The door opened, and there he was, as though she'd summoned him. Crouched at her hearth, he was poking at a piece of peat that had begun to banish the chill from the one-room hut.

Judy gasped. "I was just thinking of you."

Greyling held back and stood by the door for a moment. She had never seen the man inside the house, but his scent was not unfamiliar and the woman showed no fear, so she went to her usual place by the fire.

Cornelius was broad-shouldered, thick-necked, and pure African in his face. Nearly six feet, his height frightened most people who saw him. Too bad none of them got a good look at his eyes, Judy thought, which were dark as the new moon and ringed with a tight curling of petal-like lashes.

"I was thinking that this place would be a sorry sight without your help," Judy said.

He nodded and got to his feet, his eyes still fixed on the fire.

"I've been at Easter's all day."

The fire hissed.

"It was good of you to fetch the Wharf boys from town," she said, as a dark suspicion entered her mind. "I know you didn't like Abraham all that much."

"The old man never had a good word for me," Cornelius said, his deep voice vibrating through her.

"Abraham was all bluster. Nothing so bad as John Stanwood."

"Stanwood would like nothing more than to make a dollar turning me over to some sheriff from Alabam'."

"He can't do that," Judy objected. "Mrs. Finson gave you your freedom, didn't she? And it's law now, too, so no one can do any such a thing to you."

"Don't put it past him," Cornelius said. "For a Spanish dollar, he'd set a bounty hunter on me in a tick. They got their own rules, those devils."

"Abraham wouldn't have done anything like that," Judy said firmly.

"Huh," Cornelius snorted, and he sat down to poke at the fire again.

"You didn't want to go home tonight?" she said. "To your books?"

The African had been sleeping in a corner at Widow Lurvey's for some months. Every time he brought her a rabbit or a pail of clams, the old woman doled out a book from her husband's moldering collection of histories.

"Stanwood is over there," Cornelius said.

"I'll thank him for that."

"You'll thank him for nothing," he snapped.

"I don't mean anything by it. But if it's true you're here because of him, I'm glad of it." She took a breath. "You don't visit me anymore, Cornelius."

He went back to staring at the flames.

"Nobody ever knew," she whispered.

"It was too dangerous," he said.

"I can take care of myself."

"Dangerous for me," Cornelius said. "You're just another crazy Dogtown witch. I'm the one who'd catch it. Especially with the likes of Stanwood around."

"You credit him with too much courage."

"Nothin' to do with courage. He's a liar, bred in the bone. Letting all those people call him Captain? He never served a thing but himself. One tankard of ale and he claims to have bedded every woman in sight. You among 'em."

Judy thought about the way the men stared after her in town and joined Cornelius's study of the fire.

"Ruth was there," Judy said.

Cornelius shrugged.

"She didn't seem worried about Stanwood," she said.

For the first time that night, Cornelius looked her in the face and said sadly, "You don't know what you're talking about."

Judy blushed at the rebuke.

"It's late," he said. "I'll bring the bed over."

He took the four posts from their corner and set them standing in the notches he'd cut in the floor long ago. Then he got the key from its nail on the wall and turned it until the ropes were taut and tight between the posts. Judy carried the mattress and together they unfolded it over the webbing. Without a word, he reached for the quilt and together they laid it out. The dog woofed softly in her sleep by the fire, and Judy felt a ripple of gratitude for having two extra souls in her little house. The moment passed as Cornelius stepped outside, coatless.

She removed her dress quickly and got into bed, holding her breath. Would he come back for his coat and leave? Would he sleep on the floor? Would he join her in the bed and turn his back to her? Or would he reach for her as he used to?

It was seven years ago, on a bright April afternoon, that Cornelius had walked past her door with a couple of mallards over his shoulder.

Like everyone else on Cape Ann, Judy knew who Cornelius was by sight. "You've had good luck," Judy said.

Cornelius stopped. "Luck had no part in it."

"You're a fine hunter, then."

"A better cook."

She laughed at the thought. "That would be a matter of taste."

"You got salt?"

She nodded.

"Fiddleheads?"

"A basketful," said Judy. "Early ones, the best. I found a big stand down by the creek today."

"Get some water, then," and he added, "if you please."

She brought him water, salt, and the basket of greens she'd planned to sell in town the following morning. Meanwhile, Cornelius had plucked and gutted the birds. He melted little bits of fat from under the skin, rolled the ducks in salt, and lay them on to fry, and then added every last one of the 'heads to the pan. Judy was put out at that; she wanted a needle and thread badly and that wild crop was to have paid for them. Nor did she much fancy tasting the mess simmering in her pot. Still, she had to smile at the sight of the large man sniffing over her fire, and she set to making a pan of long rolls so there'd be something tolerable for supper.

But the duck turned out to be the best she'd ever eaten. It was different from anything she'd ever put in her mouth, more salted, and more . . . she searched for a word. More flavorish was the only way she could put it.

"How'd you learn this?"

"My mother, she showed me. Back home, they cook this way."

"Virginia?" asked Judy, remembering a story about how Cornelius's mother had been bought from there.

His pressed his lips together for a moment, then said, "Virginia ain't home. My mother told me to never call that place home. She said my home is over in Africa, where she was born. She said we would go home after this life. She said not to fret about that."

Judy hoped Cornelius was a Christian. It seemed awfully unfair for his soul to be doomed to eternal misery considering how well he cooked. She had stopped going to First Parish to avoid hearing any more about burning pits and damnation.

"You're lucky to remember your mother's cooking," Judy said.

"There is no luck for the African man," he said.

"Well, at least you remember your mother. Mine died bearing

me. My father put me out for bond when I was but seven and I never saw him or my sister again."

Cornelius looked down at his plate for a moment and then reached over to her. He touched the side of her face with one finger, running it from her forehead to her cheek to her chin. So startled by the unexpected tenderness of his touch and so moved by the unmistakable sympathy in his eyes, Judy dropped her fork with a clatter that made them both jump.

He spent that night in her bed and returned after sunset the next, and the next, all that spring and summer, into fall. Sometimes he arrived so late that Judy would have fallen asleep waiting for him, naked under her skirt.

Startling awake, she would find him staring at her. On moonless nights, his eyes were the only light in the pitch-dark room. And then he would kiss her, and she saw nothing more.

Cornelius taught her how to kiss. Lip on lip, teeth on teeth, mouth on ears, neck, wrist, thigh. With velvet tongue, gently, urgently, slowly, hungrily. He presented her with bouquets of kisses, some heavy with need, some light as dandelion fluff.

She had been with a man before. She knew a little of the unnamed release and rush between her legs, the odd sense of power in getting a man to cry out in spite of himself. But not kissing. She had known nothing of kissing.

The fullness of Cornelius's lips was her delight, a silken press that calmed her, then roused her, then freed her to try and return the pleasure. He repaired her roof, dug her root cellar, built and set the bedposts, but none of those gifts compared to Cornelius's kiss, the memory of which made Judy weep and fume during the long winter months when he visited no more.

For after the first freeze, Cornelius disappeared. Judy worried that he might be sick or injured, but soon learned that he was healthy and working odd jobs here and there. Then she wondered if she'd given him some offense and tramped the main roads in and out of Gloucester hoping to find him and ask. But their paths never crossed. When she learned that he was sleeping on Ned Crawford's floor, she stopped by with an extra potato or to ask for a pinch of tea. But she never found him in. Judy shivered all that winter, unable to get warm.

Cornelius returned to her early in the spring, bearing four scrawny rabbits but no explanation for his absence. Judy had been too grateful for the sight of him to ask why he had left her or what had brought him back.

For five years that was his pattern. Cornelius would vanish for the winter, like a bear, returning to her with the spring. The cold months were hard to endure, but the prospect of April kept Judy alive.

And then came a spring without him. She waited night after night, startling at the hooting of owls, wakened by the scamperings of mice. She mended her quilt and scrubbed her floor until the knots in the boards were bleached white. She asked Easter if she'd heard any news of Cornelius Finson and learned that he was working in a Gloucester fishery and sleeping in a warehouse there.

May passed and Judy grew thin. Easter Carter made her drink a double dose of her lively tonic, thinking she was just springish. But Judy got so skinny and pale, Easter began to suspect something else was afoot and started to ask questions.

In September, Judy finally found Cornelius on the Hutting farm, where he'd been hired to butcher a hog. But there was no talking to him, not with Silas standing by, his two sons watching as well.

"Don't you go witching on our property," said the younger one, a boy of seven or so.

"We'll throw you in the water, and you'll melt," said the other, who had a harelip and was never seen in town. Silas crossed his arms and nodded at his boys' nasty fun. Judy walked away, furious. Carrying herself as tall as she could, she muttered aloud how much she'd like to shrivel their tongues with a spell, or send a bat to blind their eyes. "What makes them think a real witch would tolerate that kind of meanness without a punishment. I'd turn them into toads if I could," she said. "And then I'd run them all through with a sharp stick."

Cornelius hadn't even looked up from his bloody work when she arrived. Had he felt her humiliation? she wondered. Did he notice? Did he ever think of her?

She walked back to her house and sat in a chair, too injured to sleep, too angry to weep. In the dark of the night, she decided to put Cornelius behind her. Exhausted and enraged, she pounded the table and let the tears come. Her life was hard enough without pining for something as unnecessary as a man. "He can go to hell," she said, not meaning it in the least.

By the next spring, Judy had tamped down her hopes and wore herself out putting in the biggest garden she could manage. She weeded ferociously and carried so much water that her carrots grew sweet as sugar, her potatoes large and creamy. She set plenty by for winter and grew calmer as the days shortened: it was easier to wean her heart when the leaves fell, and the evenings grew chill. Judy had stopped hoping for his return by then, and she prayed only that the longing for him would decrease more with every change of the season.

His sudden presence on the icy winter night of Abraham Wharf's laying out seemed like a childhood dream sprung to life. Judy lay beneath the quilts, waiting for the door to open, her jaw clamped, her hands clenched, and she willed herself not to hope for anything.

The bed shuddered as Cornelius sat on it. His boots thudded to the floor and then he lay down with his back to her, slowed his breathing, and pretended to sleep.

I should not be here, he thought, eyes wide. Even though he had covered his tracks so no one would ever know he'd come. Even though the old man's death made it safer. It was a mistake, even if it was the last time.

He had stopped seeing Judy Rhines because of Abraham Wharf. The old man had been waiting for him outside Lurvey's house one night before he left for her bed. Wharf had grabbed him by the back of his arm, like he was a child. "You stay off Judy Rhines, you hear me?" he said. "You black bastard, you touch that girl again and I'm going to see to it you're killed. Or worse.

"I oughter do it now," he hissed. "I oughter tell some of the boys in town and have 'em cut you to pieces or sell you down South. But I ain't going to, 'cause she wouldn't like it. Not yet, anyhow. But I'm going to be watching and I will see you dead before I let this go on. An abomination, that's what it is."

So Cornelius had stayed away. He told himself it was to protect Judy as much as himself: after all, she'd be ruined if word got out. But that was a lie to cover up his own wretched fear. He knew how easy it was to kill a black man. And he knew that Judy Rhines was lost to him, no matter what he did or did not do.

❖

Cornelius had been born on Cape Ann under Nicholas Finson's roof. The Finsons were not entirely pleased when they discovered their new-bought slave girl, Maydee, was carrying a baby. Their farmhouse was already crowded with their own three children, but they named the slave baby and kept him, after he could walk and talk. They kept him even after his mother died, when he might have fetched them a good price. Cornelius was only ten years old when Maydee perished of fever, so Mrs. Finson had looked after him from then on and even taught him to read and figure, alongside her own little girls.

He was not quite eighteen when Mr. Finson died. A month after that, the mistress sold the farm and prepared to join her eldest daughter in Portland. Cornelius had his clothes in a sack on the day the wagon pulled up to fetch her, but after he'd helped load the trunks, she asked him to sit down and handed him her husband's belt, boots, and good hat. "These are for you, Cornelius," she said.

"Thank you, Missus."

"These are parting gifts," she said. "I cannot take you with me, but don't worry. I mean for you to be free." Mrs. Finson reached for her reticule. "The town clerk wrote it down so there'd be a record. And I have your paper for you." She got to her feet and pressed the document and ten dollars into his hand. "I wish you good fortune, Cornelius. I wish you the best of luck."

As he listened to the wagon pull away he thought he ought to be feeling happy. He was a free man, free to go wherever he wished, do whatever he wanted.

But all he felt was empty. He was a free man, but he had no idea what to do with himself or where to go. He had lost the only people who shared any memory of his mother. He laid his cheek to the table where he'd eaten every meal of his life, in the room where Maydee had coddled him and combed his hair, where he'd learned to read and to write his name. And he wept.

⟡

The next day, he left for Boston to see for himself if there were African men who owned their own shops and wore waistcoats and carried silver-tipped canes. He walked the city streets until he found the hill where there were more black faces than white, and he stared at the dark women sporting crisp bonnets and leather slippers. They looked right through him, rough country boy that he was, so he made his way to the docks, where there were others just like him working hard. The stevedores took note of his broad shoulders and agreed to try him out on the night watch, when darkness and damp made the job even more dangerous.

Cornelius was sure-footed as well as strong and was rehired night after night, but he found no fellowship there. He was just one more of too many black men jostling for a scarce job. Competition for women was even fiercer, for there were barely any of their complexion and few respectable ones, especially not in that neighborhood.

With his first wages, Cornelius followed a mustee whore down a dark alley, where fear and need overwhelmed him, and he was unmanned in a matter of moments. The heavy-lidded girl—half-black, half-Indian—would have laughed and walked away with his money, but she heard his ragged breath and, putting her hand to his perfectly smooth face, felt the tears.

"Poor thing," she said. "Follow me."

In her narrow room, she made him slow down enough to follow his own pleasure, and then she taught him how to control himself to increase it. And because Cornelius was so young and clean-smelling, she kissed him on the mouth. They slept on her cot most of the next day. As evening approached, she told him that he could come back after work, to sleep again.

She took every cent he earned that week, and in return she shared her supper as well as her bed. She took his hand and showed him the simple secret of delighting a woman, and she gave him a lesson on the proper use of the tongue. But when he returned to her room at the end of the seventh day, there was a skinny white woman in the bed.

"Where's the other one?" he asked.

The tart's face was covered with smallpox scars. She looked him up and down and said, "She's gone, but I'm just as good as her."

Cornelius left. With nowhere to sleep, he wandered the streets, glassy-eyed, until he found himself outside Tobias Smith's barbershop window, fascinated by the sight of four well-fed black men, smiling easily.

Smith spied Cornelius through the glass and motioned him to come in.

"Look at that nappy head," he said to his friends, not unkindly. "You want a trim?"

Cornelius looked at his shoes.

"No money, eh?" Smith said. "We'll put it on your account. Or you can sweep up to pay it off."

Just then, his daughter walked in. Twelve years old but tall, her eyes were bright and quick.

The barber turned to Cornelius and asked, "Young man, do you know your letters?"

"Yes, sir," answered Cornelius from the barber chair, though he addressed his words to the girl. "And my numbers."

"Well, well," said Smith. "Perhaps I should hire the boy as my assistant. Can you cut hair?"

"I could learn," Cornelius said, showing far too much eagerness and need.

Smith considered. "Maybe you should come by tomorrow, and we'll see what you can do."

As soon as the barber pronounced him done, Cornelius grabbed the broom and swept up a storm of dust and hair. After ten minutes, Smith reached for the handle. "No need to wear it out, son."

As he left the shop, hurrying to reach the docks in time to be hired, Cornelius looked around him and realized that Boston was a beautiful place. The windows had all turned gold in the sunset, and a fresh wind out of the harbor sweetened the air. He had never been in the presence of a free African girl, so clean and bright and close to his own age. He wondered what her name was and if he'd get to meet the girl's mother, and whether the daughter favored her. He was so suddenly full of hope, he thought he'd never last until the following morning.

When he arrived, though, the door was locked and the windows were shuttered. A man wearing the white jacket of a porter saw him waiting across the narrow street and told him that Tobias had been attacked the night before. A gang of white thugs had clubbed him, robbed him, and left him bleeding.

"Is he dead?" asked Cornelius.

"Not yet," he said. "The black man takes his life in his hands walking these streets. You best be careful."

Cornelius kept watch as people came and went. A white man carrying a black leather bag spent a few minutes inside and then hurried away. After noon, he heard the sounds of wailing from inside and started back for Cape Ann.

He worked on the docks in Gloucester Harbor for a little while, but he felt ill at ease close to so many other men. He trusted none of them and grew weary of looking over his shoulder. His only pleasure came from long Sunday tramps along the shore or through the deserted hills surrounding Dogtown's fading common, where he finally took shelter in one of the half-wrecked houses, which he made habitable. He'd lived in one hovel after another or flopped with some other poor souls, moving into Mary Lurvey's house after one freezing winter that nearly cost him his toes. In Dogtown, he was able to sleep through the night and if he was not happy, at least he was not always afraid.

But after he'd been with Judy Rhines, he was more frightened than he could remember. Cornelius had no illusions: failure would always conquer hope and loss would always devour possibility. Every autumn, Cornelius decided to leave Judy before she could be taken away from him. There was more dignity in ending it himself. But with the return of the spring, his heart got the better of him, and he returned to her. Until Wharf had found him out, and fear won out.

✧✧✧

Cornelius felt the warmth of Judy's body behind him, reproaching him. This is the last time I will be so close to her, he reminded himself.

Judy stared at Cornelius's back, a dark hill in the firelight. Her throat was raw with swallowed tears. She wished he'd never come, wished he'd never shared her bed in the first place. Better not to miss him the way she would have missed her right arm.

She should have thrown him out when she first walked in from Easter's. She should have shown some pride. Even now she should shake him and demand an explanation, an answer, something. But she said nothing. She inhaled the familiar woody smell of him and took comfort from the warmth of his body under her blanket.

Judy stared at the back of his head and willed him to turn and face her.

She had survived without him, of course. She had fed herself and cleaned her house, earned enough money to get by, and even acquired some new acquaintances in Gloucester. She showed herself to be self-possessed and self-sufficient, so no one would suspect how her heart beat only half the time, waiting for Cornelius. If he had turned to face her, she would have begged him to return the next night and the next. She would have wept and pleaded.

But Cornelius remained still. She knew that they had no future together and that his presence in her bed was a fluke of some sort. And finally, she preferred his silence to hearing him say good-bye.

Judy tried not to fall asleep. She thought of small things she had wanted to tell Cornelius, like how she'd begun cooking in his mother's fashion, putting blackberries and ramps into squirrel stew. And how the cellar he'd dug for her was so dry and cool, she could store butter as well as turnips down there. And that she'd made him a pair of stockings years ago and still hadn't unraveled the yarn for another purpose.

Worn out at last by her long day, Judy slipped into a shallow pool of a dream. She walked with Cornelius, barefoot, through the warm water of a low tide on the beach at Little Good Harbor. It was a sunny day, and other people were strolling there, too. Ruth walked arm in arm with Easter, and the Dogtown pups chased one another.

Judy woke up at dawn, shivering. The heat from the fire that Cornelius had carefully banked did nothing to warm her. She was alone. Even Greyling was gone. She turned her face to the mattress and pulled the blanket over her head and tried to think of a reason to get out of bed.

Greyling

GREYLING HAD stayed on the floor rather than take her usual spot behind the woman's knees, unsure of her place with the man on the bed. She watched him rise before first light, keeping perfectly still as he ran his hands over the chair and table. When he put her cloak to his nose, he caught the dog's eye and held her gaze long enough to show her that he belonged there, even if he never returned.

She slipped out the door behind him as he left, and stood beside the house while he hurried away. Greyling shook herself head to tail and raised her nose to sniff the new day. The frozen ground was painful beneath her feet as she padded in the direction of the smallest of the pack's many warrens, a tunnel dug below a rocky outcropping near the now-frozen swamp.

She would stop at certain houses if she caught the scent of cooking, but there were others where she did not bother. Generous or indifferent, gentle or cruel, people were features of the landscape, as important as the location of fresh water. One by one, men and women represented either a threat or a meal; survival required that she remember which was which.

Greyling spent most of her days outdoors, like the other dogs. But she was not fully a member of the Dogtown pack, and never would be. She had not been born there. She held no rank. She would never bear a litter, and she was not even permitted inside the oldest burrows, which had been dug by a generation of dogs long dead.

When food was plentiful, the grey dog ate what they left for her. On summer days when all of them lay together in the high pasture, basking and panting in the sun, she positioned herself a little distance away. There was no shame in being the lowest among them. That was simply the order of things.

Greyling had turned up in Dogtown not quite fully grown, starved and skittish. She found her way up from the harbor to the hills and hid in the woods, watching the way of things, learning her manners. The dogs rarely went inside a house in the summer, but when it grew cold, they scratched softly at doors. They did not show their teeth and took what was given to them with a soft mouth. They left no droppings near the houses, nor did one dog enter when another was inside, except on the bitterest days, when all animals huddled together as a matter of life or death.

In Gloucester, there was wild talk about one hundred dogs roaming the hills, fierce and dangerous, in thrall to the witches. The truth was, there were never any more than twenty in the Dogtown pack, even at its largest. There were far more mongrels skulking beneath the Gloucester wharves, tearing one another's ears over scraps of maggoty fish and dying of their wounds among the reeds. In town, they were killed by drunken seamen who kicked sleeping dogs for pure spite, and by boys who drowned puppies for sport.

Up in the hills, the dogs rarely growled at one another and people left them alone. On hot days, they hunted mice and munched on bugs and grass, keeping cool in shallow beds they dug in the dirt. A litter was born every year or two, and many of the pups survived. Back in the days when there were children in Dogtown, boys would scout out the whelping spot, but as children became scarcer than deer, that warren remained a secret.

The people gave the dogs names. Greyling was christened in honor of her singular coloring, as the others all were shades of brown: Brindle, Coffee, Little Russet, Big Brown. There was always a Brindle and always a Bear, who was the biggest and thus the lead dog. His consort was always Marie, though no one knew how she came to get such an unlikely moniker. It was one of the lighter mysteries of the place.

The dogs had no need of names, of course, but they recognized them when it was useful. Greyling certainly knew hers. When she heard it in Judy Rhines's mouth, her ears flattened with pleasure. She frequented the woman's house from early on, and not only because of her open hand. There was something about the voice, low and tranquil, that settled her. Greyling slept soundly near Judy Rhines, even on that one odd night when the man shared her bed.

Tammy Younger's Toothache

THE SOUND was animal: low, dangerous, and close by. It was not quite a growl. Or perhaps it was. Oliver's eyes flew open. He was already sitting up, panting and afraid in the pale dawn hush.

There it was again. But now that he was out of the nightmare, he recognized it as nothing more than Tammy, groaning in her sleep. Oliver lay back on his pallet, letting his feet extend out onto the floor; in the two years since Abraham Wharf's death, he'd grown a good six inches.

Tammy had been so drunk the night before, Oliver thought she'd be senseless till midday at least. He'd unloaded her from the chair to the bed, her swollen face wrapped with a red cord. The loops, tied on top, made her look like a rabbit. If rabbits could swear about their teeth. There were two of them giving her trouble this time, one on each side, midway back on top.

For most of her sixty-four years, Tammy Younger had been nothing but healthy. She never suffered the ague, not even during the bitterest winter, not so much as a sneeze. No weakness of limb or lung, no broken bone, no female trouble, no aching joints, no stoppages or flux in the bowels. When Oliver was six years old and racked with fever, she turned him out of his bed, flushed and glassy-eyed, to fetch her some water.

"You gotta be tough as me," she said. "Too mean to get sick."

Oliver had managed to get himself to his feet and promptly fainted to the floor, where Tammy left him.

But the day finally came, in her sixty-first year, when Tammy's teeth started to go bad, and it made her furious. Anyone who crossed her path was treated to a loud harangue, as though there had been some kind of mistake. Easter listened to her grievances, put a thumb inside her cheek, and pulled back her lip to reveal a long, dark gap.

"But it never happened to me before," Tammy declared, outraged.

"Well, I suppose you just joined the rest of us," Easter said.

"Damn you," Tammy said. "And damn the rest of your teeth, too."

Tammy dosed herself with every remedy and recipe ever applied to toothache. She tried leaf poultices and chewed the bark from an ash tree that grew in Sandy Bay. She traded a session of palm reading (she had a small following of women who swore by her predictions) for a measure of imported thyme, which was supposed to ease the throbbing. She sent Oliver out to hunt for rattlesnake plant to brew a tea so bitter Tammy had to pour half a cup of honey and some hard cider into the cup to get it down.

But none of the cures did her much good. After a few weeks of dosing herself, Tammy would pull a long face and say, "It's nothing for me but them damned pliers." She'd buy up all the hard liquor she could and, once she'd drunk it, send Oliver down the road to fetch John Hodgkins, the carpenter. Over the years, he had pulled half a dozen of Tammy's teeth. "I'm going to have to put your name on these things," he'd say.

To which Tammy replied, "Damn you to hell and hurry it up."

She paid him in goose eggs or berries. Once he arrived to find she had nothing to give, for despite the rumors about Tammy's secret cache of gold, she lived as hardscrabble a life as the rest of her Dogtown neighbors. When he complained that half a dozen turnips to be paid after harvest wasn't enough, she swore at him so foully that he was happy enough to cause her a little pain on credit.

Tammy put off Hodgkins's visits as long as she could, which meant there would be a week of heavy drinking and cursing as she worked herself up to face the agony. Oliver looked forward to those evenings when she was getting herself ready. It wasn't that he enjoyed seeing her suffer; he'd never been the sort of boy who tortured bugs or threw rocks at squirrels. But when Tammy was hurting, he knew he wouldn't go to bed hungry.

Most of the time, Oliver's belly gnawed and ached for food, a feeling heightened by the unearthly good smell of Tammy's cooking. No one suspected this unlikely talent, for she dined alone and late. But her recipes filled the house with aromas so rich and heady, there were times Oliver wept, knowing he'd never get more than a scrap from her plate, which often reached him wiped clean of all traces. Even when she was miserable with toothache, Tammy took the time to flavor her corn mush with cooked mashed carrots and perfumy spices that turned even that humble fare into a treat.

When her head was softened by pain and drink, Tammy's appetite waned and she lost track of how much was left in the pot, so Oliver got to eat his fill. Those nights, she'd sit up drinking and after a while start telling one of her stories.

Oliver wasn't sure she meant for him to listen to these drunken rambles; she'd probably jabber away even if she were by herself. Some of what she said was nothing more than petty town gossip, and she seemed to have a juicy story about everyone in Gloucester. Oliver didn't know how much to believe of his aunt's tittle-tattle, and some of it was so far-fetched, he wondered if she were trying to set him up to act the fool. But he wasn't stupid enough to go and ask the Annisquam minister if his son was born with a corkscrew tail, and he sure as hell wasn't going to try to kiss the great black birds that huddled over on the Bass Rocks for good luck.

The stories Tammy repeated most often were about her aunt Lucy George, and Oliver knew those word for word. Lucy had studied the use of every plant and shrub on Cape Ann and the mainland, too. She knew what worked to cure, what could kill, and how to brew a spring potion that could wake the dead. She claimed some of her recipes came from Indians who once walked those parts in summer, steaming clams in a smoky pit down on the sand beaches.

"Everyone thought Lucy George was a witch," Tammy said. "Lucy half believed it, herself. Her old tomcat lived to be twenty, nasty old thing. She'd talk to that bag of fleas like he knew her meaning. Like he would turn and answer back.

"She did hear voices," Tammy nodded at the fire. "They got louder in winter, telling her which paths to take and which to let alone. Lucy said the voices told her how to charm animals and how to sour milk, how to frighten men into leaving her be." Tammy laughed about that. "Lucy was ugly as a flounder. Uglier! And no smile ever crossed that face, neither. Not that I saw. And why should it, eh? She ate no meat and drank nothing stronger than water. Why smile, indeed."

Lucy had little use for human company. She hated men most and children only a little less. When the constable knocked on Lucy's door with Tammy—orphaned by smallpox—Lucy thought long and hard about dropping the toddling girl into the millpond and having done with the bother. That's what Lucy used to say any time little Tammy asked for a bite to eat or a blanket or anything at all. "I should've drowned you then," said Lucy. "I'll throw you down there, yet."

Tammy soon discovered that Lucy wasn't going to drown her, or lock her in the root cellar, or hang her by her thumbs for taking an apple from the barrel. The girl took her share of beatings before she figured out how to sneak what she needed without getting caught, but after that, weeks could pass without Lucy saying a word to her. Eventually her aunt's threats were the only way that Tammy was sure Lucy remembered she was still there.

There was no mention of school, so Tammy never did learn to read or figure on paper, though she knew how to count what was hers. She studied the way Lucy took care of herself, and no one ever cheated Tammy Younger on a trade, either.

In those days, the main road from Gloucester to Riverview and Annisquam crossed over a bridge on Lucy's property. Her house was so close to the crossing, passersby could count the hairs on Lucy's chin through the window she'd cut into the wall so she could keep a watch over the traffic. Whenever she heard footsteps, she'd fling the shutter open so hard, it made a sound as loud as gunshot, startling the animals and rattling the men. If she spied a loaded wagon, she'd jump right through the window, quick as a fox. Crossing her arms, she'd stand with her chin out staring down the horse or ox, face-to-face, till she got what she wanted.

"Once, I watched her put a hex on old man Babcock's prize ox team," Tammy slurred one night, when she was deep into her cups. "They stood there, tongues hanging out like they might up and die. Babcock nearly shit himself, I tell you. Then he commenced to begging like a little girl. 'Oh please, oh please, Miss Lucy, let me go and I'll keep you in firewood all winter.'

"I once saw her jinx a whole load of pumpkins," Tammy said. "Fell right off a wagon and rolled against the house in a line, neat as you please. That farmer lit out of there fast as a bat.

"But the real truth is that Lucy didn't need magic to get her way." Tammy drew her shawl around her. "She would swear the dirtiest oaths and shame the men into giving her what she wanted. And for the women, well, she knew the stories that no one wanted told, like who was having a six-month baby and who was seen walking with a married man in the dark of the moon. Everyone knew to bring a few apples or a twist of tobacco if they wanted speedy passage and their secrets kept close."

When Lucy died in her sleep, peaceful as a parson, Tammy took over the spot at the window and let it be known that there was still a price to pay for crossing the bridge. And while no one ever saw Tammy charm a pumpkin or hex an ox, she inherited her aunt's foul mouth and taste for blackmail, and nobody cared to test her powers. By the time Oliver came along, the shore road had opened. There were few travelers over the bridge and Tammy found it much more difficult to extort enough to live on and rarely got the chance to scare little girls, whom she liked to grab by the wrist and invite inside "for tea."

Tammy was bred to be a mean old woman, but unlike Lucy, she did have one passion: she lived for her meals, and sweets most of all. Maple sugar or molasses, she licked the spoon, the bowl, her fingers, gurgling like a baby. A cup of chocolate sent Tammy's heart racing, and she would hold the mug upside down and lick the dregs, tears of happiness at the corners of her small, round, bluebonnet eyes.

The nights when she was in the worst agonies from her toothaches, she'd swallow four glasses of rum and talk about the first time she had sugar in her mouth. Anne Wharf had set a cup on her table, getting ready to make a pie, when Tammy walked in, grabbed it, and ran for the woods. She'd stuck her finger into the white powder and then into her mouth, again and again, until it was gone. It was her first memory of any sort of happiness. Even when her teeth were rotting and sugar caused them to throb, she would not stop.

Oliver had never seen her look worse than on that clear spring morning when Tammy faced up to the loss of two teeth at the same time. Her cheeks hung loose over the hollowed-out spaces in her mouth, and her skin was yellow. The hair escaping from under her dirty cap was white, and her mottled hands shook.

"Go fetch me that damned carpenter," she said. "And if you know what's good for you, you'll do it in the devil's own time."

The sun had begun to burn off the early chill and the woods were filled with a fine mist steaming up toward the light. Oliver stood near a bare bush to do his morning business, and then set off down the road, stewing over why he was still doing what Tammy told him.

Who was she to treat him like her slave? She couldn't really make him do anything or force him to go anywhere, anymore.

He was fourteen years old now, after all. Boys half his age had shipped out of Gloucester and returned with stories about the sights of New York and the whores of London. The sober ones returned with enough money to buy a few tools and get married. Not that he was in any rush for that anymore: he was mortified to remember how he used to pine after Judy Rhines, who faded quickly after Abraham Wharf killed himself.

There was nothing to stop him from staying down in Gloucester either, where he might find work on the docks. Or he could make his way to Salem or even Boston and learn a trade.

He kicked at stones as he walked, nearly tripping in front of the old Haskell place, where he stopped to have a look in the cellar. A shard from a green-edged plate poked up like an early crocus in the soggy char left by last summer's picnickers. Oliver spied a bit of metal in the mess and stepped down, hoping for a coin.

"Blast," he muttered, digging out a rusted buckle.

The ache in his belly set him back on the path. Maybe Mrs. Hodgkins would give him something for breakfast. Oliver worried that there was something wrong with him, the way he was always hungry. It seemed everyone else in Dogtown could go for days without food. Not him. He'd been nearly full the night before, finishing Tammy's mush and some dried apples stewed in cider. And here he was, ready to swallow a whole plate of biscuits and eggs, if anyone offered. Mrs. Hodgkins's biscuits were nearly as good as Tammy's; just the idea of warm bread set his mouth to watering.

Maybe his being hungry all the time had something to do with the difference between women and men. He'd spent so little time around others of his sex, he didn't much know about what they ate or talked about or thought. He longed to know more about the world of men, but he was shy of them, especially boys his age. He feared saying something that would give him away as womanish. He knew his looks put him in a bad light, too: skinny and dressed in rags. Some of the boys called him "Toothache" because he'd taken to selling Tammy's cures on his own. He let the insult pass, as it was those herbs and simples that bought him the clothes on his back. Without the toothache recipes, he'd be naked as a dog.

Worst of all, he dreaded being called a Dogtown puss. Last summer a gang of men outside Haskell's tavern had howled over that one, and Oliver had felt the sting of the insult even though he wasn't quite sure what it meant.

When he got to Hodgkins's place, seven-year-old Elizabeth answered the door. "Pa ain't here," said the miniature version of the mousy Mrs. Hodgkins, her narrow-set eyes beside the long, skinny nose. Elizabeth let Oliver into the warm house, which smelled of baking.

"He went to Salem to buy some nails and fancy lumber for a coffin ordered up by Mr. Sergeant. He said it was the best job he ever got. He took Johnny with him. I don't think it's fair to take him and not me. Do you think it's fair?"

All Oliver could think about was that Tammy would throw

something at him if he returned without the carpenter. "When's he coming back?"

"Mamma says tomorrow if we're lucky. Mamma says he's liable to find himself a tavern and forget all about us for a week. That's why Johnny went, to try to keep him on the straight path. But if he strays, to get him home as quick as he can.

"Mamma says Pa isn't so bad, that's just his nature and most of them are far worse, and I'm to give thanks to my Heavenly Father for having such a good provider in my father here on earth." Elizabeth barely took a breath. This was just the kind of talk that Tammy would love to hear, Oliver thought. Maybe he could postpone her anger with this scrap of gossip.

Then he saw the biscuits, piled like a heap of miniature gold bricks on a pearly white plate, set on the edge of the table to cool.

"Isn't your ma here?" he asked.

"She's over to Mrs. Pulcifer's house to borrow some syrup. She said I could stay here on my own 'cause I'm getting to be a big girl, and she says I can keep myself out of trouble long enough for her to have a cup of tea with Mrs. Pulcifer in peace."

Oliver took off his hat and started making his way across the room. Elizabeth set her thin lips in a line and didn't take her eyes off him.

"Think I can take a biscuit?"

"No."

"Your ma always gives me something."

Elizabeth thought about this for a moment. "My mamma says you are a half-starved wild 'un and that Tammy Younger is a skim-flint and a sinner to treat you the way she does. She says it's a shame and a scandal, too, because you have the air."

Oliver nodded but he was only half listening. He made it to the table and quick-as-he-could snatched a biscuit and stuffed the whole thing into his mouth.

Elizabeth frowned, but kept on talking. "Mrs. Pulcifer said it wouldn't be so much longer before they put her in the ground and then you'll get what's yours.

"I think Aunt Tam is terrible mean to you, whatever she says. Aren't you 'feared she's going to carve you up while you're sleeping in your bed and eat you for breakfast?"

"What are you going on about?" Oliver said.

Elizabeth grew uneasy. "I never know what Mrs. Pulcifer means," she whined. "Mamma says Mrs. Pulcifer likes to hear herself talk, but Mamma likes to hear her talk, too. They talk all the time, my ma and her. Pa says that Mrs. Pulcifer . . ."

"I gotta go," said Oliver.

"I'm telling Mamma about the biscuit," she called after him.

Oliver stood in the middle of the road and tried to decide what to do next. He did not want to go back and face Tammy without some kind of cure for her pain. Maybe the time had come for him to go down to the harbor and sign up for a berth on the next ship out. On his way, he could go past Mrs. Pulcifer's house, though he'd never had any luck cadging food from that tightfisted lady. As he stood and considered his poor choices, he noticed the big yellow cat lying in the morning sun, stretched out on the neatly swept pathway between the house and the carpenter's shed.

Hodgkins's spread was not even half a mile from Tammy's place, and yet it seemed like a different world. There were no cats where Oliver lived. Cats belonged to a world with barns and garden plots laid out in rows, where lilac bushes got trimmed back beside stone walls that weren't tumbling into piles. Suddenly, the carpenter's garden seemed the prettiest place on earth. Nothing like his house or the rest of Dogtown, which was a graveyard by comparison. What Hodgkins had was modest in every detail and more than a little worn for wear, but it belonged to the world where people had carpets on the floor and meals were served at the same time every day.

That was where his future lay. He was as sure of that as he was sure he could have eaten every last one of those biscuits and still had room for more.

But he wouldn't be going after his future that day. There were holes in both knees of his too-short trousers, his shirt barely covered his belly, and one of his shoes was ripped at the seam. That day belonged to Dogtown and to Tammy's damn teeth. Oliver picked up a rock and chucked it at a sapling, missing it three times before he hit the slender trunk.

Then it came to him: Stanwood had tools.

There was a shed out behind his house, a little bit of a lean-to where Stanwood had once cobbled shoes and mended the odd barrel. Surely he'd have pliers. Oliver hadn't noticed much skill in Hodgkins's surgeries: the carpenter yanked till Tammy yelled, then yanked some more until Tammy screamed, and out came the tooth, bloody root and all. Surely Stanwood, who was a far cleverer man, could do that.

Oliver set out at a brisk pace and reached the back road in no time, his step quickened by the thought that he might also get a look at Hannah Stanwood, the last unmarried daughter, though he'd overheard Tammy say she'd been seen sitting on the knee of a certain sea captain's son, and it was only a matter of time.

He left the road in favor of a shortcut that led past the Muzzy house, another Dogtown ruin, where nothing remained but a broken grindstone and a sinkhole. The sun, high overhead, warmed the brushy landscape that Oliver knew from years of berrying.

Oliver pushed his shirtsleeves up over his elbows and congratulated himself on his new plan, which not only solved his problem with Tammy but also gave him the chance to spend some time with Stanwood. He imagined them tramping back to the Younger place together, man to man. Stanwood would tell him tales of his adventures in the navy, and they would share a laugh. He might even offer some fatherly advice about Oliver's next step. Had there been anyone around to see Oliver's smile and rushing steps, he might have imagined him on his way to see his sweetheart.

The sight of the Stanwood homestead pulled him up short. The house was about the same size as the carpenter's, but that was the only comparison. The path to the door was littered with leaves and fallen branches. Clapboards hung loose, and an old brown rug was stuffed into a broken window. Off to the side of the main house, a sorry-looking pile of weathered boards leaned up against a six-foot outcrop of granite. And beside it sat John Stanwood, tipped up on two legs of a three-legged stool, eyes closed in the springtime sun like the yellow cat down the road.

Stanwood was unshaven and his greasy hair hung down his neck, though his boots were polished to a high sheen and his breeches, worn as they were, looked clean. Oliver remembered hearing something about Stanwood's undeserved good fortune in his wife.

He peered into the dim booth, which was certainly not in Mrs. Stanwood's care. The workbench clutter was covered with a layer of thick dust. Only the empty bottles, scattered about the bench and floor, looked like they'd seen any recent use. He could smell the liquor on Stanwood, even from five feet away.

Finally Oliver could wait no longer, and said, "Good morning, Captain."

"I was wondering when you'd get around to saying something." Stanwood opened his eyes to a slit and looked the boy over.

"You admiring my little boo'?" He glanced back at the dim wreck behind him. "My refuge from the hens." He winked and the effort nearly knocked him off his seat.

Oliver began to doubt his plan in asking Stanwood for help, but before he realized it, the man was on his feet with the front of Oliver's shirt bunched in his fist. "What's your business?" he said. "Or is it the old bitch?"

"You got any pliers?" Oliver blurted.

"What for?"

"Never mind."

"Damnation. You come all this way, ask me if I have pliers, and say never mind?" He took Oliver's arm in his other hand and squeezed hard.

"Tammy needs a tooth yanked."

Stanwood let go and sat down again. "She'll pay something for that, I expect."

Oliver recalled the time Tammy had nothing to give the carpenter for his efforts, but said, "Sure. She's got some nice honey."

"How about rum?" Stanwood said. "Or some of that hard cider?"

Oliver shrugged. "She don't tell me everything she's got."

"Time you grew yourself some balls." He tipped his chair back against the rock. "You go tell Tammy I'll be there shortly."

"You don't want to come with me now?"

"I'll be by shortly."

"Today?"

"Today."

"Soon?"

"I'll be there!" Stanwood grabbed a long twig from the ground and said, "Get out of here, or I'll thrash you and then leave that old horror to suffer like she deserves."

Oliver rushed back to the path. But as he had no desire to see Tammy before Stanwood showed up, he slowed down, shuffling and kicking at pebbles. He stopped at a pile of rubble that used to be a well, picked up a rock the size of his fist, and dropped it down the hole, listening to the quick, sad click as it landed on other long-dry stones.

God, he was hungry.

When Tammy finally died, he thought, and the property came

to him, as surely it must, he'd sell it to the first bidder and eat until he could hold no more. Chicken and biscuits and a whole damned cake.

The next house he passed was still occupied, and only a little better off than Stanwood's. It belonged to John Wharf, a distant relation of Abraham's and the last of the line left in Dogtown. The Gloucester Wharfs had never tired of telling John what a born embarrassment he was—a failed cooper, a failed fisherman, and a failed farmer. So after his wife died and his daughter married, he'd retreated to the hills, where no one would remind him of his disappointments.

The door to the cottage was open. Oliver peered in and smiled.

"Why, hello, Polly," he said, and ducked his head, remembering that she was Mrs. Boynton now, and that he had no right to be so familiar. Oliver had spent part of one winter in school with her. Four years his senior, she'd helped him with his letters and numbers, and she hadn't forgotten her manners around him. He'd heard that she married a widower from Riverview last summer. "You back for a visit?" he asked.

Polly shook her head.

"No?"

"Mr. Boynton died last week," she said.

"I'm sorry," said Oliver, and took off his hat.

"I'm not."

She was much changed from the pretty, well-dressed girl he remembered. This Polly was pale, her eyes swollen, and her blonde hair lay lank and tangled on a dirty collar.

"You staying here now?" Oliver asked.

"Nowhere else for me to go."

Oliver knew that wasn't so. There were plenty of Wharfs living near the harbor, even a few rich ones with daughters close to Polly's age.

"I'm better off here," she said.

"Aw, now."

They both studied their shoes for a while.

Unable to think of anything else to say, Oliver shrugged. "I better go."

She nodded.

"Would it be . . . I mean," he stammered, "could I come by to see you sometime?"

Polly's red-rimmed eyes were so full of gratitude, Oliver thought he'd bawl if he didn't take off.

"All right then," he said and hurried off, trying to remember everything he could about Polly. She used to blush crimson whenever the teacher had asked her to recite. And she'd been gentle in correcting Oliver's mistakes on the slate. Once she'd given him a whole biscuit, cold and hard, but smeared with enough bacon fat to make it eat like a whole meal.

He'd only learned about her marriage to Caleb Boynton after it happened, as had everyone else: not even Tammy knew about it in advance. She'd bet on December for the baby, Easter chose January, but neither of them turned out to be right. In fact, Polly had grown thinner, and now Boynton was dead. A man of fifty years or more, he was almost old enough to be Polly's grandfather, but not quite old enough to be dead. Oliver puzzled over Polly all the way home, where everything seemed quiet.

Tammy was probably asleep, and he was suddenly taken with the idea of sneaking inside, putting the blankets over her face, and pressing down hard enough and long enough for it to be over. He'd empty the larder and eat until he couldn't swallow another bite. Then he'd take whatever was worth selling—some tools and the knives at least—and head for Riverdale. Steal a rowboat, make his way to Salem and then on to Boston.

It was an old fantasy, but it had never before seemed so easy. He'd sell the tools and buy a suit of clothes. Sleep in a bed at a real inn. Buy passage for New York or Canada. He could get away with it, too.

Oliver's heart raced at the idea, even though he knew he didn't have it in him. As much as he hated Tammy, he had never been able to kill so much as a chicken; even fishing made him feel wrong with the world. He would never be able to do murder. That's what those fellows must have meant when they called him a Dogtown pussy. He was weak as a kitten, all right.

The noise of Stanwood, puffing and muttering, startled him.

"I get here quick enough for you, little girl?" he asked as he pushed past Oliver and kicked the door open.

Tammy was sitting in her chair facing the door. Her face was gray, and her eyes narrowed at the sight of him.

"What the hell are you doing here?" she said. "Salted-down prick."

"Aw, now, Tammy, what harm I ever done you?"

"What did you bring this horse's ass here for?" She glared at Oliver. "You fetch this sack of shit here to kill me?"

Oliver slinked over to the wall and looked at the floor, frightened that Tammy had somehow divined his thoughts.

"Now, Tammy," Stanwood soothed, "he came to me 'cause Hodgkins is away. Oliver's just looking after his aunt Tam, ain'tcha, boy?

"I'll fix you up better than that clod of a carpenter," Stanwood said, as gently as a mother talking to a baby. "You know he's dumber than dirt. You and me, Tammy, we're the only smart ones left up here. You take another sup of that cider for courage. I'll have a pull too," he smiled, "if you don't mind."

Tammy's breathing slowed as Stanwood sweet-talked her. She was barely awake as it was, worn out by pain and dulled by drink. He poured her another and fed it to her, sip by sip, and then took her by the arm and led her, shuffling, to the table. He put his hands on her waist and lifted her, grasped her ankles and brought her legs around and up, tucking the skirt under, proper and respectful. He placed a hand beneath her head and lay her down, softly. She closed her eyes and fell right to snoring.

"Hodgkins does it on the chair," Oliver said softly.

"Well, that's just wrong," said Stanwood, who lifted the jug and swallowed, two, three, four times, before setting it down. "This is the way they do it in the navy." He uncoiled a length of rope and tied her wrists to the table legs.

"Hodgkins doesn't use rope."

"Well, I seen it done this way a hundred times," Stanwood snapped, dropping the show of concern. He looped another piece of rope around Tammy's arms and waist, binding her down.

"This way, your patient keeps real still. It's easier to get a grip like this and then I can do it faster. And faster is better, ain't it, Tammy."

She moaned softly.

"You'll see if this ain't the easiest time you ever had."

Stanwood reached into the burlap bag he'd brought and withdrew a mallet and a six-inch wooden wedge. "Open up now," he whispered.

Tammy dropped her jaw.

Oliver recalled how Hodgkins would take a good five minutes poking around at the gum before he pulled, loosening the tooth before he tapped or yanked at all. But Stanwood didn't seem to have time for that and set the wedge right up against the raw-looking line between tooth and flesh. Then, as he raised his mallet, he glanced over at Oliver, winked, moved the wedge to the center of the tooth, tipped it up rather than down, and landed a hard blow that cracked it in two, splitting what was left all the way to the gum.

Tammy whinnied in pain.

"Stubborn son-of-a-bitch." Stanwood moved to the other side of the table and said, "That 'un don't want to let go just yet. I'll just try the other." He put the wedge smack at the center of the left tooth and broke that across, too.

By then, Tammy's eyes showed all their whites and she started to struggle against the rope. But Stanwood put his hands on her shoulders, held her down, and started bellowing in her face, "Where's the gold, you old bag? Where's that money?"

Tammy thrashed her head from side to side.

"I know you got it here somewhere. Everyone knows you got it. You give it to me or I'm going to let you bleed to death. So help me God, you tell me where you keep it or . . ."

Tammy couldn't speak even if she wanted to; she could hardly breathe for the blood in the back of her throat. But Stanwood took her head between his hands and started banging it on the table. "You give me that money or so help me, I'll kill you. I'll do it, you know, you stinking, ugly, hateful old hag. So help me."

Oliver backed up against the wall, unable to speak. Tammy would kill him for bringing Stanwood. And if Stanwood killed her, God wouldn't let him off. He had not only wished for this, he had gone and brought it down on her.

Stanwood was slapping Tammy now, hitting her with an open hand, back and forth, one cheek and the other, a malicious grin on his face. Oliver could see that he was enjoying himself, and it made his stomach turn. He bolted outside: it's the next ship out for me, he decided. No turning back.

But his shoe caught on a rock, and he fell face first, cutting his chin and knocking the wind out of him. He lay panting while Stanwood bellowed more threats and curses. It took a moment before Oliver made out the other sound coming from the house. As he got to his feet, he recognized the sobbing of a woman, hopeless, in fear for her life.

He stumbled to the woodpile and grabbed the ax.

The house was a mess. Stanwood had knocked the kettle and pots out of the fireplace and overturned everything else, hunting for money or, failing that, something more to drink. Tammy had managed to get loose and was crouched below the table, her dress spattered with blackening blood. Her eyes were wild and her mouth leaked bright red spots onto the floor.

Having found nothing resembling a treasure yet, Stanwood turned back to see if he could beat some clue out of Tammy. But she scuttled farther under the table and he stumbled trying to get her. If Stanwood hadn't been so drunk, Tammy would have been dead for sure.

"Get out," Oliver screamed as he lowered the flat of the ax across Stanwood's back with a blow that brought him to his knees.

Oliver stood over him, the ax raised high. "Get out or I'll kill you."

Stanwood peered up at him. "Good thing you're such a little girl."

Oliver brought the blade down hard but it caught the edge of the table and stuck there; Stanwood rolled away on the floor and snickered at the miss.

"You're down," Oliver screamed as he yanked the blade out of the table. "You're on the floor, you bastard. You're down and drunk and I'm standing here with an ax."

Stanwood smiled and slowly put his hands up. "No need to go off on me, boy," he said in a singsong voice that mocked his own apology. "I was just having some fun. You can't blame me, can you? She's got it coming, ain't she?" As he pulled himself to his feet, Oliver made ready to swing the ax roundhouse if he had to.

Then Stanwood changed his tone. "Why don't you let me put her out of her misery," he offered, as though it were the only reasonable course. "You weren't even here. Why not?"

"I'll kill you," Tammy croaked, but her words sent her into a bloody coughing fit.

"She don't have to kill you," Oliver said and raised the ax again. "If you don't get out of here I'll do it."

Stanwood, finally seeing that he wasn't going to get his way, shrugged and staggered out of the dim house into the light of a lovely spring afternoon.

Tammy held her throbbing face between bloody hands while her shoulders shuddered in uncontrollable fits.

"I'm going for Easter," said Oliver.

She shook her head. "No. You do it. You got to finish it. You."

Having created this nightmare, Oliver felt he had no choice but to obey. He dragged a chair to the wall and helped Tammy into it, tipping her head back for support as he'd seen Hodgkins do it. He felt like he was moving through water, slow and heavy, as he picked up Stanwood's bloody wedge and mallet. Both the teeth were shattered, but the left one was hanging loose, so he went for it first. With one careful blow, he got it free.

Tammy yelped, but didn't move.

The other tooth wasn't so cooperative. Part of it fell out after a light blow, but the other half stuck. The first tap didn't budge it, but when he struck a little harder, Tammy screamed.

"I'm going for Easter," he said.

Tammy spit out a mouthful of blood, shook her head, and pointed at him.

Oliver moved her head back again, tilted Tammy's chin as high as he could, placed the wedge at a sharper angle, and brought the mallet down as hard as he could. What was left of the tooth fell out in a crimson torrent. Tammy's eyes rolled back and she slumped over in a dead faint.

The mixed smell of blood, liquor, and sweat became unbearable and Oliver hardly had time to turn his head before his stomach rose up. Heaving and coughing, Oliver lay Tammy on the floor and turned her on her side so that she would not drown in her own blood. He tore strips from his ruined shirt and packed pieces into her mouth. He dragged himself to his feet, feeling suddenly like a very old man. And then he ran.

❖

Tammy woke up two days later, in her own bed, wearing a clean nightdress, with barely a trace of blood beneath her fingernails. The gaping sockets in her mouth had been packed with cobwebs and sealed with wax. Easter Carter sat nearby, smoking a pipe; Oliver had taken his blanket and disappeared into the woods.

The whole place smelled wet. The floor had been washed with scalding water, as had the table and chairs. A chilly rain held the damp inside as Tammy dozed on and off for a solid week. She woke up when Judy arrived with broth and kept her eyes open, watching her and Easter as they chatted, distracting her from the ache and smell of her wounded mouth.

The freshest gossip was about Polly Boynton's new widowhood. Word was Boynton had drowned falling out of his dinghy while fishing for supper. He'd been drinking, of course, and now Polly was back with her father in Dogtown. The girl was said to be weeping night and day.

"She must have loved him," said Judy.

"I don't know about that," said Easter. "Boynton was a drunk and died a drunk's death. I don't know why pretty Polly would be sorrowing over that."

❖

Tammy turned down Easter's offer of gin, and she never drank anything stronger than tea for the rest of her life. She never forgave Oliver for bringing Stanwood into her house. Nor was the true story of her toothache ever wholly known, not even to Easter, who nursed Tammy through her recovery.

Stanwood took his version of Tammy's toothache from tavern to tavern. Leaning his chair back on two legs, he turned it into one of his best yarns ever. Stanwood claimed that he pulled both the teeth neat and clean. "I'm thinking of going into the business," he said. "Set myself up as a dentist. Make some real money."

But if only his friends could have been there to see how he pretended to stop when the job was half done! And how the old witch turned all womanish and carried on weeping and wailing. "She's not near as tough as she pretends."

Stanwood enjoyed many a free pint in exchange for that story. The men slapped their knees whenever he described Tammy's eyes rolling around in her head, cussing him out, then weeping and begging, scared for no reason. It was sweet revenge to imagine her thus repaid for all the shakedowns and shaming she'd done them through the years.

The story that passed over the teacups lacked some of the vivid, bloody details, but there wasn't much pity for Tammy among the ladies, either. They shared a shiver of satisfaction over the comeuppance of Cape Ann's most poisonous gossip, before smoothly turning the conversation to the subject of teeth, and whose were false, and whose were rotting, and whether powdered charcoal or burnt bread made a better dentrifice.

Strange Sightings

THE SETTLEMENT of Dogtown was more and more like a cracked pitcher. In the three years following Abraham Wharf's death, the village leaked life at a steady pace: Mary Lurvey passed away, as did Granny Day and a few other unmourned widows. Hannah Stanwood married and moved into town.

Meanwhile, Oliver built himself a lean-to on the side of Tammy's house, where he slept better for the wall between him and his only living relation. Judy Rhines's hair turned gray while Easter went entirely bald under her cap. None of these small details—not even the deaths—got much notice in Gloucester, which had no need of such weak beer when there were far more intoxicating stories about indiscreet young ladies, foreclosures, and barroom brawls.

But the summer of 1817 saw Dogtown's stock rise briefly, at least in terms of gossip, thanks to a strange convergence of unusual sightings and odd visitations. Judy spotted a black swan in Goose Cove, and within a week John Wharf plowed up a stone that looked exactly like a rabbit. Oliver Younger was clamming on the beach near Wheeler's Point when he came across a huge pile of shells and ashes from a driftwood fire, prompting talk of an Indian decampment. Black Ruth made a rare appearance in town, too.

But chatter over these things and virtually everything else came to a halt with the sighting of a serpent in Gloucester Harbor.

Easter didn't believe it at first. A twisted ankle and a string of rainy days had kept her from hearing it sooner. "You're having fun with a poor cripple!" she said, her ankle propped on the bench and wrapped in an old tea towel.

"It seems to be true," said Judy Rhines, who'd brought the news along with a jar of preserves. "More people say they've seen it every day." Boats were out hunting the beast with spyglasses, hooks, and nets at the ready. A fellow named Cheever Felch had come up from Boston and was making a name for himself, claiming that the monster was 100 feet in length and dark brown in color, with white markings at the throat.

Judy had overheard Reverend Felch herself. A man of the church and a self-taught naturalist, he'd been repeating his story to a young Boston newspaperman, who scribbled it down amid a crowd of jostling boys on Front Street. A group of town ladies had been drawn to the scene, too. Judy had thought them lovely in their straw bonnets and white cotton summer frocks, freshly pressed and spotless. Soft Moroccan slippers peeked out from beneath their clean hems, prompting her to pull at her gray skirt to hide the unfashionably pointed brogans on her feet.

"You sure it wasn't a whale?" Easter said. "Sometimes those whales can fool you."

"It weren't no whale," said Ruth, who'd been standing just outside the door, listening to Judy's report. Judy jumped up from her seat, startled at the African woman's sudden appearance. Easter smiled, "You sure you ain't making this up for fun? You seen it?"

"I seen it," said Ruth. "Longer and thinner, like a kind of snake, but a snake the like of which you didn't see before." Ruth's speech was marked by extra syllables in the most unlikely words, so that "snake" came out sounding like *sa-nake*, echoing a voice from her past.

"In Ah-frica, they see such quite common," Ruth went on.

"You don't say?" Judy said, trying not to sound like she was bursting with questions for the last black woman on Cape Ann. When Ruth had arrived and the secret of her sex had been revealed, people had stared and debated the weird and oddly threatening presence of an African woman who wore men's clothing, took a man's name, and practiced a man's trade. But over the years, her reticence had worn down all objections so that eventually the minor discrepancy of "John Woodman's" gender was more or less forgotten.

"I thought you came from Rhode Island," Judy said, studying Ruth's long, impassive face and trying to catch her downcast eye.

"African woman there, she told it to me. She remembered things from over there, like horses with necks to the treetops and birds with colors like a rainbow. Sea creatures like the size of a house. But no whales. She never seen no whales before America."

It was the longest speech either Judy or Easter had ever heard her deliver. Easter grinned and said, "Well, well, well."

Embarrassed, Ruth hurried up the narrow stairs, ducking her head on the way up. Judy realized she'd never once seen Ruth sit down, not in Easter's house or anywhere else.

Judy dropped her voice. "She ever eat with you?"

"Mostly not. She takes it outside or upstairs," Easter said. "When I had the miseries last winter and we got snowed in, she did me a load of favors. Hauled water and brought in a clutch of eggs for supper. Ruined a nice piece of ham, though. She put enough pepper on the meat to make it get up and gallop right out of the pan. It was good of her, all the same."

"You never did tell me how she came to be here from Narragansett," said Judy.

"Well, I ain't sure I got the whole story to tell."

Ruth listened to their conversation from her pallet above stairs. The eaves seemed to collect words and drop them directly into her ears, so she didn't miss a whisper that was spoken below. She'd heard all manner of secrets and scandals confided in that parlor, and she'd learned that Easter repeated nothing except what was light and harmless, and already well-known.

Mimba had been right about white people. The best thing was to treat them like ghosts and cannibals, not to be trusted. But sometimes, a white ghost would look at you straight on, with a full smile, eye to eye. The smile of the eye was the secret, Mimba had taught her. You had to be careful always, but every now and again you could act as though they had souls, too. Easter was one like that.

⁘

Easter hadn't been fooled by Ruth's clothes, not from the moment, fourteen summers back, when she first walked up the path. But Easter had been just about the only one.

Ruth was surprised by how easy it had been to escape suspicion. During the long journey from Rhode Island, over country roads and through city streets, no one noticed the woman's face between the coat and the cap. The breeches alone would have been disguise enough.

When she first arrived in Gloucester, Ruth had asked a boy how to get to Brimfield farm. Following his directions, she'd taken an old walled road, past weedy fields and stunted trees and through a swamp that seemed to suck the color out of the sky and the song out of the birds. The air was so hot and thick, Ruth felt like she'd stepped into an oven. A parched, abandoned landscape where lightning or carelessness had scorched the trees and only the grasses seemed confident of the future, it was the most desolate place she'd ever seen.

Ruth set down her heavy sack and turned to study the stone walls that lined either side of the road. She bent over and, starting from the ground, ran her hands up and over the big, two-man stones, then past the smaller cobbles nearer the top. All of it had been placed hither thither, without thought as to how the whole would last. Ruth frowned at the shoddiness of the work: without a trench, it would all tumble into ruin sooner rather than later. Of course, these were mere property lines, little more than rubbish heaps where some farmer had tossed up the fieldstones he'd plowed out before planting rows of corn and rutabaga, though rocks were by far the most reliable crop in those craggy parts.

Across the road, another effort showed the difference between one man and the next. The flat capping stones on top would keep rain and snow from loosening the wall below. Much better, Ruth thought, though she disagreed with his placement of one handsome rock, pale with black seams, almost like stitching on a quilt. He'd laid it too near the ground, which was, to her eye, a waste.

It would be good to work again, Ruth thought. The two vertical lines between her eyes eased as she bent down to reach for a smooth, white, egg-shaped pebble that seemed out of place in the dust. But as she began to straighten up, the hairs at the back of Ruth's cropped head stood up: someone was nearby. She gripped the stone, ready to throw it, ready to run. With both fists clenched tightly, she turned, but found no enemy; only a brown dog of middling size.

He stood in the middle of the road, sniffing in her direction. Ruth remained braced for attack, but the cur stayed where he was, his eyes on hers. After a moment, he cocked his head to one side, and Ruth couldn't help but smile.

The dog shook himself from one end to the other, stretched his front legs out in a long bow, sneezed, and set off up the path. The dancing tan flags on his haunches seemed to invite her to follow. Ruth shouldered her burlap bag and trailed after him to a rambling two-story house. Though weather-battered and worn, it showed signs of life, with squash and beans growing helter-skelter, Indian-style, on either side of the open door into which the dog had disappeared. The next moment, a child wearing an outsize cap appeared at the threshold and wiped her hands on her apron, just like a grown woman. As she drew closer, Ruth realized it was a woman after all. And not a young one either, though she was barely more than four feet tall.

"I'm Easter Carter," she said. "And what might I call you?"

"John Woodman."

Easter put her hands on her hips. "Come, come. That's a man's name. You got a woman's name?"

"Ruth," she said and frowned. She'd meant to leave that name behind for good.

"Whither goest thou?" said Easter, grinning at her own joke.

Ruth made no reply.

"What brings you up this way, dearie?"

"I came to see Brimfield farm."

Easter cocked her head to one side, a perfect imitation of the dog in the road. "Don't see why. The Brimfields all died or moved away years ago. The fields were near the coast. Looks like someone sent you on a goose chase, dearie. You should have walked Washington Street to get there. You're in Dogtown now."

Ruth set down her sack. It had been two days since she'd slept and nearly as long since she'd eaten. A girl's high giggle issued out the door, and a man's laugh rumbled out after it. Ruth took a step back.

"I get the young ones up here for a good time," Easter said. "I got no lodgings for strange men, though." Then she winked as though they were sharing a joke.

Ruth had the feeling that the odd little woman was asking her a question, though she wasn't quite sure what it was.

"Can you pay for room and board?" Easter asked.

Ruth pulled out her last coin and pointed at a pile of rocks that had once been a garden wall. "I can fix that."

"I suppose you can," Easter said, glancing at Ruth's hardened hands. "But I got nothing worth keeping inside a wall, and I don't want to keep no one out, so that's no use to me."

"My walls hold for good," Ruth said.

"Most folks do their own fencing round here," said Easter. "But there's a cover for every pot, I always say. We'll just have to see what cover fits yours, won't we?" Easter stepped forward and reached for the burlap.

Ruth grabbed the bag and turned her glance to the ground to hide the anger on her face. Easter laughed. "I ain't stealing your pretties." Then she looked up and smiled right into Ruth's eyes. "You come with me. I got room upstairs, and I sure could use a man around the house." That set her to chuckling again.

Ruth kept her eyes on the tiny woman's back as they walked inside, past the couple dimly visible in a corner of the parlor, and up a flight of stairs to a long attic room that was too low for Ruth to stand up in. Sunlight filtered through spaces between the timbers and mouse droppings littered the floor. Still, it was as big as the whole house, and it smelled of pine.

Easter went back downstairs to her guests, leaving Ruth to shake her head. She felt as if she'd walked into one of the legends that Mimba used to tell by the fire, though in those stories characters like Easter always turned out to be flesh-eating witches, and Ruth was certain that Easter was harmless.

Within a week, Ruth had scrubbed the floor of her aerie with sand. She mixed ground clamshells with clay to caulk the ceiling and stuffed her sack with sweet straw for a pillow. Easter crept up the steps when Ruth went out, curious to see what all the hauling and scuffling overhead had been about, and found that the African had hung bunches of sedge and wild peppermint to dry from the rafters. She'd woven a floor mat from river reeds.

"Right cozy," she told Judy, who wondered if her friend hadn't acted hastily in inviting such a peculiar stranger to live in her house.

Easter did not notice the white, oval-shaped stones in the four corners of her attic, set out to protect the house against evil spirits. Ruth polished and repositioned them from season to season, and she checked them whenever there was a bad luck sign, like an owl calling during daylight or a night when a full moon was swallowed by its dark twin. On the day she saw the sea serpent breach and dive into the dark waters of the harbor, she moved the stones as close to the walls as they'd go without touching.

Ruth had never seen a worse or clearer omen of coming evil, and it had rattled her bad enough that she'd gone and flapped her gums, like a foolish old woman, in front of Easter and Judy Rhines. She wondered if Judy would pass her words around; no doubt she'd make something of the way that Ruth, silent as a post most of the day, had rattled on.

Easter's good opinion of Judy counted for something in Ruth's eyes, but she knew how much the woman liked to chew over the workings of other people's hearts. From her pallet, she'd heard Judy tease apart the motives and morals of everyone who crossed her path; not maliciously, but with an avid attention that Ruth found unsettling.

She lay back and listened to Judy tell about all the young boys camped on the beaches to catch a glimpse of the sea monster, and how some of the preachers were using it as an example of the devil's power. Finally they turned to other topics, laughing about a crop of new babies born to the residents around Sandy Bay on the northeastern limits of Cape Ann. Exactly nine months before, the area had been pounded by a three-day storm that kept fishermen ashore and farmers indoors. Ruth knew those hamlets well, having recently built a large paddock there for Tom Fletcher, who had decided he'd try breeding horses for the rich men of Cape Ann. He'd given up on farming, he said. There was no money to be made from a small place like his anymore.

⟡

Fletcher was the only white man who had ever shaken Ruth's hand, and the first person on Cape Ann to hire her on as a stonemason. She'd spent her first years there walking from one farm to the next, offering to build or mend any kind of wall, for a pittance or even in trade for food. But no one would take her on to haul rocks, much less build. Money was scarce then, and when sugar and coffee are luxuries, people don't pay for any work that can wait. Ruth was told no with shrugs, stares, and plain rudeness. She paid Easter for her lodgings with fish and berries, and laid a handsome path to the door, just for the practice.

Fletcher had said yes only as a last resort. He'd hurt himself trying to get a fallen tree off the fence around his cornfield: With sheep in the next pasture, harvesting about to begin, the neighbors busy with their own farms, and a bad back, he hired Ruth at fifty cents a day to finish clearing the tree and mending the wall. It was robbery, but Ruth threw herself into the job with such energy and skill that Fletcher was embarrassed at what he'd paid and promised to use her again.

In fact, Ruth had been ashamed of the work she'd done for him, which seemed clumsy and awkward to her. Mending a wall is harder than building one, especially one piled up as a slag heap for the nuisance of rocks plowed up, year after year. And these refuse rocks had presented her with a new kind of trial, for Ruth had learned her craft on Rhode Island schist, a soft stone that broke into two-inch slabs and stacked up neat as slices of bread. Granite was much harder and crotchety, and she'd bruised her fingers and blackened her nails as she hurried to master it. After a few bad days, she slowed down, remembering to let the stone call the tune for the heavy dance of lifting and dropping.

The night she finished Fletcher's wall, Ruth dreamed about the crisp click of granite hitting granite, and she woke up longing to build something else. But there was nothing for many months, leaving her little to do but dig clams and pick rose hips for Easter, and mend whatever she could to keep the house from falling down.

Ruth's fortunes rose when the wife of the minister at Fourth Parish at Riverview sent word that she wished a pen for a newly plowed vegetable garden beside the parsonage. As soon as the enthusiastic Mrs. Pembrooke heard that the mysterious female stonemason called John Woodman had not stepped foot in a church since arriving in Cape Ann, she made it her mission to save the African's immortal soul. Ruth, whose hands itched at the prospect of working on a project of her own, quickly agreed to the price offered by the pallid, gap-toothed woman.

As she walked the boundary of the garden, measuring it heel-to-toe, Ruth promised herself that she'd be more patient than she had been at Fletcher's. She would consider every stone before lifting it; for as she'd been taught, only a child or a fool picked up the same rock twice.

Ruth decided she would make a double wall, though it was hardly necessary to fashion anything so sturdy for the purpose. But she needed the challenge and liked the fact that it would take longer, as the days weighed heavily when she had no work.

Even the drudgery of digging the foundation delighted her, and Mrs. Pembrooke thought she detected the hint of a smile as the African knelt to carve a trench and place the heavy, flat rocks below-ground. Ruth set the ground stones an inch apart for drainage, with enough slag in between to make an even base.

While she was on her knees, Ruth hit upon the idea of building from found stone only and decided she would touch neither the stone feathers nor her sharp stone points to cut and shape. She would use nothing but her hands and her eyes.

No chocks or shims, either—those little bits and pieces that balance the bigger ones. Only stone on stone, two upon one, one upon two.

Ruth held her breath as she placed the first stones aboveground, since each of those carried consequences. After that, the wall would tell her what was needed next. As the wall grew, it filled her mind with the particular shapes it called for. Her head was full of holes, she realized, and nearly laughed at the idea.

She walked with downcast eyes, her head swiveling left to right and back again, putting Mrs. Pembrooke in mind of a lighthouse as she watched Ruth arrive one morning, carrying what looked like a man's skull under her arm.

On fine days, the parson's wife would spend several hours near Ruth, reading aloud from the Bible. Her student tried to ignore the breathy babble, and whenever the lady returned to her house, Ruth gave silent thanks and tuned her ear to the sound of stone dropping into place, each granite kiss creating a permanent home, two upon one, one upon two.

In her dreams, the stones all fell effortlessly, landing with a satisfied *tock*.

❖

When the wall was finished, Mrs. Pembrooke handed Ruth five dollars and placed a hand on her sleeve. "I trust I'll see you at church," she said. "Soon. As we discussed."

Ruth nodded, wondering what the pale little woman was talking about. Back in her room, she considered the prospect of the empty days ahead and felt a dark fogbank gather around her.

As it turned out, Mrs. Pembrooke did become a source of salvation for Ruth, though not of the sort she'd intended. A distant cousin of hers, a wealthy matron in town, was charmed by the lovely wall and declared that she must have one just like it. She sent word through Easter that she wished to hire the mason for her Gloucester garden, one of the largest in town, and made no objection when Easter quoted a price four times higher than what the clergyman's wife had paid.

Ruth finished that wall in half the time, though it was more than twice the length, using all her tools, chocks, and every stone that came easily to hand. It turned out to be a lovely piece of work, and its proud owner made all her guests admire the clever way that Ruth had set a rosy-hued stone near her pink rosebush, and how care was taken to set off the tansy with a showing of green-tinged granite. With such an endorsement, several of her friends decided that they required similarly cunning masonry in their gardens, and Ruth had work waiting for her, months ahead.

The women liked having her in their gardens, not only for the quality of Ruth's creations, but also for the mystery of her person. Africans had become almost as rare as pumpkin flowers in May, and it was a novelty having one so close at hand. A black woman in trousers, as strong as a man, was an oddity of the highest order.

Children tried to imitate her odd accent, young girls wondered if she had any knowledge of the spirit world, and people with abolitionist leanings guessed at lurid hardships that must have attended her life to the south. A few of the braver ladies tried to engage her in conversation, but the African barely said "thank you" for the draughts of water and the occasional biscuit she was offered. Her face betrayed no gratitude or impatience, nor anything else for that matter, and eventually, people stopped trying to peek behind the stolid mask she presented to the world. Soon enough, Ruth was as unremarkable as any other servant, and she began to feel just as invisible as them.

That changed on the day a roughly dressed young stranger stopped to watch her work. He stared for a good half hour until the mistress of the house came out and asked him to state his business.

"That nigger looks like a runaway I heard about in Virginia," he drawled, loud enough for Ruth to hear.

"This person is not a slave," said Martha Cook.

"I suppose you can prove that, Mistress?" he said, bold as a fox.

Martha's voice grew icy. "Sir, if you are calling me a liar in my own home, I shall thank you for your name and lodgings so that my husband, Judge Cook, can call upon you to settle the matter."

The blackguard removed his cap and backed off, sullenly begging her pardon even as he glared daggers at Ruth, watching his cash bounty slip away.

Ruth kept her head down during this exchange, but after she'd finished Mrs. Cook's wall, she accepted no more assignments in Gloucester and eked out a small living up-country, repairing pasture walls and building animal pounds.

But when Martha Cook requested that she return to extend her wall a little, Ruth agreed. As much as she dreaded returning to town and the feeling of pale eyes on her skin, she could not deny the lady who had defended her against a bounty hunter. It was on the last day of that job that Ruth caught a glimpse of the sea serpent that had set all tongues to wagging.

Back in Easter's parlor, the debate raged: Was it real or not? A fish or a fish story? A harbinger of the end of days? Everyone who walked across Easter's threshold announced an opinion, one way or another. Everyone, except for one particular fellow who came knocking early one morning, when no one else was about.

Most of Easter's visitors were spirited boys and girls from town, or sailors wishing to flee the sight and smell of water before shipping out again. The summer usually fetched up a small assortment of eccentrics, too: Englishmen in search of the unsullied American wilderness, or awkward fellows from Boston and New York who made the trek carrying sketchpads, paint boxes, or leather-bound notebooks.

But Easter had never had a guest like this one. He wore the drab, cassimere wool coat favored by traditional Quakers, though his white silk stockings were grimy from the road and the silver buckles on his shoes were coated with dust. Doffing a large flat-brimmed hat, he revealed a head of white curls stuck to a high damp forehead. "Pardon the intrusion, Mistress," he said. "But may I trouble thee for a drink of water?"

"No trouble, dearie," Easter said, tickled to be addressed so biblically. She gestured for him to follow her inside, limping on her still-sore ankle. "Take a seat. I'm Easter Carter and this is my place. You're welcome to a draught of ale if you're of a mind."

"No, thank thee. Water will be ample blessing," he said, blinking at the indoor dimness. He drained Easter's cup and then mopped his face with a large handkerchief. "But perhaps thee could be kind enough to provide me with guidance. I am in search of the home of Abraham Wharf who was married to Anne Wharf?"

Easter leaned forward. "You knew the Wharf family, did you?"

He nodded. "The family did me a good turn long ago, and since I find myself nearby, I thought to stop and pay my respects."

"Well, Abraham passed some three years back," Easter said.

"God's will be done," the visitor said, gravely. "And Mrs. Wharf?"

"Twenty-three years dead."

"So young!" he cried.

"A canker in her breast."

"A terrible thing," he said. "Foolish of me to imagine that she might still be among the living."

"Abraham buried her behind the house," Easter said. "Scandalized the minister who wanted to plant her in sanctified ground. But Abraham had to keep her close."

"His angel," said the stranger.

"That's what Abraham called her, all right," she nodded.

"Even so, I should like to pay my respects, but I seem to have lost the way. Would thee be so good as to set me on the right path?"

"I warn you that there ain't much left to see up there," said Easter. "But if you're set on it, just follow the road the way you were headed till you get to a hard bend to the right, Mr.—" Easter paused. "You ain't told me your name!"

A momentary panic passed over his face. "It's Mr. Henry," he stammered and got to his feet. "Thee have been a gracious hostess, Mistress Carter."

"Nobody calls me anything but Easter, dearie. Stop by on your way back. I hope to have something stewing by then."

"Good day, Mistress Carter," he said. "God bless thee."

Above stairs, Ruth lay on her bed. She had no work that day, which was just as well since her back ached all the way down both legs. She pocketed a long, narrow iron chisel, winced her way down the stairs, and was gone before Easter had a chance to call out to her.

She hurried until she got the black coat in her sight, then kept a safe distance as the man made his way to the old Wharf place. Ruth watched him wander the tall grass until he found the hole that had been the cellar. He removed his hat before he stepped down, as though there were still a difference between inside and out. Turning slowly, he shook his head and frowned.

After a few minutes of this, he stepped out of the hollow, replaced his hat, and began circling the overgrown boundaries of the house, thrashing at weeds and brambles with a stick until he found what he was looking for. He crouched and set to pulling the grass and saplings away from a thin slab of a headstone. He ran his fingers across a name still visible, clasped his hands, and bowed his head.

Ruth bit at the inside of her cheeks as she watched the Quaker finish clearing the grave. He took a small packet from his breast pocket, laid it near the marker, and piled some stones on top of it. Then he stood, brushed himself off, and walked away.

As soon as he was out of sight, Ruth sprang from her hiding place and ran to Anne Wharf's grave. She tore the small cairn apart, tossing the stones aside like a digging dog, to reveal a square of brown paper, no more than three inches across. Unfolding it slowly and carefully, she found a twisted scrap of cloth, a lock of crisp, black hair, and a narrow silver band. Ruth stared at the three oddments for a long moment before replacing them in their paper, pocketing them, and rushing after the Quaker.

He was nearly to the Commons Road, but instead of heading back toward the harbor, he forged down an overgrown trail that was known only to locals. Ruth knew who she was following now, and where he was going.

Brimfield's pasture overlooked blue water on three sides, with views of 'Squam River, Goose Cove, and Mill River. But the Quaker did not stop to admire the sparkling scene. With his head down, as though he were leaning into a strong wind, he made straight for a large, flat boulder, where he finally stopped.

A loud groan startled Ruth, who watched as he commenced shaking his head back and forth, faster and faster, from side to side until his hat fell from his head and another moan escaped him. He pulled his shirt open and beat at his chest with clenched fists, hand over hand, until red marks blossomed on the pale flesh.

A shudder ran through Ruth and released her from her hiding place. She sprang out and ran up behind him, taking him unaware. Grabbing his long hair with one hand, she placed the sharp edge of her chisel against his throat and said, "Murderer."

He gasped and struggled so that he pricked himself against the blade. At that, he dropped his hands and whispered, "Heavenly Father, Thy will be done."

"Who are you?" Ruth demanded, her voice a low growl.

"If you accuse me of murder, you must know," said Henry Brim-field, dropping polite address and speaking to his attacker as he would to a horse. He pointed to the great, tablelike boulder. "That is where I found her, weak and bleeding."

"You *found* her?" said Ruth, pulling his head back farther still. The stranger's eyes were the color of water.

"You must think that I killed her. They all did. They believed that I was the father of the child, too. But I swear upon my eternal soul that it was not me. I did not kill the girl, nor did I . . . nor was that child mine."

Her lips at his ear, she said, "Liar."

"My father was the guilty one," Brimfield said. "I have spent my life trying to puzzle out what happened here, how it came to mur-der. I have rehearsed it a hundred times and it must have been that she threatened to reveal him.

"Pride was my father's greatest sin," he said, a brittle bitterness in his voice. "He treasured his good name above heaven itself, and if she would not swear to keep his secret, he might well have traded his soul for his reputation."

"You were there."

"It was my first day home from Harvard," he said, rushing to complete his confession. "I was not yet one-and-twenty, a new physi-cian, like my father. I hurried here, where I knew she pastured the cows. I wanted only to declare my love for her. Though now I doubt if it was love at all, or only lust.

"This is where I found her," he said, glancing over at the boulder. "The dueling sword—my sword—thick with her blood."

"Dead?" Ruth demanded.

"Not quite," said Brimfield. "Doomed. She begged me to save the child and once she died, I opened the womb with the sword that killed her and delivered my father's bastard, my half-sister. No Greek drama was ever more perverse."

Ruth changed her grasp on Brimfield, twisting his arm behind him and putting the chisel between his shoulders. "Why did you come back?"

Brimfield closed his eyes. "I am old," he said. "This memory has haunted me, and I hoped, well, if I might have spoken with Mrs. Wharf, there might have been some peace. But she is gone. Your vengeance is proof that my guilt is still current, hereabouts. But the murderer is gone, I tell you. Died in his own feather bed, eighty-seven years old, though there will be no repose for him in hell."

Sure the mortal blow would follow next, Brimfield struggled to keep his bowels within him. But the moments passed without any change in his attacker's grasp.

"What of the baby?" Ruth whispered, at last.

"Mistress Wharf warmed it in her own shawl and gave it a cloth teat. She dressed me in her son's coat and said to take the poor creature to her cousins in Providence. From there I went on to their brethren in Philadelphia, to the Society of Friends, where freeing the African has been my life's work."

Ruth heard the expectation of thanks in his voice and knew him for a fool.

But Brimfield sensed that something had changed; there was a loosening of the lock on his arm, and he no longer could feel the pressure of the blade on his back anymore. He changed his tone, speaking as he would to a child that might be coddled out of a bad temper. "I wanted to thank Anne Wharf," Brimfield said. "Without her, I might well have left Phoebe's child out in the woods, and for such a transgression I would have been doomed for eternity."

Ruth discovered that she could not draw a full breath as he continued. "I am convinced beyond argument that the African is endowed with a God-given soul. I will give Mistress Wharf my thanks in heaven."

Sweat beaded on her face and the chisel fell from her fingers.

Hearing the thud, Brimfield peeked behind him and saw the crude iron weapon on the ground; the black man's eyes were squeezed shut. At that, Brimfield started to tiptoe away, slowly, tense as a cat. As soon as he had reached the trees, he broke into an awkward gallop and did not stop until he saw ships in the harbor.

Blood pounded in Ruth's ears. She had never felt weaker or more confused. This was the moment she'd been living for, but the only thought she could muster was that her mother had not been Phyllis, as she'd been told, but Phoebe.

The only time she'd ever heard that name before was from Mimba. "The African names came with the mothers," she said. "Cato is from Keta. Phoebe is from Phibbi. Most of them here don't remember. The mothers be dead. But I remember."

"Phoebe," Ruth whispered. "Phoebe," as though Mimba were still there to hear. "Waking and dreaming, not big different," Mimba used to tell her. "Now-days and times-past, not so different."

❖

Brimfield had provided Ruth with one piece of the puzzle that had always eluded her. The slaying of Dr. Henry Brimfield's slave girl was an old tale, but such a juicy story that it was repeated whenever any murder was mentioned. When Gloucester had first discovered that the younger Brimfield had disappeared on the very night the corpse was discovered, covered in his coat, killed with his sword, the court of public opinion pronounced him guilty. That turned out to be the only form of justice ever meted out as Dr. Brimfield, the father, had friends in the law. No warrant was ever issued and no search ensued, a breach of fairness that remained a shocking and satisfying detail of the gruesome story. Long after the slave girl's name was forgotten (she was "the slave wench" or "Brimfield's girl"), the locals continued to tut-tut about the murder: "Respectable is as respectable does."

But of all the times Ruth had heard the tale repeated at Easter's hearth, there was never any mention of a baby. That knot was unraveled for her, but there were new mysteries now, and there was no way any of them would be solved.

She unfolded the paper packet again. The lock of hair was tied with a pink ribbon faded nearly white. Had he cut this from her head after she was dead? Did he use the saber that killed her to remove it as a souvenir?

The silver ring would not pass over the first knuckle of her littlest finger. Were her mother's fingers so small? Could a Yankee slave have owned such a thing? Was it a reward from her master, a gift from her mistress, a stolen secret? Did she wear it on her hand?

The twist of fabric was tight as a nut and hard, the size of a thimble. Ruth pried it open carefully, but there was nothing inside but a pattern of yellow flowers. She put the scrap to her nose, but it held no scent. What was this? Why had it been saved?

The questions buzzed like bees inside her head. She put her treasures away and laid her chisel on top of the boulder where her mother had perished. And then she walked down the steep slope to the water's edge.

Ruth turned her face to the south and started along the banks of the 'Squam River, putting one foot in front of the other along the muddy shore. She kept her eyes on the ground ahead of her, with no thought to where she was headed. She saw nothing of the lingering golden sunset nor did she notice the rise of a nearly full moon. She succeeded in forgetting herself altogether until she found herself in Gloucester Harbor. Ruth crouched under the wharfs and hid behind pilings, hurrying silently between shadows to avoid detection, running from the fouled water and greasy smells until she reached the quiet of Wonson Point.

From there, she scrambled over the Bass Rocks, trudged the white Good Harbor sand, and clattered across Pebblestone Beach.

From dry granite to slick granite, skirting low tide and soaking her boots at high tide, she let her legs make the case against death.

Only when she arrived at the farthest reach of Halibut Point did she stop and allow memory to have its way. Brimfield said he'd returned to Cape Ann to make peace with his past. She had come for the same reason, after all. And because of Mimba.

❖❖❖

The short, wiry, coal black woman had been Ruth's mother from the moment Ruth had appeared in the Prescotts' kitchen. Mimba pulled the frightened four-year-old onto her lap and kissed her on both cheeks. "You gonna be my dearest-dearest?" she whispered. "You gonna be Mimba's apple-sweetie?" Her words bore the stamp of the West Indies, where she'd learned housekeeping and English, but she never forgot the African names for "milk" and "home," for "honey" and "memory," which found their way into her stories.

Mimba was born to tell stories: old wives' tales from Africa and Barbados, gossip about whites and blacks alike, family histories of all five of the slaves on the Prescott plantation on Narragansett Bay, in Rhode Island's South County. Mimba told Ruth a story about her life, too, or as much of it as she could and would.

She always began the same way. "Your poor-dear mother was called Phyllis Brimfield, as I heard it, and she got a sad-sad story, because she didn't get to love you long-time like Mimba." Standing between Mimba's knees while her hair was brushed and braided, Ruth learned that her poor-dear mother had died giving her birth, "up there in the north, on a cold island with a lady name. There was a tall man fetched you to Mistress Naomi and Hiram Smith, Providence-way, and Mr. Hiram give you name of Ruth, to make honor on his wife, I heard."

It was their black servant, Nance, who'd done the work of caring for Ruth. The Smiths had set all of their slaves free, but Old Nance refused to go. She said her masters wanted to throw her out because she was too weak to lift the wash kettle. "She say they suck the marrow dry, and wants to throw the bone away.

"But then Old Nance passed on and them Smiths fostered you over to Queen Bernoon, that big-smart free African lady who sells oysters to eat."

Ruth stayed with Queen and her large family of daughters and sons-in-law and grandchildren. For three years, Ruth ate, slept, and worked among the Bernoon children, picking through oysters and clams as soon as she was big enough to stand. But after the smallpox sickened all the little ones save Ruth, Queen got a spooky feeling about the quiet foundling, so she sold her to a fellow named Cuff, a half-breed African-Indian peddler who claimed his wife was pining for a little girl.

"Cuff was a bad 'un," said Mimba. He took Ruth to Narragansett, where prices for slaves were higher and the law was distant. William Prescott bought the child for a large wheel of cheese and three silver dollars.

"You got a sad story, Ruth," Mimba said. "But not sad-sad. You here with me and Cato and all us together now. You have a happy-sad story. Best you can get in this life is happy-sad. But you always gotta remember your own mamma that birthed you. Even though you only got a crumb of her story, you still got to say her name out loud. You always honor your dead, else you get trouble from them, sure."

That story would keep Ruth awake at night; she had enough imagination to picture a sad-sad ending to her story, with her sold to some other master. The idea of a life without Mimba or Cato terrified her into nightmares, and Mimba finally stopped telling it to her. Meanwhile, Ruth did everything she could to ensure that she would never be parted from her Mimba. She was obedient, polite, and quick to learn the kitchen work from Mimba. She followed Cato into the fields and studied how he tended the cattle and fixed the long stone fences, too.

From the first, she preferred the outdoors to life in the house, where the white people kept her always on edge. Cato told her to be grateful for the kindness of owners who rarely struck them and had never sold anyone off. But she heard the false voices he and Mimba used when the master or mistress was near. And she knew that Mimba and Cato had jumped the broom in secret, so Prescott would not know they were husband and wife and hold the threat of separation against them.

But it wasn't the master who pulled them apart. Mimba died when Ruth was seventeen, and she cried all the tears she hadn't cried as a child. She refused to be separated from Cato after that, becoming what Mistress Prescott called "willful." She refused to stay in the kitchen with Patricia, the other female slave who could not remember Mimba's recipes as well as Ruth did. Master Prescott tried changing her mind with a switch; that didn't do it, and neither did a real whipping with a belt. After he threatened to sell her, one of the wheels on the buggy fell off as the family was driving to church, and the cows kept escaping their pen. When the parlor curtains caught fire before dinner one day, Prescott realized what he was up against and told his wife she'd have to make do without Ruth.

She moved into the barn with Cato, who taught her everything he knew about stones and masonry, and then he told her all the bad-sad stories that Mimba had kept him from repeating to their broody girl. Mimba had been the noon to Cato's midnight, and once she was gone, he recounted the bad-sad memories of his youth on a large Maryland plantation. And he told Ruth, "Your mamma didn't just die borning you." Cato whispered so that Mimba would not hear him from the other side. "She was killed by a white man. Murdered by her master in a cow pasture is the truth of it.

"I heard it from Queen Bernoon herself," said Cato. "I'm only telling you so you stay clear of the men. White men are worst, but the Africans ain't much better, like that Cuff who lied to Queen about wanting you when all he wanted was money.

"I didn't tell you before 'cause Mimba didn't want to break your heart," he said. The taste of her name in his mouth always set him to grieving. "I miss her first thing in the morning. I miss how she used to heat up milk for my tea. I miss her in the bed every night." Tears washed his cheeks. "I miss her on Sundays when we would sit together." Finally he missed Mimba so much, he walked into the ocean, his pockets filled with stones.

When they found his body on the beach, Ruth had been shocked by the gray shards and rough slag he'd used to weigh himself down. Cato had taught her to look at stones the way other people looked at flowers, beautiful and varied. How could he have gone to Mimba without bringing her something pretty? Smooth white eggs, or the striped, sparkling "coins" that were his favorite?

Once Cato was gone, Ruth cut off her hair, put on his trousers, and came inside the house only for food. Prescott let her be, not only because she was his most able worker but also because as the youngest of his slaves, she would be his last.

Word of emancipation had finally reached the Africans of the South County plantations. Ruth heard it in church, where the slaves were crowded into the narrow balcony called nigger heaven. "Newport is full of free Africans," someone behind her whispered. The man to Ruth's left leaned over her and said he heard that all the Rhode Island–born slaves could claim their freedom if they were twenty-one, but a woman on her right warned that the masters were fighting it one by one, arguing how this man was born somewhere else, or that girl was too young to count. Worst of all, you needed a paper to prove it, and what master was going to put it on paper?

The talk upstairs got so loud, the parson slapped his hand on the lectern to quiet the noise. Three times he pounded, but it did no good. Ruth saw proof that the news was true from the looks on the upturned white faces; some of them seemed scared, some sad, all of them plainly unsettled.

That night, Ruth watched the full March moon rise over the bay and felt herself grow lighter. Until that morning, being a slave had seemed a lot like being a woman: something you got born into, hardships and all. Ruth knew that she was smarter than her mistress and that she could run the plantation better than her master. But now, the notion that they owned her was no longer merely cruel—it had always seemed cruel. Now, it was nonsense. The Prescotts might as well claim to own the sea or the sky as Ruth or anybody else.

She hugged her knees to her chest and decided to leave as soon as the traveling got easier. She would head north to Cape Ann and visit her mother's grave. Mimba used to sorrow over the way her own mamma's bones were all the way across the sea in Africa, and she fretted that no one there would go to cheer her spirit with food and conversation. Surely a murdered mother needed more consolation than most. Ruth knew that Mimba would have approved her plan, even though it meant her own grave would be lonely. She took a little comfort knowing that Mimba had Cato right next to her.

On a moonless May night, Ruth put Cato's extra clothes into an old burlap sack, along with Prescott's best stone chisels, wedges, and his good mallet. She left one of the four silver dollars she'd found sewed into the corners of Cato's mattress by way of payment and never looked back.

She walked until dawn, when an old African man in a buggy stopped and offered her a ride. There was a paper pinned to his shirt; he pointed to it. "Says I own myself and this wagon and no one can take me." Ruth slept in hayricks by day and traveled by night, eating whatever she could find, wearing out her shoes on the way to Cape Ann.

From a chilly granite perch on Halibut Point, Ruth held her head in her hands and measured her days since that long trek fourteen years ago, from Narragansett to her meeting with Henry Brimfield. In all that time, she had found neither comfort nor satisfaction. Even her freedom had provided her little more ease or consolation than the moon above warmed her tired bones. Ruth had come so far and lived so lonely only to learn that she was the daughter of a rapist and a murderer. She was half-sister to a smug fool who would probably have used Phoebe as ill as his father, had he been given the chance. And even though she finally knew where her mother's blood had been spilled, Ruth still did not know where her bones were buried.

The sound of barking startled Ruth out of her reverie. A wet, hoarse bawl rose from the rocks not a hundred yards from her, where a dozen otters lay, their sleek pelts gleaming in the moonlight. One of them had rolled onto one of his fellows, who had made the loud, doggish complaint. The animals shook themselves and settled, much like the pack she knew so well. Ruth realized that there had been no sea monster in Gloucester Harbor, just flashes of these glossy backs in the water, tricking the eye into imagining one big creature that did not exist.

There had been no portent of Brimfield's arrival, or of anything menacing. Otters were uncommon visitors in those waters, but nothing unnatural or ill-omened and they would disappear back into the sea, without explanation or consequence. The way of the world, she thought. Whales breach and vanish. One slave girl is killed and another is born, and both are forgotten.

The wind cut through Ruth's spray-soaked shirt. With numb feet and aching knees, she suffered the last miles back to where she'd started out the day before.

The boulder seemed insignificant in the dawning light. It was just a large rock, flat as a table, but nothing as grand as the natural monuments considered odd enough to be christened. "Peter's Pulpit" and "Whale's Jaw" lured the tourists who speculated about visits by ancient Viking travelers or some other nonsense.

The rocky altar where her mother died was nothing but one more of the countless stones that gave rise to the hoary joke that Cape Ann was the last place that God created, since it was where He dumped all the rocks that were of no use elsewhere.

Ruth lay her cheek on that granite table and shivered. She was ashamed of herself for letting Brimfield go. He might have been lying about the murder, but even if he'd been telling the truth, what difference did that make? Father or son, an act of vengeance might have provided a fitting end to her mother's tale and her own. But it was out of her hands now. She'd lost the chance to make him tell her what Phoebe looked like, what her voice sounded like, what she cared for. She would never unlock the riddle of the lock of hair, the ring, and the scrap of yellow cloth.

She would wait for death, whenever it came for her. She would live day to day. She would not wonder anymore. Ruth closed her eyes and slept.

❖

When Ruth had rushed out of her house in pursuit of Brimfield, Easter sat down by the door to wait. She'd kept her vigil there long after dark, feeding scraps to Brindle so she wouldn't have to sit alone.

"She should be here by now," Easter said as the moon started to set. The dog pricked up his ears. "She likes that room upstairs. She's walked miles in the snow rather than sleep somewheres else. Even if there was a dry barn or a warm kitchen floor, she'd make it back." Brindle snorted and put his head on his paws.

The following evening, Oliver Younger had stopped by to tell Easter about Henry Brimfield's visit. One of the old-timers in town had recognized him getting back on the Boston-bound coach, and within hours the taverns were buzzing as though the slave girl's blood was still fresh. It didn't take long for word to filter up to the parlors on High Street. "Guilty as sin," "bold as brass," and phrases less genteel were passed from mouth to ear as news of "young" Brimfield's visit made the rounds.

Easter didn't let on. "The rogue," she said. After Oliver left, she patted Brindle and muttered, "Good riddance and thank goodness."

Ruth returned midmorning the next day, wet and limping. She did not even nod at Easter, still sitting by the door, and made straight for the attic without a word. For the first time in all the years they had shared a roof, Easter followed her up the stairs.

Ruth was on the bed, her face to the wall.

"It's good that you let him go," Easter said gently. "Not that he don't deserve a horse-whipping," she added. "The Brimfields were a rotten lot. The men, I mean. The women were just ninnies."

Ruth lifted her head and stared.

"I had a feeling when you first showed your face at my door, all those years back," Easter said, sitting on the floor in a weary heap. "When Henry poked his head in yesterday, I was sure."

"Did you know her?" Ruth asked.

"Brimfield's Phoebe? No, can't say that I did. Though I caught sight of her, from time to time. But I never had cause to speak to her. A little twig of a girl. Fourteen she was at the time. Far too young for, well, for . . ."

"Was it the son?" Ruth asked.

"No, dearie. You can put your mind at rest on that score. It was the old man, for true. I had the story from Anne Wharf herself. Young Dr. Henry brought the baby to her, all bloody and squalling, poor thing. Anne sent that baby off to her people before anyone tried to sell her. Or drown her, more'n likely. If Abraham found out what she'd done, he'd have, well, I don't know what. He loved his Anne, but he hated the Africans. Don't know where that poison came from, but lordy, he had it in for 'em all." Easter shook her head.

"Anne never told a soul until it was her last breath, and it was me nursing her at the end. That secret gnawed on her all them years.

"Did they take care of you all right in Providence?" asked Easter. "She sent you there, to some cousins she never met. Anne wondered after you all her days. She never quite trusted that Henry would do what she'd told him."

"He did," Ruth said.

"Well, that would have given her a measure of comfort," said Easter. "Knowing you grew up with them, free and all."

Ruth turned her face to the wall. She was too tired to talk, and besides, there was no point in burdening Easter with that bundle of sorrows.

Mimba would have told Easter the whole of Ruth's story, accompanied by sighs, and tongue-clucking, and tears. Easter would have listened, keen and respectful, and then she would have filled Mimba in on what had happened to Ruth since she'd arrived in Massachusetts. Easter would talk about the fine walls that she had built and about her stubborn silence, which was just as hard on the shins as granite.

They would get a laugh out of that. Indeed, the two of them had the same kind of laugh: a high and girlish *hee-hee-hee*. Easter would ask Mimba if there really were sea monsters off the coast of Africa. They would look Ruth in the eyes and, with a single voice, tell her that it was time to rest.

Easter put her hand on the sleeping woman's back. "This is your home, Ruth," she said. "Long as you want it. Long as I've got breath, anyway. You got that, at least."

Stanwood Reformed

S AMMY STANLEY perched on the branch of a beech tree and stared at the sea. The timid child of six who'd trembled at the thought of Abraham Wharf's corpse had grown into an eleven-year-old who would climb thirty feet up without a moment's hesitation. Sammy scanned the horizon north to south, wondering if this might be the color "sapphire," a word he knew from the Bible. Under a milky sky, the water looked like a whole summer's worth of blue had been collected before him. But then, quick as a blink, a gust of wind changed everything, sapphire turned to ink, and a ruffle of white lace foamed across the waves. The air in the forest turned over, too, and fall arrived for good.

Until then, the day had felt more like April than October, though there was no mistaking the autumn smell. A yeasty mulch of oak leaves carpeted the forest floor and quieted the woods to a dry hush.

Sammy rolled down his sleeves and gathered the white apron over his shoulders for a little extra warmth. He reached for the five new dimes in his pocket, a sensation that soothed him more than anything. The night before, when everyone else was fast asleep, he'd counted seventy-eight dollars in the old strongbox hidden under the floorboards beneath his bed. Some of it he'd earned doing odd jobs for the widows of Sandy Bay, who doted on his good looks and nice manners. But much of it was stolen from the men who passed through the whorehouse that was his home.

He was an object of fun to many of them, who mocked him for the apron his grandmother made him wear and the long, blond hair she forbid him to cut. But others stared at him and asked Mrs. Stanley if Sammy was "good for a go."

The first time she heard that request, she let a full minute tick by with Sammy's ear pinched between her thumb and finger while he guessed at what the question meant. She'd finally let him go and whispered something into the fellow's ear, causing him to turn crimson and hang his head till Sally Phipps came over and pulled him into her curtained corner of the room. Sally was the smiling, fair-haired whore that the sailors liked better; the farmers favored Molly, who was taller, dark, and had less to say.

Ever since his arrival on Cape Ann, barely out of diapers, Sammy's blond curls, dark blue eyes, pink cheeks, and rosebud mouth had attracted attention and desire. He still turned heads when he walked Gloucester's streets or the rougher paths through the villages on the northern reaches of Cape Ann. Women would stare and then turn to whisper about the shame of a boy like him trapped in a Dogtown brothel.

If Sammy was embarrassed or sorry for himself, he never showed it. He carried himself tall and reminded himself that he could climb a tree faster than most boys, was quicker with figures than the merchants' sons, and knew his Bible better than any preacher's daughter. It was simply in his nature to master whatever he tried; he even kept house as well as the best local wife. Indeed, Mrs. Stanley's linens were cleaner than might be expected of such a place, and the floor was swept right to the corners, every day.

Sammy was also an accomplished thief. He was barely into his first trousers when he found three cents under Molly's bed. He hid them under his pallet, savoring the feel of the wreath pennies and liberty caps between his fingers.

Sammy waited for more coins to appear, but men were not so careless with their money and when he realized that happy accidents would be too rare to count on, he took to stealing. He'd wait until the last candle was snuffed and the only sound was snoring. Then, rising from his place against the wall, he slipped beneath the burlap sacks hung to make a separation between the "parlor" and the tiny bedrooms. There might be a man lying on the cot with Molly or on the mattress with Sally; sometimes there'd be one with each. Sammy was quiet as a shadow, and the slightest rustling from either bed would turn him to stone. He could swallow a cough or kill a sneeze or squeeze off the need to piss for as long as it took for the silence to thicken and settle again. Only then would he move toward wherever a coat had been flung. No mouse could tread lighter than his fingers as they slipped in and out of pockets.

Sammy took only one coin at a time, and while he sometimes stole a half-dime from a full pocket, he usually went for pennies. No man set off a fuss over a lone penny, though he'd never pinch a man's very last cent as that would be asking for trouble. Sometimes a week would pass when he found nothing at all. Mrs. Stanley's guests were not a wealthy crew, and some paid for their pleasure with a half-full bottle of gin or a gutted rabbit.

Mrs. Stanley did not entertain as many guests as Molly or Sally, and when she did, she took her callers to the closet-size room she called her "salon." It was not much better than the rest of the cramped little house, but it did have a real door on it. Sammy had no interest in trying his luck there, even though those pockets were more likely to yield nickels. He was born more cautious than greedy, and besides, slow-and-steady was working fine.

From his roost in the golden beech tree, Sammy squeezed his dimes tightly. He wanted his own business, and a granite house with a banister and a staircase, and a parlor with a piano in it. He'd be rich enough to pay someone else to do his laundry, too, and his linen would be spotless every day.

The boy in the tree was so absorbed in these plans that the sudden groan from below nearly cost him his footing in the tree, and his neck. He grabbed at a branch just in time and spied John Stanwood on the ground, only a few feet away. He was on his hands and knees in a pile of leaves, retching a stream of yellow bile, a display that ended in a fit of coughing and panting, which was immediately followed by another long, disgusting puke.

Sammy's eyes narrowed. Serves him right, he thought. Stanwood liked to make sport of the boy's hair. The last time Stanwood spent the night, he'd set out his foot to trip Sammy, who'd split his lip in the fall.

Stanwood moaned and heaved again, though nothing issued forth. He hung his head for a moment and then sprang up, struggled with his trousers and crouched to loosen his bowels in a noisy torrent. It was a sight that would otherwise repulse Sammy, but as it was Stanwood, a smile flickered across his lips. Perhaps the greasy bastard would empty his guts from end to end until there was nothing left but a sack of dry bones. There might be a coin in the scoundrel's pocket yet, he thought, eyeing the stained waistcoat flung over a bramble.

The wind kicked up again and hit Sammy full in the face so that before he could catch himself, he sneezed a high-pitched, "Achew," a sound that alerted Stanwood, who was still crouched like a dog in the bushes.

He struggled to his feet, pulling up his trousers in front, and turned so that Sammy could see his narrow backside. Had Sammy not trained himself to silence, he would have laughed and revealed himself for sure. But the breeze did it for him, blowing dust up his nose and making him sneeze three times in quick succession.

Stanwood heard a treble voice above calling, "You, you, you!" and glared up into the green boughs of the fir trees. Seeing nothing there, he turned and scanned the half-bare oaks until he faced Sammy's autumn-gilded birch, glowing like a blazing candle in the midmorning sun. Sammy retreated to a branch on the far side from where Stanwood stood and was still as stone. But the wind had loosened his hair and blew it around his face, billowing the apron as well.

Peering through eyes addled by a long drunken binge as well as the curtain of yellow leaves, Stanwood saw a gauzy shimmer of white and gold. He squinted up, shading his eyes, to figure out what he was seeing. In the past week, he'd swallowed enough brandy, cider, rum, and beer to kill a larger man, and he suspected that his eyes and judgment were not completely trustworthy.

Much as Sammy tried to stay out of sight, the breeze conspired against him, ruffling the branches and revealing glimpses of his golden hair, his white shirtfront, all through a veil of shifting, sparkling leaves. As Stanwood stared, the image came to look more and more like a snowy robe and a floating halo. He fell to his knees and started blubbering words that Sammy couldn't make sense of until he heard, "Thy will be done in earth as it is in heaven . . ."

Stanwood stopped, unable to summon the rest of the prayer. His eyes bulged in fear and his jaw hung open, making him appear even more an idiot than usual. Which is what set Sammy off: only that much stupidity could make him angry enough to risk his safety.

Shifting his weight against the tree trunk, Sammy cupped his hands around his mouth and crooned, "Oooh." In the highest note he could reach he sang, "Oooh, thou sinner. Base sinner, art thou."

Stanwood clasped his hands at his chest and squeezed his eyes shut. "Mercy," he squeaked. "Oh, angel, have mercy!"

"A sinner who loves his sin shall burn in hell forever," Sammy warbled, drawing out the words in a broad imitation of the British accent. "Fornicator," he chanted. "Drunkard. Gambler. Thief. Thy sins are manifold."

Stanwood dropped to his knees and flung himself facedown into a pile of leaves, his naked ass to the air.

"He that sinneth against me, wrongeth his own soul," said Sammy, trying to sound menacing and angelic at the same time. "Ooh. The man that hateth me loveth death. The pit shall be his portion!"

He knew that he was not being the sort of Christian that Reverend Jewett described in his sermons, but Sammy couldn't stop himself. Stanwood was vile and crude, and Sammy was afraid of him. Perhaps it was even God's will that he be an instrument of Stanwood's instruction.

Stanwood raised himself up to his elbows, hands clasped, and wailed, "Oh, angel, you're right. I've done bad things. But I repent. I swear it. I'll mend my ways."

"The liar finds no home in heaven," Sammy trilled. "Ooooh."

A dark cloud moved over the sun, extinguishing the birch's ethereal light and plunging the woods into an autumnal gloom.

Stanwood shivered and peered up, searching for another glimpse of his vision.

Sammy hugged the trunk, willed himself not to sneeze, and prayed mightily that Stanwood wouldn't have the gumption to circle around to the other side of the tree. Silently, he prayed, "Lord, make him go away."

But Stanwood stayed where he was, his pants around his ankles, openmouthed and pop-eyed. He wasn't so sure that he wanted the angel to return. Perhaps it would be best if this vision were just one more phantasm of drink, like the flying pigs and ghastly green faces of past sprees.

But another part of him wished for it to be true. He'd never heard voices before and the angel's words had been thrilling. Perhaps this messenger was sent to save him from the pit, and wouldn't that just be a poke in the nose to the high-and-mighty nobs that stepped off the curb when they saw him approach. A personal visitation would be quite an impressive proof of his worth, wouldn't it?

Stanwood got to his knees and drew up his pants, woozily unsure whether to stay or run. For nearly an hour he kneeled, craning his neck upward. "Angel? Are you still there? I heard your warning and I'm repenting. I swear it. Do you hear me, angel? God save ye."

The clouds thickened and a steady drizzle began to fall, but it took a thunderclap to finally convince Stanwood to leave.

Sammy waited a long while before he climbed down. Tucking the soaked apron under his shirt and tying back his wet hair, he decided he didn't want to be there if Stanwood stopped in to tell Mrs. Stanley about his "vision." He'd better spend the night with one of the widow ladies for whom he often did chores.

The farther Stanwood walked, the more convinced he was that he'd seen an angel, and while he couldn't recall them precisely, the angel's words seemed increasingly sublime, her voice a whole blessed choir. Stanwood's amazement grew as he began to sober up. He stopped in the middle of the path, clasped his hands and whispered, "Our Father Who art in heaven, hallowed be Thy name, Thy kingdom come, Thy will be done in earth as it is in heaven.

"Give us this day our daily bread. And forgive us our trespasses, as we forgive them that trespass against us." As the words came to him, he recited the prayer faster and louder until he bellowed, "For Thine is the kingdom and the power and the glory. Forever and ever, Amen."

Stanwood shook his head and blurted, "Goddamn it to hell and why the blazes couldn't I have remembered it back there and shown her. Or was it a him?"

A gust of wind sent a cold shower down on his head and Stanwood looked skyward in horror. Maybe the angel was still near enough to overhear that fresh blasphemy. Frightened, he put his head down and barreled straight home, not even glancing at Mrs. Stanley's door as he passed.

Stanwood knew that he was a lucky sod. For all the times he'd been drunk and fallen, he'd never broken a bone. As much as he drank, he rarely paid for a round and even so, the fellows in the pubs always greeted him warmly. He was their local scamp, a bandy-legged rascal who got away with things they'd never dare. He'd been a handsome youth, and his flashing black eyes and thick black hair had survived the years of hard drinking, which had stamped his face with a craggy map of worldliness—or depravity, depending on the light.

Stanwood was Mrs. Stanley's lure, drawing the men far out of the city and into Dogtown for pleasures they'd not soon forget— not the way he sold it. He spoke of Sally and Molly with words that turned men into tense knots of need, describing their smells and their skills so vividly, no one even laughed or challenged his worse lies. They listened and leered and got to their feet every so often to adjust their trousers, and the younger ones would sometimes retreat outside for a little while.

"They got tongues like silk, mouths like satin. You don't know what I'm talking about? Brother, you are going to thank me." And he was thanked, with drinks and coins, and in kind from Mrs. Stanley herself.

Though he was a favorite with the men, Stanwood was detested by nearly every female on Cape Ann. In Gloucester, ladies met his wanton stares with daggers and even his own daughters cringed at his company.

Stanwood had never been in doubt of his own wickedness. He'd been on his way to hell since childhood and figured there was no point in trying to change. Why bother with church, or charity, or Christian pieties when the devil had long ago spoken for his soul?

Stanwood had never wasted time thinking about his eternal destination, until the day that the angel appeared to him and he decided that he'd been given a chance at heaven. He'd never heard of anyone, not even a minister, claiming a visitation from on high. Didn't he recall something about Jesus talking to whores? His Mary would know, he thought, and rushed to ask her.

Grabbing his startled wife's hand, he declared, "I've seen the light, Mary. You're looking at a new man."

Mary saw nothing new in the unshaven, bloodshot, wet, and coatless man before her. The stench of liquor barely masked the bodily odors that had filled the room with his entrance. It would take a daylong airing to clear out the smell of him.

"No, no," Stanwood said, seeing the disbelief on her face. "God sent an angel to warn me against the pit. I've been given a chance at salvation," he insisted. "That would make me one of the elected, wouldn't it?"

Mary frowned. Her husband had come home with a hundred excuses, and all of them lies. There was a time he'd been able to get her hopes up a little, but those days were long past. He had never tried blasphemy before, though.

"Be careful what you're saying, John," she said.

"I ain't lying," said Stanwood. "I swear. Where's that Bible? I'll swear on the Bible."

"You sold it."

"What?"

"Last year. You took the Bible and the hymnal that my mother got from her mother. You sold them." Mary said this calmly enough, though that indignity had finally freed her from the notion that she owed her husband any feeling at all. She'd stopped being hurt by his absences, or upset by his language, or surprised by the latest tale of wantonness. Mary Stanwood was certain John could do nothing to shock her anymore, until she saw the tears in his eyes.

"Poor Mary," he said, taking her hand again. "To have put up with me all these years. But God has seen fit to give me another chance and now you must, too." He knelt before her, pressed her hands to his heart, and presented her with another surprise. "Mary. I am not just telling you this to get out of a scrape. I'm a sorry sight of a man, I know. I've done you every wrong a husband can do, but I'm changed. I swear it."

She had never heard him admit to lying or any other failing in himself, and without thinking, she squeezed his hand in return.

Looking up, he noticed the deep lines etched above her lip and on her brow and said, "I've turned you into a wrinkled crone, haven't I? When did your pretty brown hair get so gray?"

Mary pulled her hands back, grabbed the bucket, and walked out.

Stanwood rushed after her. "I saw an angel, Mary," he said. "So help me, and may God send me straight to hell this minute if I'm not telling you true." He couldn't get the words out fast enough. "The angel, I tell you, the angel was floating up in the air, high up above me. Twenty feet up.

"First I heard the voice calling out to me. Like a heavenly choir, it was. And there was organ music, too. So sweet, Mary. You never heard anything like it."

Mary tried to ignore him as she walked to the creek, but Stanwood insisted, flitting around her like a no-see-um, taking no notice of how she winced at the heaviness of the pail. Nor did he take the burden from her hands, even though she had to stop and catch her breath more than once while carrying it back up the slope.

"She was on a ladder, Mary, a golden ladder. Hey, ain't there a Bible story like that, Mary? The angel with the ladder?"

Mary knew the story of Jacob's ladder, but she'd be damned if she'd give her husband that satisfaction. She set about making dinner, putting a sliver of salt pork in the pot to sizzle, and scraping a knife over a turnip while Stanwood hovered at her elbow, talking away. "Mary, it's a wonder, ain't it? You know the Scripture well as any. Doesn't it say that Jesus loved the sinner? Doesn't it say that?"

Mary pressed her lips together as she stirred and wondered if her husband would complain if she didn't make biscuits, too. Stanwood, annoyed at the lack of wonderment or praise from his wife, fell silent. The heat from the fire reminded him of the stiffness in his neck and knees after a long day of looking heavenward.

"I want a hot bath," he said, and instantly repented of his sharp tone and added a chastened, "Please."

The courtesy startled Mary, but the prospect of an evening of Stanwood wheedling for attention and praise had become completely unbearable: it was time for one of her little holidays with her daughter in Gloucester.

"Get your angel to heat the water," she said, and took off her apron. She got her second dress down from its peg, put it in a basket, and left without another word.

"I'll see you over at Rachel's, then," he called. "We can all go to church together on Sunday."

Exhausted from his encounter with the divine and parched after long hours without so much as a glass of ale, he turned back into the empty house, stepped out of his filthy trousers, and was snoring before his head touched the bed.

Stanwood's next recitation of his heavenly vision was entrusted to Easter Carter. He delivered it in a rushed whisper as though he was imparting a great secret, but she said only, "Well, dearie, that's a new one on me."

Feeling misunderstood and greatly unappreciated, Stanwood decided that he needed a more devout audience and went to see the Reverend Reuben Hartshorn, pastor of First Parish. The cleric motioned him to a chair on the far side of his study, arranging himself as sternly as possible for a man with apples for cheeks, who would not be thirty for another six months. "The purpose of your visit, sir?" he demanded.

Hat in hand, Stanwood said, "I have seen an angel."

A furrow appeared between the young minister's eyes. "An angel," he repeated sourly.

"It was in Dogtown Woods," Stanwood said. "An angel appeared to me from up above, sitting high up on a golden ladder. First I hear an organ, or something like it, and it was playing a hymn. It might have been 'How Long Wilt Thou Forget Me, Lord?'

"And then she warned me of the error of my ways, but she said if I quit sinning I'd go straight to heaven and I figured I should come to you, so you can spread the word."

Reverend Hartshorn's face had puckered into a scowl. "This, er, passionate experience of the divine to which you lay claim is not necessarily evidence of salvation," he said, choosing his words carefully. According to his theology, election was an absolute mystery; however, the notion that this foul-smelling lout could lay claim to revelation seemed monstrous.

"The surest and most substantial proof of divine love is sober and well-behaved obedience to the commandments of God," Hartshorn said. "The stronger God's love, the more uniform and steady the obedience."

But Stanwood was not as thickheaded as the pastor thought him. "So if I get steady and become obedient, that would clinch it, right?"

"Mr. Stanford," said Hartshorn.

"Stanwood."

"God's grace is a mystery, but so is the bottomless depravity of mankind. If you wish instruction in the doctrines of the church, to learn the perseverance of saints in the paths of holiness, and to study the truth that salvation is available to us only through the atonement of the Redeemer, I would suggest you begin with attendance at divine worship."

Stanwood did not understand that he was being dismissed. "But since I was visited by the Holy Spirit, you want to study what she said to me, don't you? It's a miracle, it is. A kind of proof, eh?"

At that suggestion, the young minister lost the last of his composure. "Your presumption is evidence of utter depravity," he shouted, loud enough to be heard in the kitchen. "Indeed," he continued, regaining control, "you are insolent proof of the worst corruption and degeneracy. Good day."

Stanwood was not much chastened by the minister's screed, as he knew all about Hartshorn's famously dark views. Mrs. Stanwood had often returned from his Sunday service trembling at the prospect of certain damnation, which had been described in great detail and length during the sermon.

His next stop was at the parsonage attached to Second Parish, which was inhabited by the Reverend David Fuller, an elderly cleric whose great claim to fame was his selfless patriotism during the Revolutionary struggle and the merciful brevity of his service. That extremely bald gentleman was eating his dinner when word came of an urgent visitor who insisted upon waiting. Ever since his seventieth birthday, some seven years gone, Reverend Fuller had distrusted his fading memory and feared offending a parishioner, if not a patron, so he hurried his meat, staining his waistcoat in the process, and postponed his port to attend to the troubled soul whose name was not immediately familiar.

Fuller permitted himself an audible sigh when he recognized his visitor as one of the more wretched fellows of the community. Regretting his haste and his wine, he called for his wife. The stout little woman, who had been waiting outside the door, stepped in immediately.

"Mrs. Fuller, give Mr. Stangood something from the kitchen, would you? He's just leaving."

"But I have to tell you of my meeting with the angel."

Reverend Fuller shook his head sadly, feeling an imminent bout of dyspepsia due to his miscalculated rush. "In these fallen times, the angels do not make themselves known to us," he said. "Good-bye, Mr. Stangood."

Mrs. Fuller was glad to give her full attention to Stanwood's story, while he consumed a chicken leg and two biscuits. She knew how well it would go over, when she served it, reheated, to her friends at tea later that afternoon.

Stanwood ran into the Reverend Elijah Leonard on the street as he approached the Third Parish parsonage, his next destination. The Universalist minister imposed upon Stanwood to tell his tale out of doors rather than inflict the fellow's pungent company on his wife. Upon hearing it, Reverend Leonard broke into a beatific smile and said, "Oh, my good fellow, the Lord loves us all equally and makes no special case for you or me. Talk of revelation must be suspect in these modern times, for it is reason itself that reveals our Maker. As for angels," he said, not letting Stanwood get in a word edgewise. "If wagering were not a sin, I would bet that you had been deep in your cups. I can see that the conscience that God has placed in the breast of every man, woman, and child has finally gotten the better of you." As he closed the door behind him, Leonard wished him a breezy, "Good afternoon, Mr. Stanhope."

Stanwood felt his mood darken. He pulled his hat down hard and walked away. After three ecclesiastical meetings and nothing stronger than milk to drink, Stanwood's head ached and he wondered again if his vision had been nothing more than a rum dream. Still, the memory of that bright light and sweet voice was strong enough to get him past the taverns that had, only two days before, been his most familiar haunts. Ignoring the invitation of an old acquaintance who hailed him from one of those dark doorways, he went directly to his eldest daughter's shabby room, where he also found his wife.

Rachel spooned out a helping of hominy for her father, which was all she would eat for dinner until her seafaring husband returned. The two women braced for complaints about the lack of meat, the size of the portion, and nothing but tea for a beverage. But Stanwood bowed his head over the gruel, gave thanks, and talked eagerly about their attendance at holy service come Sunday. After a short, awkward evening, Mary got into bed with Rachel, leaving Stanwood to nod off on the chair.

The following morning, he was turned out of the house so that the women could spread the sheets Rachel took in for hemming. With nothing to do, he walked the streets until he found himself near the docks and one of the rougher public houses. As he opened the door into the dim, sour room, wide smiles greeted him.

Someone said, "I'll buy the drink if you can make me forget my troubles." Heads turned in expectation.

When Stanwood said, "Nothing but water for me," the room erupted in laughter and a crowd gathered around. Delighted to have an audience at last, he started with whatever he could recall of his drinking exploits the evening before his revelation, and where memory lapsed, filled in with details from other soggy nights and days. After a well-received recital of cups and carousing, he launched into a long and colorful description of the bodily price he had paid for his fun. "Out both ends." He winked and gestured. "First one and then the other," inviting the crowd to laugh.

Without changing his demeanor or his tone, Stanwood continued, "And then, on my knees in the ugliest state you ever did see, God Himself sent an angel to save me from hell. So I'm here to show you my salvation, so you can follow my lead."

After a moment of silence, his host slapped the table and doubled over in laughter. "You son-of-a-bitch!"

But the superior smirk on Stanwood's lips remained fixed. "I am speaking the truth here," he said.

There followed an uncomfortable scraping of chairs, clearing of throats, and draining of cups. "And then what?" someone prompted. "Did she come down and do what Mrs. Stanley does for you?"

Stanwood grabbed him by the collar and shook him. "I am talking about an angel of God, you codpiece," he said. "That's just the sort of blaspheming that's going to send you to hell while I'm singing hymns with the saints."

The fellow pulled free and joined the rest of the company, which had shuffled a retreat to the far corner of the room, peering at Stanwood and whispering like a bunch of schoolgirls.

❧

On Sunday, he woke his wife and daughter early and hurried them into the church before they could finish their tea. They were the first to arrive and Mary had to pull him out of a front pew, which was reserved for wealthy parishioners. But Stanwood sat tall in his seat near the back, anxious to hear how the minister would serve up his redemption for the edification of the unfortunate sinners around him.

Reverend Hartshorn began his sermon in high dudgeon. "The miracle of this day is that all of you have not been snatched into hell since you awoke. It is only God's hand keeping you from that awful place, and even more so that you sit here in the house of God, provoking Him by your sinful and wicked manner of attending His solemn worship."

A shudder ran through the congregation, which recognized the tone and knew it was in for one of their pastor's more violent perorations. "Consider the fearful dangers you face," he warned, "the great furnace of wrath, a wide and bottomless pit full of the fire of wrath. You hang by the thinnest thread. Flames of divine wrath are flashing all around you, ready at every moment to singe that thread and burn it asunder."

Hartshorn continued in this vein for a solid hour, painting pictures of a scalding future while the sanctuary grew steadily colder. Stanwood chewed his lip and crossed his arms and tried to follow the preacher's thoughts, but his mind wandered and he was nearly dozing when he realized that Hartshorn was shouting, signaling the climax and conclusion of his address.

"Let every one of you who is still without Christ, you who hang over the pit of hell, whether old man or old woman, or middle-aged, or young people, or little children, listen to the loud call of God's word. For a day of great favor to some will doubtless be a day of vengeance to others. Man's heart will harden, and his guilt will increase apace if he neglects his soul. Never was there so great a danger.

"The wrath of Almighty God hangs over the greater part of this congregation. Let everyone fly out of Sodom: 'Haste and escape for your lives, look not behind you, escape to the mountain, lest you be consumed.'"

The minister closed his book with a flourish, at which point Stanwood got to his feet, climbed over Mary, and marched up the center aisle. Every hat and bonnet turned to watch him fling the door open and slam it shut. And then, one hundred pairs of damning eyes turned upon Mary and Rachel, the mother white as a sheet, the daughter glowing crimson.

Stanwood strode out of the city and back to Dogtown, grumbling all the way, and did not stop until he reached the scene of his miracle. He stared up into the once-enchanted tree, now barren and bleak against the low-hanging winter sky.

"God damn me," he muttered, and then clapped a hand over his mouth. If the Holy Spirit had come to him here, might not the place itself be sacred? He bowed low and then scurried to his cold Dogtown bed, where he covered his throbbing head with a blanket and tried to stifle his awful thirst.

❖

Accounts of Stanwood's misadventures with the clergy and his behavior in church traveled the length and breadth of Cape Ann quickly, delighting everyone except Mrs. Stanley, who saw her business fall off by more than half. Sally and Molly didn't mind the slowdown. They spent their days together under the covers, looking at old newspapers, whispering, and occasionally asking Sammy to cook another pot of cornmeal mush.

Sammy had hardly slept and bit his fingernails to a bloody quick. He was certain that Stanwood would wake up one morning and realize that it had been no angel up in that tree. He jumped whenever Mrs. Stanley's door opened, and was relieved as that happened less and less.

But after four straight days without a single guest, Mrs. Stanley told Sammy to seek out Mr. Stanwood. "Tell him I wish to see him," she said, adding coolly, "Tell him nicely."

Sammy went to town, but made no effort to find him. In fact, he'd been keeping a careful watch on Stanwood, who made daily visits to the tree where he'd been tricked into salvation. He approached on tiptoe, cringing with his hat in his hand. He never got any closer than about twenty feet, where he'd bow his head for a few moments and then slink off, glancing up over his shoulder as he went.

On the day Sammy made a pretense of running Mrs. Stanley's errand, he went by Stanwood's house and, hearing tapping from inside, crept around to the back window and felt his insides freeze. Stanwood was at the table, a chisel in his hand, working on a granite tablet that was precisely the size of a child's headstone. Sammy ran all the way back home and pulled the blanket over his head, complaining of stomachache.

His fears were laid to rest the next day when he walked to Stanwood's tree and noticed that a flat marker had been pounded nearby. Sammy smiled as he ran his finger across the inscription:

JMS

1819

Within a month of his angelic visitation, Stanwood had become a pariah in Gloucester. Without liquor to lubricate his tongue or paint a new flush over the roseate wreck of his face, he looked grizzled, old, and pasty. Once a welcome sight at public houses and bachelor quarters, he had become a whinnying parody of a preacher, smug and grim. After several unpleasant scenes, the town publicans decided that Stanwood's presence was bad for trade and banned him outright.

Shut out of every other pub and tavern, Stanwood became a fixture in Easter Carter's sparse parlor. She had few guests in winter, which made it easy enough to turn aside any tensions when Stanwood waxed odious. She refilled the cups, told a joke, and steered the conversation away from the eternal fire that awaited the unrepentant.

As the short afternoon passed into the longest night of December, Stanwood sat with a mug of tea, nursing a cold. Coughing into a filthy kerchief, breathing hoarsely through his mouth, he stared into the flames, uncharacteristically quiet.

Easter's other guest that day was a shy sailor named Joseph, a British gob who called upon her whenever his ship made port in Gloucester, bypassing far more convenient pubs in town. "She puts me in mind of me mum," he told his mates, who thought him mad to trek so far for cabbage and weak beer. For an extra dollar, Easter mended his stockings and washed his shirts.

Joseph was whittling and watching Stanwood suffer through another loud, racking coughing fit. "Hot rum is the best thing for the catarrh," he said.

"I have sworn off strong drink," Stanwood said, wiping his nose.

"Admirable," Joseph said. "But for medicine, there's nothing better to tame the cough. I knew a chap who broke his ribs coughing like that. The pain was something awful."

Stanwood's mouth watered at the idea of a dram of rum, which had always been his favorite spirit. He recalled the way it had warmed him, from tongue to belly, and the taste, sweet as smoke from a wood fire on a cold morning.

"Joseph is right, dearie," Easter agreed. "It's a good cure, 'specially with a little drop of honey in it. I got a little bit hidden away," she said, "just in case I come down with something, but as I'm feeling fine, I'd be glad to put the hot poker in a cup for you. It makes the nicest toddy. Just for the cure of it, of course."

Stanwood's thirst sidled up to him like an old friend. "Just for the cure," he said.

As Easter poured, the smell penetrated Stanwood's stuffed head. He smiled in relief and recognition as the heat intensified the scent, wafting it into his grateful eyes, which watered in anticipation. He took the warm cup between his hands and held his face over the steaming surface for a moment before taking the first, slow sip, paying reverent attention to the effect of the heat and alcohol as they opened his nose, soothed his raw throat, and eased the knot in his chest. After another sip, the dull headache he'd suffered for two months melted from his brow. He was home.

Stanwood beamed at his hostess as he drained the cup and held it out for more. "Easter," he said. "Your name suits you. I am resurrected."

Easter thought that was a good one and laughed as she emptied the bottle for him. Stanwood swallowed the second serving a little less carefully, smacked his lips and pressed his last quarter into her hand. "That deserves a chaser," he said. "Bring on the beer, my good woman, though cider would do. I'm still parched."

Easter poured, feeling only a little guilt for ending Stanwood's dry spell. He was no treat drunk, but sober he'd been as bad as a swarm of fleas.

Stanwood's head grew lighter by the moment and it occurred to him that the best thing about sobriety was the way it punched up the effect of a drink afterward. Three glasses of ale followed the rum, and Stanwood felt like a great weight had been lifted from his neck

"You all right now, Johnny?" Easter asked, watching his face regain its old glow. "That angel of yours won't be angry, will she?"

"Don't you meddle with that," he snapped.

Easter shrugged. "I don't mind, dearie. Not me."

Stanwood stalked out in a hurry. Walking at a brisk clip, he passed his own house and thought about the mess inside, frowning at the thought of having to fetch his wife back to clean it up. As he neared Mrs. Stanley's house, he smiled and tipped his hat in the darkness but did not stop until he arrived at the foot of the tree where he'd had his vision. There was a crunch of frost underfoot, and the moon silvered the silent, bare branches. He listened hard for a minute, and then he unbuttoned his trousers and watered the tree. Giggling, he turned and ran over to piss on the marker he'd set out. Stanwood tucked himself, pulled himself up to his full height, cupped his hands around his mouth, and shouted, "I'll be damned."

Pleased with himself, he muttered, "I'll be goddamned," all the way back to Mrs. Stanley.

Although it wasn't long past sunset, her windows were already dark. He cracked the door silently, planning to take his old friend by surprise. The only light came from a candle stub in Sammy's corner beside the stove. The boy's back was to the door. Stanwood stole across the room, thinking he'd give the boy a good fright first. But when he reached the bed, he saw what looked like a king's ransom in coins laid out in rows on the blanket.

Stanwood put a hand over Sammy's mouth and whispered, "What have we here?"

Sammy tried to get free, but Stanwood held him where he sat. He reeked of drink and sweat. "You're a real little bastard, ain't you? Holding out on your grandma like this."

When Sammy tried to twist loose, Stanwood gripped him around the neck so tightly, he thought Stanwood meant to choke him. But he let go and swooped down and filled his pockets with every last cent it had taken him years to acquire.

Stanwood swayed a bit as he straightened and fixed Sammy with a menacing smile: he put a finger to his lips and ran his other thumb across his neck. Sammy nodded and Stanwood went into Mrs. Stanley's room, where murmurs were heard, then laughter, then hurried rustlings, then silence.

Sammy's limbs felt like lead. He stayed perfectly still until the familiar honk of Stanwood's snore startled him into motion. He pulled on his boots and coat and ran all the way into Sandy Bay, straight to the home of Widow Linner, where he knew he'd find the door unbolted. Inside, he wrapped himself in the hearth rug and curled up before the fire.

When Margaret Linner found him the next morning, she didn't know whether to shake him or kiss him. Her floor was tracked with mud but Sammy's face was so angelic, she pulled up a chair and watched him sleep while her kettle boiled. When he woke up, he crept to her side and told her that John Stanwood had arrived at Mrs. Stanley's house with a sailor who wanted to use Sammy as he used the girls. Sammy said that he'd put up a fight and escaped, but having no family to turn to, he'd hoped for refuge from the kindest woman he knew.

"Please," he begged, "don't make me go back there. I'm afraid."

With pretty tears glistening in the corners of his sapphire eyes, he said, "I'm afraid they might still be there, waiting for me."

With a few more hints, he had the old woman believing that his youth and beauty had often put him in similar jeopardy and that Stanwood had been the biggest threat to his virtue. Mrs. Linner swore he'd never return to that wicked place and that he could stay with her. Later that day, she paid a call on Reverend Jewett, the minister at Fifth Parish, who made an unprecedented visit into Dogtown. He told Mrs. Stanley—in very worldly, if not to say vulgar terms—of the consequences should she or any of her minions come after Sammy, who was now a member of his flock and under his care. The old whore smiled up at the handsome clergyman and said only, "My dear grandson is fortunate to have you for a friend."

❖

Though Sammy's lodgings were larger and far more pleasant than ever, he felt dull and listless. Being penniless did not suit him. Mrs. Linner considered his labors a fair exchange for his board and gave him nothing extra for doing her laundry, heavy cleaning, and sundry errands and tasks.

It would have been most peculiar, and even a little scandalous, for any other boy to be washing a lady's dresses and shifts and emptying her chamber pot. But even the keenest gossips were forgiving when it came to Sammy, who remained the polite and appealing ward, with his impeccable manners and his golden locks tied back fetchingly in the old Revolutionary style.

He was, in all respects, a model servant, and he never once took advantage of Mrs. Linner's carelessness with her change purse. She often remarked how much kinder Sammy was than her own nephews, who showed no interest in her. This gave Sammy the idea that acting the part of her loyal grandson might be his quickest route back to solvency. The widow was seventy-five and short of breath. If she were to leave him her cottage as a legacy, he'd be in a position to invest and make his fortune. The plan cheered him up and set him back to scouting out a likely scheme.

He considered fishing; cod, pollack, and scale-fish were plentiful, and the market for oil on the rise. But Sammy didn't care for the uncertainties of the sea, having heard too many stories about ships and fortunes lost in mighty gales. Granite seemed a safer bet, with businessmen as thick as seagulls in Folly Cove, ruining their shoes on the shore ledge. He might even work in a quarry for a while, if the wages stayed high.

But the truth was, Sammy disliked the company of men. Life in the brothel had made Sammy contemptuous of them all. The old ones had been desperate, the sailors loud and vulgar, the quarrymen filthy and rough. Sammy had been befriended by the wives of the farmers and fishermen he'd seen follow Sally or Molly through the curtain. Worst of all were the boys barely older than he, who'd showed up at Mrs. Stanley's in pairs or threesomes, the money jingling in their pockets, teasing each other in booming voices and strutting like roosters. They left in silence, carrying their heads lower, and regained their voices only after they reached Gloucester, where they lied about the wild times they'd had in Dogtown.

Sammy was most comfortable among old women, and it was they who gave him the idea about how the summer trade might be a safe ticket to a wealthy future. Mrs. Linner's friends all rented rooms to Boston lawyers and bankers, charging them a few dollars more every season. "The city folks spend all this time oohing and ahhing over the sunsets and the fresh air," said Mrs. Linner, while Sammy poured their tea. "As if the sun don't set every blessed day." With more and more cottages and ocean-facing rooms being let from one summer to the next, Sammy decided if he ever got the chance, he'd buy property with a view to the water.

The hope of an inheritance and a future as a landowner buoyed Sammy's spirits through Mrs. Linner's long, miserable decline. For the better part of a year, he spoon-fed her, washed her soiled sheets, tended her little garden, and kept her accounts. But when she finally died, the house, its contents, and all her savings went to the negligent nephews who did not visit once during her last illness, even after she sent Sammy to fetch them. No one expressed surprise or sympathized about the fact that he'd gotten nothing. Blood was thicker than water, and that's all there was to it.

Three days after Mrs. Linner's funeral—which Sammy catered and cleaned up after—he made himself a money belt out of the old lady's best tea towel and walked to the barbershop in Gloucester, where he got two silver dollars for his long, yellow braid. He carried Mrs. Linner's silver service—a secret treasure she'd kept under lock and key—to Ipswich and sold that for a good price, too.

With a new nest egg strapped around his waist, Sammy found a room with another widow and pursued every odd job he could find: carting, running errands, even doing laundry. He returned to stealing, too; just a little bit and with great caution. In Sandy Bay he was known as "the little businessman," a term of endearment among the ladies who followed his progress. "He'll own the whole town someday," one would cluck to another whenever Sammy Stanley's name came up.

To which the usual rejoinder was, "He'll make his mark, or I'm the Queen of England."

The Lost Girls

WITH SAMMY's departure, life grew colder, hungrier, and dirtier for Molly and Sally. But even though they missed his cooking and hated having to haul water for themselves, neither of them missed having the boy in the house.

Sally had treated him as she might a cat, petting him and even calling him "puss" when the mood took her, then ignoring him for weeks at a time. Molly kept her distance from him; he looked a bit like one of her nephews and she disliked any reminders of the family she'd left. There was no knowing what Mrs. Stanley thought about Sammy, even though she'd been in charge of him and was the only one who required that the house be kept clean. By the time Sammy left, her interests and attentions had narrowed to keeping a reliable stock of rum in her house, and for that, all she needed was John Stanwood. "Such a nourishing beverage," she said every time he brought her a bottle. "You know that molasses is excellent for the digestion."

That the house was known by Mrs. Stanley's name testified to her expansive sense of herself, and to the effect she had on men. Few people remembered that Molly and Sally had been doing business under the same roof for several months before she even appeared. But then, neither of them was in any way as memorable as Mrs. Stanley.

Molly and Sally were certainly nowhere near as pretty, nor had they been, even as girls. Molly Jacobs had once owned a beautiful head of raven hair, which helped soften the downward turn of her thin lips and the birdlike effect of close-set eyes arranged beside her long, narrow nose. She was thin in every aspect, with arms that seemed oddly short for the rest of her.

The fifth of six daughters born to a hardscrabble Plymouth farmer, she understood early that she was unmarriageable and doomed to serve as a permanent nursemaid to her sisters' children. Once they grew up, she'd be the kind of maiden aunt that no one needed or wanted underfoot.

After her second sister bore her third son, Molly realized she didn't like children, so at fourteen, she ran away to Boston and got her living the only way she could. She walked the streets near the waterfront and made a little name for herself as mistress of the French trick, which she learned from an older member of the sisterhood, as a sure way to keep from getting the clap or, just as bad, a baby.

Molly had been at it for a few years when she crossed paths with Sally Phipps. The barman, who kept an eye out for his regular girls, motioned her over and said, "Watch out for that ginger-haired bantam over there." He nodded at a potbellied fellow who was drunk as a fiddler. "He's underselling you something terrible, trading his poor little niece for the price of a rum punch." Adding, "Niece, my arse."

A moment later, a sailor slammed the door wide and said, "Set the fellow up."

A slip of a girl crept in and stood in a corner, where she could lean up against one wall and stare at the other. Her white-blonde hair was wet from the rain, slicked down to her skull. Her chest rose and fell quickly, as though she'd been running, and Molly noticed the unmistakable swelling at her waist. When the red-haired "uncle" went outside for a piss, Molly hurried over to the pale, soaked girl and said, "Follow me."

Sally looked into Molly's sad face and considered the invitation. Ned had taken to slapping her for just about anything, including talking to strangers without his say-so. But he was out of the room, and she sure as hell didn't want to lie down for anyone else that evening.

"Aw-right," Sally drawled, and turned on a smile full of milky teeth and blind trust.

Molly led her out the back door, down the alley, and up a flight of stairs into her room, which was bare except for a plank bed, a stool, a couple of pegs, and a chamber pot. Sally headed straight for the cot and within a minute, a soft whistling sound came from her upturned nose. Sleep was by far the best time of the day for a street-walker.

Poor thing, Molly thought and sat beside her, trying to decide on a next step. The barman wouldn't tell the pimp where she lived, but there were others who might. Once that Ned sobered up, they might want to be somewhere else. Maybe this was the sign that she ought to leave Boston.

When she first left the farm, Molly had loved being on her own. Her sisters had made her feel invisible and unimportant. Being a woman alone—even a bad woman—meant that she could claim her own time, as well as her price. She'd chosen a new name, too—switching from Mary to Molly—and had picked out "Jacobs" as a surname, from the store where she had her first taste of pineapple.

But she'd turned against Boston, which now seemed nothing but dirty and dangerous. She'd heard it was quieter up in Portsmouth and the prospect of a traveling companion made the journey suddenly seem more like a holiday than a retreat.

Of course, she didn't even know this girl's name or where she came from. Molly wondered if her slow way of talking meant she was bottle-headed. Or maybe it was because she came from Georgia or Virginia or someplace where everyone talked like that. She'd find out in the morning, she decided, blew out the candle, and squeezed herself into the narrow space on the bed beside Sally.

At dawn, Molly tiptoed out to see about the next coach to Portsmouth and returned to find Sally sitting up, watching the door.

"I put in some sugar for you," said Molly, offering her a mug of tea.

"Ain't you a sweetheart."

"I'm Molly Jacobs."

Sally nodded, and then turned her attention to the tea. "Mmmmm."

"Well, what's your name?" Molly asked.

"Sally Phipps."

"Where you from?"

"Bal'mer."

"Is that south?" Molly asked.

Sally shrugged and beamed.

Not the sharpest knife in the drawer, Molly decided. "How far along are you?"

"Eh?"

She pointed to Sally's belly. "You're carrying, ain't you? You got a baby coming."

Sally looked blank.

"Oh, no. You can't be that simple. How long since you had your courses?"

Sally dropped her eyes. "I don't know," she said at last. "A while now."

"First time you get caught?" Molly asked.

Without her smile, the light went out, and Sally was plain as a box, with no chin to speak of and blue eyes so light they seemed almost blank.

"Well, given the size of you, it might be six months, might be less."

"Less?" Sally said, hopefully.

"You want to leave town with me?"

"I suppose. I sure don't want to see Ned no more."

"We'll have to, well, work for a living when we get there, you know."

Sally's face fell again. At least she wasn't that stupid, thought Molly. "Or maybe we can hire out at a dairy, or maids for some rich lady in a big house?"

Sally's expression didn't change much at those suggestions.

"Well, never mind that now," said Molly, and set to stuffing her extra shift and stockings into a sack. "Fold up the blanket. We got to get moving. The first coach is going to Gloucester, which is as far as I can afford to get us right now."

Sally slept through the whole bone-rattling journey, her head on Molly's shoulder. Molly, who had trouble falling asleep in a feather bed, could have pinched her for spite. But the last leg of the trip perked her up. The North Shore was nothing like the coastal lands of her childhood: the boulders seemed to lift the whole landscape up into the sky, and a honeyed brightness in the air put a keen edge on every hummock. The April trees were budding in red and gold, and the marsh grasses seemed to be waving at her. She had a good feeling about making a fresh start here. Maybe she and Sally could hire out as housemaids after all. Maybe she could stay clean in this tangy air.

The coach finally stopped at the battered public house on the green. The publican's wife stepped out of the tavern to greet the travelers and eyed the two girls warily. "Who might you be?"

"Molly Jacobs, ma'am."

"I'm Sally Jacobs."

"You two sure don't look like any sisters."

"Same pap, different mamas," Sally fibbed so easily that Molly suddenly wondered if "Phipps" was also a lie.

"Huh," she said, pegging them as strumpets from the state of their shoes and the color of their skirts. "Well, you two sure as hell ain't coming in my place. Get yourself down to the harbor or up to Dogtown where you belong. And by the by," she said to Molly, "your 'sister' don't look so good."

Sally's face was pale green. "My down-belows are in a twist," she said, and doubled over.

"I got to get her somewhere to lie down," said Molly, suddenly panicked at what she'd done in taking a perfect stranger, pregnant at that, to a place where she knew no one.

"Who needs to lie down?" said John Stanwood, emerging from behind the house, buttoning his pants.

"My," Molly fumbled, "sister?"

"You my kind of sister?" He winked and Molly dropped her eyes. "You come with me. Easter Carter never says no to visitors." He picked up Molly's bag.

"Where's the wagon?" she asked.

"No need. We can manage her," he said, and put his arm around Sally's waist and hoisted her to her feet. "Get over on the other side."

It was slow going as Stanwood and Molly half carried, half dragged Sally up the Dogtown road, stopping every few minutes so she could bend over and retch.

Easter saw them coming and walked out to greet them wearing

her usual smile. But when she got close enough to see the state Sally was in, she turned into a mother hen. "Go fetch some water, Johnny," she said, and got the ailing girl settled inside.

The baby came that night, a tiny stillborn boy with a clubfoot. Sally didn't make a sound through it all, and she slept for three days after. On the fourth day, she sat up, melted Easter with her brightest smile, and asked, "You got any porridge, Missus?"

Easter made a big pot of corn mush and put the last of her currants in for a treat. She gave the girls a pallet in the back corner of her big drafty parlor while Sally recovered and Molly did everything she could to be of use, weeding the garden and washing up after Easter's young people stopped by to drink and flirt. She learned a few of the Dogtown paths and was working up to ask Easter about building a second chicken coop so they could sell eggs down in Gloucester. The fact that Easter let the strange black woman live in the attic fed her hope that Easter might take them in, too.

But one sweet-smelling evening when the three of them were sitting at the table, Easter said, "It's been fine having you girls here, but now that Sally is up and around, you got to be thinking about moving on."

The look on Molly's face gave Easter a moment's pause. "I'm sorry, dearie, but your business is, well, I just can't stand to have that going on under my roof. Not that I judge you for it, but it's just too sad for me to be anywhere near it. Too sad by half."

"Couldn't we do something else for you?" Molly asked, without much conviction. "You know I'm not afraid of hard work, outside or inside. And I'm real good with chickens. Or we could hire out as housemaids, Sally and me. We'd give you half of what we earn. More than half."

Easter shook her head. "Stanwood already spread the word about you two, and you know, good as me, that there's only one way a girl's reputation can turn, and it ain't from black to white."

Sally took her finger out of her mouth. "Johnny told us we could live in one of those empty houses."

"Or we could try to head north," Molly said. "I was thinking of going all the way to Portsmouth. This was the only coach I could afford."

"That's a thought, dearie," said Easter, who felt bad about turning them back to whoring. "Let Sally build up her blood and you can try again. Meanwhile, I'll loan you some things for housekeeping." Easter made the offer on her way down to the potato cellar, returning with an armload of chipped cups, wooden ladles, ironware, chamber pots, and some forks. "Just some odds and ends I saved over the years."

Sally smiled. "Ain't you a sweetheart?" She turned to Molly. "Ain't she?"

But Molly was barely able to nod.

Stanwood brought a wheelbarrow for Molly's few possessions and Easter's rusty gifts. He led them up an even rougher road to what used to be the Pierce house, which was set off in a hollow, on the way to Sandy Bay.

"Real private," he said.

The house was small even by Dogtown standards, with two cramped rooms, front and back, and all of it a mess of pine needles, mouse droppings, and broken glass. Molly groaned, but Sally rolled her sleeves, hitched up her skirt, and started sweeping with the broom they'd borrowed from Easter. "Johnny?" she said, stretching out his name so long, it was like she was sucking on it. "You go ask Easter for a bucket and a mop, won't you, Johnny?"

Johnny was leaning up against a wall, trying to figure out which girl he'd have first.

"You know it will be worth your while." She winked at him.

He moved up to her and put his hands on her breasts and said, "It better be, because I don't fetch for women. Not even my own damn wife!"

As he left, Molly stared openmouthed at Sally.

"What the matter, darlin'?" Sally asked.

"I don't understand you one bit. Where do you come from?"

"I told you," Sally said. "Bal'mer."

"I can't decide if you're simple or evil, or some of both."

"A girl has to live," she said seriously, her finger pointed up in the air like she was quoting scripture.

"Who taught you to say that?"

"My mamma, I think."

"Your mamma? Was your mamma a . . . was she like us?"

Sally turned away and picked up a shard of plate from the floor. "This had a pretty border on it."

"Listen," said Molly, taking her by the elbow. "That weasel is going to be back in a tick, and I need us to agree about what we're going to do and what we won't be doing. And we ain't going to be spreading our legs for anyone."

"What do you mean?" said Sally. "You want to kill Johnny? Is that it?"

"Christ almighty, I wasn't talking about killing anyone. I just want us to be clear about what we won't do for these johns. I ain't given up my cunny but two times." She grimaced. "Almost made me go back to my sister's. But then I seen how you can make a living without. All you got to do is play the pipe, if you know what I mean."

Sally's face was a perfect blank.

"Playing the pipe?" Molly said, lowering her voice. "You take 'em in your mouth. Get 'em off that way. That way you don't get a baby, and you don't get the pox."

Sally clapped her hands over her mouth and squealed. "Ooooh. That's horrible. I don't think I could ever . . . Do the men like that?"

"They think they died and went to heaven. I make 'em wash it first, but mostly they don't mind, and if you wash it for 'em, it's

part of the fun. There were some fellows down in Boston who
swore they'd never have it off any other way," Molly said. "When
Johnny gets back, I'll go with him, and you can watch how I manage it. Some of the johns, they like being watched, but that's extra.
I'm telling him it's the only trick we do, and if he don't like it, then
we're off."

"And if he ain't fair with our money, then we kill him," Sally
said.

"Are you teasing me?"

Sally smiled and went on with the sweeping.

Stanwood returned carrying a bucket, a mop, and some boiled
eggs from Easter. Molly took him outside to talk business. He agreed
to supplying johns for half the take and when Molly explained their
services, he said, "I got no problem with it," and tried not to appear
too eager. There wasn't any of that sort of thing to be had elsewhere
on Cape Ann, and he was just the one to sell it. "But I gotta make
sure that you two know what you're doing first."

"Nothing's free," Molly said.

"Free?" he bellowed. "You bag of bones. Here I been carrying
and carting like some kind of mule. You owe me for that, and for
what it's going to cost me to get you some kind of beds in there."

"I'll do you twice for it," she said.

"The other one, too."

"Sally will go you once."

"Twice."

"Once."

Stanwood shrugged. He was aroused and ready to go, and he followed Molly into the woods like a dog trailing a plate of meat. Sally
snuck up to watch as Stanwood leaned up against a tree and unbuttoned his trousers. Molly knelt before him and, using one of the flan-
nels she'd brought from Boston, started rubbing his skinny stalk
with the cool, damp cloth.

"Goddamn," he roared, but in a moment he was moaning a different tune.

Sally couldn't really see the mechanics of the act, only the back of Molly's head, pumping in and out. It was over fast. Stanwood whinnied and leaned against the tree as Molly bent over, spat, wiped her mouth, and started back for the house. When he returned to the house, he looked at Sally up and down and said, "You as good as your sister?"

He spent the rest of the day sitting and watching as they cleaned the shack and hung paper over the empty windowpanes. Molly felt his eyes on her, like a wet wool coat. When he finally left, she sat on the floor and put her head in her hands.

Sally sat beside her and pulled her close, stroking her hair until she calmed down. As the sun started to set, she said, "Let's go to sleep."

Silently, they made a nest of blankets and cloaks, and burrowed into each other's arms. As she drifted off, Molly remembered the perfect safety she'd felt as a little girl in her mother's lap, and hugged Sally tight.

Stanwood woke them up midmorning with the tip of his boot. A red-faced youngster in a dirty uniform stood at the door.

"My turn," Sally whispered. "Outside," she ordered the cabin boy, found a flannel, and was gone before Molly was fully awake.

When she returned, Molly was still in bed, the blanket over her face.

"It's not so bad," said Sally. "Salty. He was a baby, that one. I don't think he'd been with a woman ever, not that he has now, either. It's the quickest money I ever made." Sally's voice was flat, lower than usual. Molly felt her eyes burn with tears.

"Now, don't you get to feeling bad," she said, as though she'd heard Molly's thoughts. "You ain't the one turned me out. You saved me from Ned, and now I have me a sister and a roof."

Molly pulled back the covers and stared.

"Don't be scared if I rattle on about what's going on in your head," Sally said. "It's my gift. I always know when a pot's about to boil over, and sometimes I can tell when there's going to be trouble in a room so I clear out first. It don't work all the time, though. And I'm better on girls than boys.

"I ain't smart in the other ways," Sally said. "Can't sign my name. Can't read, though I reckon you can."

"Yes," said Molly. "I can read."

"That might come in handy. But this here is going to be all right for us, so don't fret. I saw some berry bushes outside so come summer we'll have fruit and there are rose hips for tea and jelly. But right now, we need to see about getting us some tea and cornmeal and such. That Johnny-boy brought nothing with him. We might want to buy a chicken or two, soon as we suck off a few more gents, eh, my dear? I could eat an egg right now, if there was one to hand."

Molly burst out laughing, and Sally smiled her sunniest, pleased to have lightened her friend's mood. They walked arm in arm to Easter, whose guilt was still fresh enough to give them three baby chicks as a gift.

By the time the chicks were laying eggs of their own, there was a regular pattern to their lives in Dogtown. Stanwood would bring two or three sailors on Saturday nights, sometimes Friday and midweek too, depending on the dockings and which day the quartermaster paid out. He was an excellent salesman, sidling up to men in the taverns and whispering, "I've got some mouth whores up there in Dogtown. Suckstresses. You ain't lived till you tried it.

"Worth a walk in the woods, I can tell you. And no risk of the pox," he winked. He'd get the gobs so worked up, some of them would race ahead of him, half-cocked and unbuttoned when they walked in the door.

Most were far too drunk to notice the misery of the place until they came to the morning after. One sailor opened his eyes and declared it the saddest excuse for a whorehouse he'd ever seen, and swore it was enough to put a man off harlots for good. No one stayed for long.

The house was stark as a jail. Stanwood had scavenged a wormy table and a bench with wobbling legs, just so he'd have somewhere to bend his elbow. Molly filled a few of the chinks with mud, but there wasn't much clay to it, so the stuff crumbled onto the floor. The chickens roamed in and out as they liked.

There were eggs most days, and corn mush and game, which some of the local boys offered instead of money. Sally did the gutting and plucking but wouldn't cook. With only one pot in the place, Molly boiled everything to a tasteless mess. They rinsed their shifts once in a while, letting them dry in the sun while they waited, naked, under dirt-stiffened dresses. There wasn't a speck of beauty in their lives, and Molly tried not to think about what would happen to them come winter.

But Mrs. Stanley moved in before the first snow, and everything changed.

Stanwood saw her on her first day in Gloucester, sitting in a tavern where her alabaster throat and corn-silk hair seemed to light up the dim room. When she fixed her eyes on him and smiled, he was a goner. He brought her to the cabin with three crates filled with clothes, bedding, and china.

"These are the girls I told you about," said Stanwood.

"The dark one is Molly?"

Molly stared at the deep-bosomed woman, wearing kid gloves and a silk skirt.

"Who the hell are you?" said Sally.

Stanwood slapped her face so fast, she barely knew what had happened. "You never talk to Mrs. Stanley like that."

Mrs. Stanley watched this exchange without comment, and then

walked the four steps up and down the front room. Her lips tightened. "The chickens go outside," she said. "Build a pen, or a coop,
or whatever you like. I will not live in a barn."

She turned to the back room. "I'll be wanting a real door there,"
and pointed to the blanket tacked over the empty frame. "You'll be
wanting a door, too, if you want to see any more of me."

Stanwood scowled but knew he'd do anything she asked. In the
full light of day, Mrs. Stanley was older than he'd first thought, with
fine lines around her eyes and blue veins starting to show on the
backs of her hands. Still, he was dazzled by the straightness of her
nose, the curl in her hair, the throaty pitch of her voice, the way she
touched her finger to her lip as she considered her next move.

"Now," said Mrs. Stanley, pointing to the door and tapping her
foot.

"You do what she tells you," he said to Molly and Sally as he hurried away.

"Help me with the trunks, ladies," Mrs. Stanley said with a bland
authority that quickly became the ruling force of their lives.

⬥

Within a week of her arrival, she had a door for "her" room and
moved the girls into the front room, with blankets hung from the
ceiling to separate their chamber from the parlor and kitchen. She
got Stanwood to put glass in the windows and rehang the front door
so it closed properly. One of her crates produced a few curtains and
sheets enough for three beds. A sturdy table and two chairs appeared
soon thereafter, and by Christmas she acquired a small chest of
drawers and a real bedstead for her room.

All of this was paid for by whoring, though Mrs. Stanley was
never heard to use the word. She behaved as though the three of
them were merely women of reduced circumstances. "I myself am a

widow," she'd say, softly. "Lacking any family, I have been blessed by the charity of dear friends, gentlemen, all."

No one ever learned her Christian name—not even Stanwood, who over time became familiar with every inch of her. No one ever called her anything but Mrs. Stanley for all her days in Dogtown. Sally never even called her that, managing to avoid using any form of address. "You there" was as much as she could squeeze out. With Molly, she referred to her as Beelzebub.

"What?"

"That's the devil's first name, don't you know? I get the feeling she's run away from something," Sally said, with the glassy look that tipped Molly to the fact that Sally was having one of her visions.

"Well, there's nowhere farther to run than this," Molly said.

"I figure she kill't a man."

"Oh, Sal, you have murder on the brain."

But Sally shook her head with conviction, and Molly felt the hairs at the back of her neck prickle. There was something icy and entirely calculating about Mrs. Stanley, which was as plain as the nose on her face. But men didn't see past the flattery and fluttery glances that promised more than any woman could deliver, and they gladly paid her twice what it cost to have it off with Molly or Sally.

Mrs. Stanley led her customers to her tiny bedroom like she was showing them into a gilded drawing room, and she used the words "lady" and "gentleman" so often that Molly wondered if the old tart actually believed her own lies. She and Sally rolled their eyes when the bass groan, baritone howl, or tenor hoot issued from behind the door, where Mrs. Stanley made quick work of them. They stumbled out minutes later, faces still flushed, with boots, trousers, and coats in hand.

Few of her callers returned for a second visit. Sally said they didn't come back because "Beelzebub" smelled so strongly of brimstone, but Molly said it was because her price was so high. Whatever they thought of her, Mrs. Stanley's johns were satisfied enough to send plenty of others, so there was often meat on the table as well as sugar for tea, and even a banana when the madam had a hankering.

Mrs. Stanley spoke to Molly and Sally as though they were her servants. She expected them to do as they were told, and in return gave them her old shifts and dresses, which meant they were better dressed than either had ever been before. On cool, sunny days when she was inspired to go shopping, Mrs. Stanley insisted they attend her, and led the way with stately, measured steps, holding her head so high her hat seemed to float above her shoulders. Walking the Gloucester streets, she fixed a knowing half smile on her lips, which seemed an insult to any woman who recognized her and a greeting to any man, whether he'd made her acquaintance or not. Sally and Molly trailed behind her wide wake, huddled against each other, barely noticed.

They hated those excursions into town; Molly wilted under the glare of the women on the street. Sally couldn't bear the smell of fish, which permeated the whole city. Mrs. Stanley made a show of paying for their shoes and buying an orange for them to share. This prompted the most forgiving souls in town to credit Mrs. Stanley for looking after the two simpleminded women.

One day, when Mrs. Stanley announced an outing to town, Sally claimed she had a headache, "something terrible," and Molly begged to be left to take care of her. Mrs. Stanley considered: without them, there would be no need to buy a second orange and she might even get a cake for herself. "As you wish," she said, and went on her own.

No sooner was she gone than Sally threw her arms around Molly and giggled.

"You're not sick?"

"You are the most believingest girl," Sally said. "Now, come over here and read me the papers."

Tucked in a nest of clothes and blankets on the mattress, they leafed through cast-off newspapers and magazines, stopping at every advertisement for skin cream and kitchen soap, patent medicine and farm machinery. Sally could not believe that there were people stupid enough to think that Mrs. Philby's milk tonic would remove freckles or that Hanson's thresher would double the yield of a rocky field. "And them's people smart enough to read!"

On the day of the feigned headache, Sally took the newspaper from Molly's hands and kissed her on the mouth. Molly hugged her and kissed back, but when she felt the advance of Sally's tongue, she was startled and drew back. There was a new slyness in Sally's eyes, and something else, too. Longing. "My Mol," she said, and kissed her nose.

Molly felt the rise and fall of Sally's bosom through their shifts: her own breath quickened to match. Eyes locked, Sally took Molly's face between her hands and began covering her eyes and cheeks with soft, running kisses, returning again to her lips.

"Are you game, my darling?"

Molly still had no idea what Sally was driving at.

"Didn't you never make yourself, well, feel nice?" Sally whispered and reached under the covers, cupping Molly's breasts, and lightly dancing her fingers over her belly and on down to her sex. Molly clamped her legs together and pulled away.

"It's not like with them," Sally promised. "It's nice. Nice as kissing me."

"Then let's just kiss."

Sally sighed and turned her back to Molly.

"Don't be angry," she begged. "I was just surprised is all. You know that I love you, don't you?" Molly threw her arm over Sally's side and pressed up against her, making spoons. Sally took Molly's hand and kissed each finger.

"That's my dearheart." Molly sighed with relief.

"Shhhhh," said Sally as she took her friend's hand and led it back under the covers, under her shift, to her need.

Molly kept her eyes closed and let her friend do what she wanted. Feeling Sally pant and gasp, Molly felt an odd pressure between her legs, and an urgency to go somewhere, though she didn't quite know where. Finally, Sally sighed, let go of her hand, and fell asleep.

Molly rolled to her back and stared up at the ceiling, happy and frightened and suddenly resolved. She didn't know what to think about what they'd done, nor how to speak of it, but it had changed something between her and Sally, and she couldn't remember when she'd been so happy. She would never again suggest that they leave the quiet of Dogtown for Portsmouth or anywhere else.

Molly dozed off, too, waking up to the sound of Mrs. Stanley's return. She leapt to her feet, afraid that the madam would be able to tell that something had happened in her absence, terrified that she would send the two of them packing.

But Molly had no cause to worry. Mrs. Stanley paid little attention to anything that did not directly touch upon her own needs and comforts. Once Sammy left, Sally and Molly had the whole of the front room to themselves and looked forward to long winter nights when business was dead and they could bundle without fear of discovery, warm and content in each other's arms. In truth, there was no one on earth who cared what Sally and Molly did, which suited them just fine.

Oliver Younger's Heart

THE COURTSHIP of Oliver Younger and Polly Boynton began on the day he brought John Stanwood to yank out two of Tammy's rotten teeth. Oliver was fourteen at the time, and though he'd gotten his height, his voice was still changing and he was far too shy to look Polly square in the eye as she stood, half hidden, in the doorway of her father's house.

She had retreated to Dogtown, planning to remain a widow the rest of her days, but Oliver's visits seemed harmless and she appreciated having a little bit of company besides her father. He found a hundred reasons to stop "on his way" from one place to another, and he always brought her a gift: a bucket of clams, fistfuls of lilacs or bittersweet, or at least a few sticks of kindling.

While he was there, Oliver fixed broken clapboards, carried water, pulled weeds from the kitchen garden, and whittled a new walking stick for Mr. Wharf. In exchange for his help, Polly insisted upon washing and mending his clothes.

Sundays became their regular day together. Polly stopped walking to church so she could stay with her father, who claimed that his swollen knees would carry him no farther than Easter's place. Oliver would appear midmorning—as clean and combed as he could manage—and drink a pot of tea with father and daughter. He would bring whatever news he had from Tammy or from town and then spend the better part of an hour while Mr. Wharf dissected the weather as though it might contain the secrets of the universe. "Rain this early is usually a good sign," said Mr. Wharf and Oliver agreed heartily, though he didn't quite know why that should be so.

Polly would prepare the Sunday meal while the men talked, serving apologies alongside the burned fish and gummy bread. Oliver protested that it was the most delicious food he'd ever tasted.

"No need to fib, son," Wharf said, laughing. "Though it would all taste a fair sight better if we had something to drink."

After living with Boynton, who had rarely been sober, Polly refused to permit any spirits in the house. So after dinner her father invariably pronounced himself "parched," patted Polly's cheek, shook hands with Oliver, and hobbled to Easter's for refreshment. Oliver dried the dishes and lingered while Polly took out her sewing basket; her clever dressmaking earned enough to keep the last two Dogtown Wharfs fed and clothed.

Polly asked Oliver to read aloud from the Bible while she worked, gently guiding him over the words he'd never seen before and helping him to pronounce the impossible Israelite names. It took them two years to work their way through the scripture, both Old and New, and by the end Oliver was as fluent as Polly.

"Should we get another book?" she asked.

"I think we better start over on this one," he said, trying to figure how they might skip right to the Song of Solomon, which did not seem at all pious to him but was a treat to share with Polly, who blushed all the way through it.

Reading wasn't their only entertainment. Once Oliver's voice found its bottom, Polly taught him all the hymns and lullabies she knew. One day, he offered up a sea shanty he'd heard at Easter's, pruned a bit for decency. Polly was delighted. "What a wonderful gift."

"I'd rather give you some ivory combs for your hair," he said, thinking of the displays in the dry goods shops in Gloucester. "Or a silk paisley shawl."

"But a song never wears out," said Polly.

Oliver believed that was the wisest and sweetest thing he'd ever heard. Indeed, he thought Polly the cleverest and kindest girl who ever lived and agreed with everything she said. Or nearly. When she mentioned her longing to hear the pastor up in Sandy Bay, who was said to have a fine baritone voice, he grimaced and shrugged. He had never been inside a church and was sure that he'd do something stupid and prove himself a backwoods simpleton in front of Polly and the whole congregation. He knew he'd have to go to a church to marry Polly, but that would be worth it.

⊰⊱

Oliver brought Polly blueberries whenever he could, knowing they were her favorites. "I should bake a pie," she said.

"Why bother," Oliver said, delighting in her pleasure as she ate them two at a time, no more and no less.

Three years into their friendship, he found a thicket of the sweetest blueberries he'd ever tasted and picked a brimming pail of them for her. He hurried to get them to her house while they were still warm from the sun, imagining the bliss on her face as she took the first two into her mouth.

When he arrived, no one answered his knock. Disappointed, he opened the door, thinking to leave them for her and sad that he would not be there to watch her enjoyment.

But Polly was at home. She was alone, washing her hair, her

dress hanging over a chair. Her long blonde tresses dripped over her bare shoulders.

"The berries look wonderful," she said, as though she wasn't naked to the waist.

Oliver stared at her small rosebud breasts, and the brown birthmark on her right collarbone.

"Bring them here," she said. "Put the pail down."

Oliver did as he was told.

"Take off your shirt." She dipped the flannel in cool water and lathered it with a small cake of lavender soap. Oliver closed his eyes, inhaled the scent of flowers, and felt the strength of her short, tapered fingers beneath the softness of the cloth. She circled behind him and washed his back and neck, running her hands over the muscles in his shoulders, down his arms to his hands, first the left and then the right. He had been touched so little in his life; he trembled at the tenderness of her hands on him.

"Should I stop?" she whispered.

He opened his eyes and turned to face her. They were both breathing as though they'd run a race. "You are so beautiful," he said.

Polly touched the soft, new beard on his face, and said, "You are so good to me." She leaned against him, and he was overwhelmed by her silken flesh, the press of her lips, and the damp perfume of her hair. Oliver thought his knees would have buckled without the support of the table beside him.

She took his hand and led him to the bed, but it was not an auspicious beginning. Oliver tried not to think of all the rutting pigs and cattle he'd watched, and struggled against the howl that filled his mouth almost as soon as Polly's legs opened under him.

Polly tried not to think of the times her husband had pushed his way inside her. After Boynton had finished, he'd roll over snoring and she would walk to the river where the cold water would numb her chafed skin and raw heart.

When Polly and Oliver were done, they lay still, sticky and afraid. Polly turned away and started to rise, but Oliver reached out. "Wait," he said and fetched the berries. Sitting on the bed, he fed them to her, two at a time, until she swore she could eat no more.

He walked his fingers up her arm and down her back, softly tracing the miniature peaks and valleys of her spine, the height and pitch of each perfect bone from her neck to her waist. His hand was so light, Polly sighed and leaned against him.

They embraced a second time, slowly. Polly kissed every inch of Oliver's face as he tangled his hands in her hair. He saw the dimples on her shoulders for the first time and like an explorer discovering a new country, claimed them for his own. She admired the strength of his arms and the beauty of his back. They stared into each other's eyes as Oliver rocked against her and into her.

They slept through the sunset and woke up in the darkness. It was raining hard and the world smelled new. Polly lit a candle, and they held each other, shyly at first. When Oliver's need became apparent again, Polly smiled her assent and they closed their eyes and lost themselves in the shared rhythm of their young bodies. In the middle of their union, they understood what they were doing as love.

Oliver and Polly were different people after that. The gnawing hunger that had plagued Oliver since childhood vanished and he seemed to grow another inch for the way he held his head up taller. She refused to answer to her married name and told people that she was Polly Wharf again.

There was a light around the two of them, and had they been spotted together by the ladies of Gloucester, there would have been a storm of talk. But only John Wharf really knew what was afoot, and he died happier knowing his daughter was in good hands.

After the old man passed away, Oliver spent all his nights with

Polly and woke early enough so that he could lie beside his beloved and bask in his good fortune. During waking hours, she became uncomfortable under his worshipful gaze, but he could stare and adore as much as he liked while she slept.

❖

In the morning light, Oliver studied his darling's face, enchanted and amazed, and tried to master the lump in his throat. Polly's puckered slightly at each exhale; her hair fell across her face, a pale blonde web shot through with the strong spring sun. As usual, he was helpless to stop his tears and thoroughly ashamed of himself. At seventeen years old, it was unmanly to weep so easily and yet he seemed to have a bottomless supply of tears. Perhaps it was because he'd cried so little as a child: Tammy used to taunt him mercilessly for any sign of weakness.

But these tears worried him because they seemed like an affront to his good fortune, a threat even. He had to be stronger, he told himself; he should count his blessings, pinch himself, and get on with things. But then Polly sighed in her sleep, and he was overwhelmed at his own luck: she was his antidote and his salvation, his light and his hope. There was just no point in waking up if she wasn't there.

It was a heartbreak every morning to leave his Polly, awake or asleep. Oliver pushed away the thought of where he was supposed to be and what he was supposed to be doing. Oliver no longer lived in Tammy's house, but he hadn't quite severed his ties to her. Her legs had grown too painful for her to take the cows to pasture or to get her butter to market, and these tasks fell to Oliver.

He was already late that morning, but then, he really didn't see what difference it made where Tammy's cows grazed. "Damn," he muttered.

Polly opened a lazy eye. "Have you been awake long?"

"Hours," Oliver said.

"Well, then, where's my tea?"

"You haven't a crumb in the house. But I figure there'll be enough for both of us when I take you over to Dora Stiles's."

"I thought you couldn't walk to town with me today," she said.

"I'm damned." Oliver sat up and shook his head. "I was supposed to get those damn cows of hers to pasture at dawn, and it's getting near noon."

"Oh, it's nowhere near that late," said Polly, putting her finger to the tip of Oliver's nose. "But it's getting later all the time. And you know Aunt Hannah wants to marry me off to Silas Ridge."

"Does she now," Oliver mocked. "A man with a harelip and a mortgaged boat?"

"A man who owns half of the biggest fish market in town, and a house on Main Street," said Polly, imitating the superior tone and nasal phrasing of her aunt.

"Why don't you marry him, then?" Oliver shrugged, making a show of not caring one way or the other.

"Because I'm going to marry you."

"Yes, you are."

"And when might that happen?" she asked wearily, knowing full well what he'd say next.

"When I can buy you a proper dress," Oliver insisted. "When we can stand every last one of your damned cousins to punch and a cake. When I can . . ."

Polly threw off the covers and got out of the bed. "There won't be any tea left at Dora's if I don't step lively."

"Oh, Polly," Oliver sighed. "Don't make a fuss. I love you more than all the tea and all the coffee and all the biscuits. . . ."

Polly laughed. "And all the blueberries, too?"

At the mention of blueberries, Oliver pulled her back down beside him and began to kiss her in earnest and it was another hour before the two of them said their good-byes and went their separate ways: Polly to Dora Stiles's elegant Gloucester home, where a basket of mending awaited her; Oliver to face Tammy and her cows.

With Polly's scent on his skin, he had no fears of the foul tirade that awaited him, but even so, the smile drained from his face as the house came into view. The cows were grazing by the front door.

With better roads and quicker routes elsewhere on Cape Ann, the traffic over Tammy's bridge had slowed to almost nothing. Without her tolls, she'd taken up dairying. Oliver couldn't quite fathom how she'd paid for the two huge, brown creatures, but Betsy and Bertie did what Oliver would never have believed possible: they made a mother out of Tammy Younger.

Although she tried to hide it, he knew she doted on those animals and spent hours brushing them, her eyes half-closed, her forehead against their great bowed bellies. She even sang to them in her piercing, reedy voice; weird lullabies: one song for Bertie, a different one for Betsy.

When Oliver caught her putting dandelion wreaths on their necks, Tammy spat at him and called him a dim-witted son-of-a-bitch who didn't know his ass from his elbow. "I'm working a charm," she said.

No one could argue that the milk wasn't the richest on Cape Ann, and it churned into the sweetest butter anyone could remember. Even so, no one would buy it from the foul-tempered crone who insulted the housewives and shopkeepers who were willing to pay double for her perfect yellow-gold logs.

So Oliver became the go-between, welcomed at general stores and bakeshops in Gloucester, where Tammy's butter gained him a large circle of acquaintances and a few friends. He kept half of what he took in for himself, deciding that when Tammy discovered the extent of his thievery, he'd quit and be done with her forever.

❖

Tammy was scratching at the dirt like an angry rooster when Oliver appeared. "You bastard no-good muttonhead," she shrieked. "You lying sack of shit. The girls had their hearts set on the high pasture this morning."

The cows seemed happy enough, nibbling and chewing where they were. He shrugged.

"You dunderhead, I oughta . . ." But she had no idea of what she ought to do to Oliver. He was taller than she and her knees were much too sore to chase him. She knew he was keeping part of her profit, but assumed the gutless fool wasn't taking more than a trifle. Not that she spent any time pondering her nephew's habits or choices; she hadn't even noticed that his clothes fit him properly and that his shirts were always clean.

The girls had her full attention. Bertie was twice as good a milker as Betsy, but Betsy's milk was so rich and fat, it ran yellow from the teat. Between the two of them, Tammy was assured of her sugar and cocoa. The nuisance was that it should come by way of Oliver, but she had no choice, as no one in town would speak to her.

Toothless, breathless, and lame as she was, outrage was still strong in Tammy. When Oliver hadn't shown up, she'd cussed and spit and undertaken such a furious fit of churning that there was an extra log of butter in the cooling bucket. "You ought to be horsewhipped," she said. Oliver laughed at that, another proof of her weakness.

"Take your backside into town and bring me some tobacco from Mansfield," she ordered. "And a pound of sugar, and another packet of cocoa, and three of those bananas if he's got 'em." She tried to come up with an order too big for Oliver to skim anything from the transaction. "And don't be leaving my linen there this time. You lost me the best wrapper last time."

"That was a year ago, old woman," Oliver said.

"You think you're smart enough to pull something over on me?" she shrieked.

Oliver shook his head and poured away half of the water to make the pail lighter for the journey.

"Don't think you're fooling Tammy Younger. You ain't got the brains or the balls."

Tammy's abuse followed him out of the clearing and a few yards onto the road, where the sky finally swallowed up her noise. The calm of the day put him in mind of Polly. A bird set up a racket above him and reminded him of how Polly liked birds. She liked dogs, too, and wanted one for a pet, just like the little gray one that looked up at Judy Rhines with such devotion.

"Don't I love you enough?" Oliver had asked.

"I want a dog to love me, too."

"What about a pig?" he teased.

"Pigs, cows, chickens, dogs, everything but cats," said Polly. "They give me the shivers."

"No cats," Oliver promised.

Thinking about Polly set him to humming. It was a sunny day and going into town was better than herding Tammy's damned cows. He might even try to visit Polly again, even though she wasn't keen on their being seen too much together. Oliver didn't quite understand why she worried so about her reputation. Widows were above suspicion as far as he could tell, and she was born a Wharf, which set her even higher. But he would never argue the point with Polly, or any other, for that matter. He'd had enough cross words to last the rest of his days and he was determined to keep things between them peaceful.

With Polly to think about, the walk to Gloucester was nearly over before Oliver remembered that he hadn't eaten breakfast. He wondered what Everett might have on hand.

Everett Mansfield was Oliver's favorite customer. Even though the ladies at the bakeshop were always good for a free loaf of day-old bread, Everett would set two chairs together and sit down for a friendly man-to-man about business, local politics, and his two little girls. He was sweeping out the shop when Oliver arrived. Reaching for the butter he said, "Well, if it isn't young Mr. Younger. I didn't expect to see you back so soon."

"Tammy got a bee up her arse and churning is how she settles herself."

Everett laughed. "I got someone waiting for this. Too bad it sells so high," he said, as the two of them headed behind the counter. "I got some of my Susannah's finger rolls here today and they would do it justice. How about some marmalade instead?"

Oliver grinned. Wouldn't Tammy turn green if she knew he was eating English jam on her account?

Everett was right to brag about his wife's rolls and the marmalade was a revelation of tartness within sweetness. Oliver wished there was a way he could save a spoonful for Polly.

His host was quieter than usual, chewing on his pipe instead of regaling him with stories about his Abby and little Ella. Everett pulled on his chin, trying to fix on a way to talk about what William Allen had said to him the other day. Allen had been in the store looking for a log of Tammy Younger's butter. "The wife wants it," he explained, as Allen himself was famously tightfisted.

"Why not buy it direct from Tammy?" Everett asked, as Allen was Tammy's closest neighbor, and he might have saved himself some money that way.

"I haven't talked to the old bitch in fifteen years."

"Well, I don't expect Oliver back here for at least a week."

"Humph," Allen snorted, filling the air between them with the smell of strong drink. "Do you think that boy is slow or stupid?"

Everett shrugged. He rarely expressed opinions about people: you agreed with one fellow about the meanness of his neighbor, and the next thing you knew, neither of them would buy from you, nor their wives. With the bakery and a dry goods store on the same block, a general storekeeper had to be careful about losing any trade.

"You mean Oliver Younger?" asked Everett, as though he was trying to place the name.

"Don't give me that," said Allen, picking at the dirt under his thumbnail. "I seen the two of you in here, drinking tea like a pair of old ladies."

Everett knew that Oliver wasn't dull or lacking in ambition. They had talked about his moving out of Dogtown and debated the various ways a fellow might earn a living in Gloucester. He asked, "What makes you think he's stupid?"

"What's he doing her bidding for then? That land belongs to him, not her," Allen said.

"Well, I expect he'll come into it when Tammy dies."

"Nah. It's been his for a while now. I witnessed that will myself. Poked a hole in the paper when I signed."

"Oliver's got a legal claim now?" Everett asked.

"So what?" Allen shrugged. "The place is useless."

"You ever tell him about this?"

"That was for Tammy to do."

"You figured Tammy would tell him?" exclaimed Everett, and deciding he could afford to forgo Allen's trade, added, "And who was it you just called stupid?"

❖

While Oliver licked the last of the marmalade from his fingers, Everett cleared his throat and said, as lightly as he could, "William Allen was in the other day and said he had something for you. Said you should stop by his place."

"Allen? He's never given me the time of day."

"Well, he wants to talk to you now," Everett said, relieved at the arrival of a customer, who put an end to the conversation.

Oliver pocketed his commission and, with Tammy's supplies in hand, headed for the Stiles house on High Street. He wondered what on earth Allen would want him for: perhaps he needed an extra pair of hands to pull out a stump or move a boulder.

As he passed the great houses of the city, Oliver's attention wandered. The bright blue of the harbor blinked in and out of view between clapboards and blossoming bushes. A man on a ladder applied a fresh coat of green paint to some shutters and Oliver was overwhelmed with the desire to give Polly a home as big and elegant as one of these.

Hurrying past the Stiles's imposing front door, he entered through the kitchen gate and found Polly on a shaded bench, frowning over a snowy napkin. She hated hemming linens, feeling it was beneath her skills. Any ten-year-old child could do it, but if someone was willing to pay top dollar for straight-stitch, she wouldn't turn it down.

The sight of Oliver's adoring face lifted her spirits so quickly, she almost felt dizzy. But her happiness was quickly eclipsed by fear when the Stiles' little dog started yapping. "Oliver. You shouldn't have come."

"I was nearby," he said. "When should I come back for you?"

"I'm staying the night," Polly said. "And tomorrow, too, most likely. There is so much to do." She lowered her voice. "Dora needs a bridal trousseau for her Emily. In a hurry."

"Who's robbing that cradle?" he asked, as the girl was barely fifteen.

"She's marrying Thomas Pearce, that colonel's son. The wedding's set for Sunday next," said Polly, who figured there'd likely be a christening well before Christmas. She pointed to the heaped basket at her feet. "There's a mountain of sheets and tablecloths inside."

Polly's stomach pitched, and she realized that her dizziness might be a sign that she was in the same boat as Emily. Her own courses had been due last week, and it was only a matter of time before she and Oliver got caught. She was not afraid for her future. Even though Polly had no hope of a dowry, she counted herself luckier than Emily, who had all the linens a girl could want but did not love her baby's father. The only question would be how to get her cousins to the wedding. They had been furious when she moved to Dogtown, ignoring their objections that she was too young, pretty, and well connected a widow to live among the degraded females of that neighborhood. As far as she could tell, they still knew nothing about Oliver.

She looked up to see tears in his eyes. "Oh no," she said, and bit her lip to keep from smiling. "I'm not deserting you, dearheart. I'll be home tomorrow, or the day after."

Oliver cleared his throat. "I know," he said and tried not to dwell on the prospect of waking up alone the next morning. Happiness had made him too tender for his own good.

"You'd best be going," Polly said. "They don't approve of my having visitors. Especially not dashing young men."

Oliver kicked at the gravel and hung his head.

"Just think of our reunion," she said.

He doffed his hat, brushing it across Polly's lap, up her chest, and under her chin. She kissed the air in his direction, and he marched himself away.

In the street, Oliver felt newly orphaned. He started back up the road to Dogtown, dragging his feet at the thought of facing Tammy without the reward of Polly's smile at the end of the day. After a few paces he turned back and started down toward the harbor, kicking at stones until one landed in the water. Oliver looked up to find himself beside a large pile of old planks and pilings at the harbor's edge.

"What's all this?" Oliver asked of a man dragging the wood into piles.

"A new wharf," said the dark-haired fellow, grateful for the chance to stop and mop his brow. "Mr. Bates wants to salt his mackerel right here instead of taking it into Boston. We're going to make this dock big enough to set up the flakes to dry the fillets right here. See, Bates got burned by the Boston market last year when the price dropped and he had to dump a holdful. Nearly lost his boat. He figures on salting his own fish and shipping it out west in his own barrels."

"Can he make money on that, do you think?"

"I'm counting on it. My name's Grady. I'm the foreman," he said, eyeing the shape of Oliver's forearms and the weary state of his boots. "I'm going to need a crew. The work ain't too hard but you got to be able to stand the smell."

"I might be interested," said Oliver.

"Well, if you want to get off the farm, you come see me in a couple of months."

Oliver tipped his hat and wandered back up to Front Street. One trip across the bay in rough seas had cured him of any seafaring dreams, but the smell of fish didn't bother him. And he thought that Polly might just as soon live in town, closer to her customers and a steady supply of thread and ribbons, and female conversation.

Passing Peg Low's tavern on Front Street, the smell of bacon snagged Oliver's attention. In the past, he'd steered clear of public houses. A scant glass of Easter's weak beer made his head ache, and besides that, Polly hated to see him drink so much as a glass of hard cider. But he was feeling sorry for himself and he knew that taking a drink or two was exactly the thing that men did when they needed cheering up. Then he remembered that Peg put out free crackers for her customers, which was reason enough.

The tavern was a long room with a low ceiling, filled with empty chairs and tables. At midafternoon, there were only two other patrons, who glanced up as he entered. One was an ancient fellow with a marked tremor in his hands and dark clothes that gave no clue to his occupation or status. The other was a sailor whose odd scarf identified him as a foreigner; his leg was propped on a chair beside him, splinted and bandaged from ankle to knee.

After four hard crackers and half a tankard of strong beer, Oliver's mood had lifted. His talk with the foreman down at the wharf seemed a good omen: with a steady job in town he could marry Polly. They would move out of Dogtown and live in town, like other people of their age. With a drink in his hand, he surveyed the room and felt like a grown man who belonged there. Oliver drained the mug with three gulps and got to his feet—with barely a wobble—fortified to face the empty house and the cold bed.

Just then, the injured sailor called, "Young men."

Oliver looked toward the door for the incoming crowd.

"You," he pointed to Oliver. "I vould speak vit' you."

He was one of the largest men Oliver had ever seen, tall and broad, with a dark red beard and a gingery fringe of hair around a shining bald dome.

"I am Ladimir," he announced. "I am only Russian you meet, yes?" he said, with a great rolling of his *R*'s.

"I am Oliver Younger." He reached out to shake hands.

"You are sailor, Oliwer. Yes?"

"No," he said. "I am . . ." What was he? He herded cows for Tammy and hired out at planting and harvest time. "I'm a farmer, I suppose."

"My father, too. He gots hundred hectare with barley and wheat. Many geese. You got so much land, also, Oliwer?"

"No," said Oliver. He had nothing. No property, no livestock, no tools. Calling himself a farmer was a lie; he was still nothing but a Dogtown pussy. A joke among men. A failure before he started.

"No land?" Ladimir boomed. "Too bad for you. But I still buy you fleep, yes?" and called for Peg to bring them the drink.

Oliver had never tasted flip, which smelled of rum, lemon, and spice. "Bottom up," said Ladimir, clinking his glass against Oliver's, who swallowed the sweet stuff like it was lemonade. When the arrack and brandy hit Oliver's throat, he was seized by a coughing fit that lifted him out of his seat.

"Farmer Oliwer don't know how to dreenk the fleep!" said Ladimir, delighted. He ordered another round and launched into the long story of his travels.

Halfway through his second glass of flip, Oliver began to chuckle. "You were on a 'woyage'?"

"In big wessel," said Ladimir.

Oliver covered his mouth.

"There was wery big willage," said the Russian.

"Willage?"

"Yes," Ladimir said, suddenly suspicious.

"Was . . . it . . . in . . ." Oliver took a breath, "Wirginia?" Laughing out loud he gasped, "Or maybe Wermont?"

"You laugh at me? You are willain."

"Willain?" Oliver hooted. "I am willain?" He doubled over, holding his sides, repeating, "Willain, I am Oliwer the Willain."

Ladimir's face turned purple. He pulled himself up to his elbows and punched Oliver, knocking him off his chair and onto the floor.

"The pup's a cheap drunk," croaked the old man in the corner.

Peg materialized above him. "Out," she hollered. Grabbing Oliver by the ear, she led him to the door and pushed him outside. He staggered into the middle of the street and stood, dizzy and dazzled by the suddenly bright light.

Peg threw his hat out after him to the delight of four half-grown boys, who kicked it back and forth and then made a show of accidentally knocking into Oliver. At that, he doubled over and threw up, a display the boys greeted with whistles and catcalls.

Cornelius turned the corner just in time to witness the scene. He hesitated only a moment before stepping forward, retrieving Oliver's hat, and pulling him up. The boys kept on hooting and clapping, while a few men gathered to watch the African gather up the crumpled packets of tobacco and cocoa, and stuff them all into Oliver's pockets.

"Will you look at that?" said one of them. "The nigger comes to the rescue of the Dogtown idiot."

The boys walked away, slapping one another on the back. The men disappeared inside the tavern. Oliver hung his head, feeling like a whipped dog. Before he knew it, Cornelius was gone, too, and he had to run in order to catch the African, who had walked on up Washington Street, his back as straight as a pike. As the houses gave way to weeds and dusty fields Oliver tried to say thank you, but every time he tried, Cornelius hurried his pace.

Oliver's aching head echoed with Tammy's sour voice calling him an idiot, a nit, a dolt. Once Polly heard how he'd gotten drunk and stupid in front of the whole town, she would finally see him for what he truly was: a hopeless case and a waste of her time. When he groaned, Cornelius glanced back over his shoulder, but this time Oliver turned away.

The two men slowed as they reached the path leading to Tammy's house. Oliver reached out to shake Cornelius's hand; for a moment he thought the African might take it, but he hurried away.

Oliver was relieved to see that Tammy was in the barn, talking to her cows. He tiptoed to the door, threw the provisions on the table, and ran as though he'd been stealing rather than making a delivery.

Back at Polly's house, he fell into bed, where he lost the rest of the day and the whole night. He woke with a dreadful headache, thinking about Cornelius. As a boy, he had never given the man any more thought than he would a dog. He'd idolized John Stanwood, the worst rotter on Cape Ann. Oliver covered his face with his hands and swore at himself. Why had he walked into that damned pub in the first place?

When he finally got up, the sight of his blackened eye in the looking glass made him glad that Polly was in Gloucester. After a few hours of holding his head in his hands, the notion that he'd lost her began to plague him again, and he thought he'd do himself some harm if he didn't get out of the house. There was no going back into town so soon after that public humiliation, and he would not let Tammy get a chance to laugh at his face. Easter would ask him what happened, if she didn't already know. Then Oliver remembered Allen's message and decided he might as well find out what the man wanted.

"Who gave you the beating?" The farmer was sitting on a bench outside his house, mending a broken barrel, when Oliver arrived.

"I fell," he mumbled.

Allen smirked, but said, "Figured I'd try my hand at this before paying some damned cooper to do it."

"Everett Mansfield said you wanted to see me."

Allen glanced up at Oliver, took another whack at the bent spoke, cleared his throat, glanced at the horizon, chewed on his lip, and said, "It's near supper. You might as well come inside."

Mrs. Allen was not happy about the sudden arrival of a guest. "Just give me a minute," she said and whisked the two plates from the table to divide the beans and brown bread into three smaller portions. The Allens ate quickly, without exchanging a word. As soon as the last bite was swallowed, Allen led Oliver back outside, lit a pipe, and said, "Good to have company at the table."

Oliver wondered about the purpose of that lie and dug his toe into the dirt. "You got some work for me?" he asked.

Allen puffed. "That parcel of land you're on," he said, "too bad it's such a pile of rocks. No hope of a crop up there."

Oliver shrugged.

"That stream is about dried up, too, ain't it?"

"No," Oliver said. "It's still running sweet."

"Huh," Allen said. "How long it take you to walk to the harbor? An hour?"

"Nowhere near."

"The berries give out yet?"

"The berries are fine," Oliver said, losing patience. "Everett seems to think you have some sort of commission for me."

"Actually, son," Allen dropped his voice, "I figured you'd have worked it out for yourself by now, how the Younger place belongs to you. It's yours. Been yours for a while, as I count it."

"What are you talking about?" said Oliver. "Tammy inherited the place from Lucy."

"No, sir," said Allen. "That's Younger land, belonged to your grandfather and then your father. Tammy was sister to your grand-dad, but when he died and left it to your pa, Tammy was already set up in the house. Your pa was off at sea, but your ma wouldn't have nothing to do with Dogtown so he stayed with her people whenever he come ashore."

"But it's hers till she dies," Oliver said. "Isn't it?"

Allen sighed. "A few weeks before he died, your pa come to me with a piece of paper he wrote up. Your mother had the fever real bad, and he wasn't looking any too good himself. Maybe he had a feeling his time was coming, I don't know. But he wrote it up so's you'd come into your rights at sixteen."

"You saw a paper?"

"I signed it," Allen muttered. "I was witness."

Oliver knew very little about his parents. The last of his relations died when he was a boy, and no one in Dogtown or Gloucester had ever volunteered a word about them. He'd been too shy to ask, or afraid of what he might learn. If Tammy was the best he could do for a guardian, maybe there were worse secrets in the family cupboard.

"Does anyone else know this?"

"I doubt it," Allen shrugged. "Maybe."

Oliver felt as though a wave of icy seawater had broken over his head. His eyes burned, his ears rang, and he gasped for breath. When he surfaced, his hands were tight around Allen's neck.

"You son-of-a-bitch. You goddamn son-of-a-bitch, you didn't tell me?"

Allen twisted loose, but Oliver grabbed his arm and pinned it behind him. "I'd come here begging for food, and you'd turn your nose up at me. Your daughters laughed at my clothes." Oliver tightened his grip. "All that time you knew this, and you didn't tell me?"

"I didn't need Tammy mad at me," said Allen.

"You aren't stupid enough to believe she's a witch, are you?" Oliver said. "Are you as dumb as all that?"

Allen had his reasons for keeping on Tammy's good side. She'd made it clear long ago that his silence about the Younger will would keep her quiet about his regular trips to the harbor's whores. It had been a good enough bargain, till now.

"I'm going to break your arm," Oliver said. "And then I'm going to break the other one."

"It ain't me you want, boy," Allen said. "It's Tammy that did you the harm. Go settle up with her. Go find yourself that will, that's what you need to do. It's probably in the house somewhere."

Oliver twisted Allen's arm one last time before rushing headlong into the woods. He moved as quickly as he could, kicking at the underbrush as the whole of his hungry, lonely boyhood came back at him. He had been a slave in his own house and he could have been his own man years ago.

But the truth was that Oliver could have become his own man

long ago. He could have moved out of Tammy's house. Easter would have taken him in if he'd asked. Or he could have bound himself to a blacksmith or a cooper; by now he'd have a trade and the means to marry Polly.

But he had been too weak and too afraid, as Tammy had made him. Maybe she was a witch, after all. Oliver might appear to be a grown man, but in fact, he had the spine of a jellyfish. It was past time that he found his nerve.

Oliver thought of the long knife in Polly's kitchen and ran all the way back to the house, to find her there, waiting for him with a big smile and arms open. He walked past her without saying a word.

"What happened to your eye?" Polly cried.

Oliver brushed her hand aside with what felt like a slap.

"Ollie!"

"I fell," he said as he found the knife and set to sharpening it.

"What is it?" Polly said. "What happened to you? What do you want with that?"

He turned the blade over and started on the other side.

"Please, Ollie," she begged. "Tell me what happened. What are you doing?"

Polly was terrified. As she'd walked home, she had prepared a funny speech to tell him the news of the baby. But there was no talking to this wild stranger. Just a few days ago, the remoteness of the house had made it seem a haven of privacy and safety. Now it felt like a kind of prison, with no one to summon for help and nowhere to turn. The barking of a dog sent her outside to see Greyling worrying a squirrel up a tree.

Judy Rhines appeared a moment later and waved. But when she saw Polly's tear-streaked face, she hurried over. "What's wrong?"

"It's Oliver," Polly was sobbing. "He's not himself. He's got a knife, and he looks so strange and he's been hurt, too. He won't talk to me. And, oh Judy, I'm going to have a baby. I'm sure of it now."

Judy took her arm and led her inside, where they found Oliver testing the knife on the edge of the table.

"What's that for?" Judy said.

But Oliver set his jaw and kept working.

"Oliver, dear," said Judy. "You must talk to us. You may not have secrets from Polly now. She's carrying your baby."

That stopped him. "What?" he said, and looked up.

"I was going to tell you today," said Polly. "I was hoping it would make you happy." Had it been any other day, any other hour, he would have covered her face with kisses but at the moment he could not meet her eyes. There was nothing inside him but anger.

"What is the knife for?" Judy said.

"Tammy."

Polly shook her head. "I don't understand."

"Nor I," Judy said.

His knuckles white around the shaft of the knife, Oliver told them what William Allen had said about his inheritance and the way Tammy had cheated him out of what was rightfully his. "I'm done being the coward," he said. "I'm a grown man now. It's time to act like one."

Polly tried to put her arms around him, but Oliver pulled away.

"She is a spiteful old horror," Judy said. "But you're not going to murder her. It isn't worth the risk to you, or to Polly. And besides, you don't have it in you."

He glared at Judy. "You don't think so, do you?"

She was suddenly ashamed of the excuses she'd made for Tammy over the years. Judy had made light of Tammy as a character, uncouth but essentially harmless. She had known that Oliver hadn't had it easy, but she had never put herself in his place, and for the first time, Judy had a feeling for just how bad it must have been for him.

Polly took his face between her hands so he had to look at her.

The sight of her tears undid him. "What the hell is wrong with me?" he cried.

"There is nothing wrong with you," said Polly. "There just isn't a killing bone in you. I love you for that."

"Did you know about the will?" Oliver asked Judy.

"No."

"Did anyone else know?"

"I don't think so," said Judy, whose mind turned to Easter. Would she have kept such a thing to herself?

"You need that paper," she said. "Do you have any idea where it might be?"

Oliver knew. Tammy's house was as bare as any other in Dogtown: a bed and a table, a few chairs and a stool, a row of pegs for a wardrobe. But she had one extra piece of furniture, which Oliver had always figured she got through blackmail. A dainty little lady's writing table, with turned legs and a carved shelf, it sat tucked between her bed and the wall. Now chipped and stained, it was crowded with empty pots that once held jam, clouded spice bottles, broken pipes. Once, as a boy, Oliver had peeked inside the drawer and found a mass of wrapping papers from every fondant and nougat that Tammy had ever eaten.

"Wait until she's away from the house," said Judy.

"That doesn't happen anymore," he said. "She can hardly walk to the stream and back."

Judy thought for a moment. "I'll get her into Gloucester then, and give you a chance to find what's yours."

⬧

Judy set her plan in motion that very day. After a quick visit to the Allen farm, where she browbeat William into loaning her his wagon, Judy made for Tammy's house. She was churning butter in the shade by the side of her door. As soon as she saw who was com-ing up her path, Tammy said, "You can go to hell."

"Hello to you, too, Mistress Younger."

"I know you got a soft spot for that half-wit nephew of mine," Tammy said. "You see him, you can tell him I'll shoot him if he comes back here."

"Is Oliver missing?"

"I ain't seen a hair of him for two days now. My girls are pining for the meadows while he's having at it with some strumpet or other. Or maybe he fell into a well and drowned. Good riddance, I say." Tammy looked Judy up and down and, realizing that she needed someone to get her to market, changed her tone. "Except that I've got a whole lot of sweet butter to sell, and no way to get it into town."

"Then it's lucky that I happened by," said Judy. "I'm aiming to take a bunch of rushes into town on Monday. Mrs. Cook wants three chairs mended and a new broom. I got William Allen to loan me his wagon. I could take you with me."

Tammy screwed up her face. "Allen is making a loan? That horse's ass does nothing for nothing."

"You're right there," Judy agreed. "I fixed him up with some spring tonic a little while back, and I'm calling in the favor. I figure I might get some of that famous butter out of you, in exchange for the ride."

"Why should I give you anything?" said Tammy. "You won't be going out of your way."

"I could pass on by without stopping."

"And what would people think of you when I tell 'em you left me here to starve?"

"How about if I take half a log of butter for doing you that favor?" Judy said.

Tammy thought Judy a ninny for asking so little, but she scowled to hide her satisfaction at the bargain.

❖

Oliver rose early to gather enough reeds to make good on Judy's lie, and for once he didn't regret cutting short his morning with Polly. He was skittish about rolling over on her now that she was carrying a baby, though he barely slept for worrying. What if Tammy decided not to go into Gloucester? What if she had destroyed the will? What if he couldn't find it? What if he did? And what kind of difference would it make, anyway? There was no way to get back what had been taken from him.

The mist was starting to burn off as Judy stopped at Tammy's place. She was waiting, smoking a pipe and tapping her foot, with three full buckets ready to go. She had churned so much she'd had to wrap some of the butter in strips of yellow gingham instead of white linen, and she'd been rehearsing ways to insult the shop-keepers if they made any complaint about the difference.

As soon as the cart disappeared, Oliver stepped out of the woods and headed straight for the writing table. It was more cluttered and dustier than he remembered, piled with all sorts of rubbish: lengths of string and ribbon, buttons and nails, shells and bent spoons. The drawer was so full, it took him three tugs to get it open.

He sat down at the table with the drawer and set to removing the scraps and wrappers, reading every label and advertisement, and then laying each paper flat to make sure he missed nothing. Beneath the last yellowed slips of tissue, he found a small wooden box that rattled with promise but contained nothing but a dozen pale pebbles. On second look, Oliver realized that they were actually the brittle remains of Tammy's teeth. A shiver passed through him as he remembered her bleating cries at John Stanwood's hand.

There was no will. He had been so certain that the desk would yield it up. He was wrong again. Polly would be better off married to anyone else—even Caleb Boynton. Hating himself for thinking such a miserable thing, Oliver returned to the desk and kicked it as hard as he could, breaking one of its legs and toppling the whole thing onto its side. The back split apart, and he saw the piece of parchment stuck between two thin panels.

Oliver held his breath as he teased it, yellow and dried, out of its snug hiding place and unfolded the creases slowly, so the paper would not tear. The whole document was but two lines of writing.

This is to state that all of the Younger lands, including the house on Cherry Street to the stream below and to the road above, as well as the pasture to the north and west as noted in town deed, are the sole property of Oliver Younger, son of Daniel Younger. This to take effect 12 September 1818, sixteen years to the day after his birth, when he shall come into his inheritance.

[Signed] Daniel Younger and William Allen
27 June 1806

Oliver had never let himself wonder what his life might have been like had his parents lived, but there was no way to avoid the thought now. His father seemed to be standing in the room with him. He stared at the handwriting, which slanted to the left. And at his birth date, which he had never known. He was a year older than he'd thought.

Oliver stood up and kicked the desk again, breaking another leg. He grabbed the broom and swept all the papers he'd piled on the table down to the floor. He picked up the little box that contained the dry nubs of Tammy's teeth, dumped it on the hearthstone, and ground them into dust with his heel.

He surveyed the mess he'd made, nodded once, and closed the door as he left.

When Tammy saw what had been done to her house, she shrieked and cursed so loud that she set her cows to lowing in fear. Judy, who had jumped back into the wagon and taken off at a trot, could hear her a half mile down the road.

The next morning, Tammy managed to limp to the Allen farm. Puffing and sweating, she arrived before dawn, walked into the bedroom, and yanked William Allen out of a sound sleep. "You're taking me to see the judge, and you're taking me now."

At the clerk's office she demanded, "I want the magistrate. I want to see a judge."

"Judge Philpot is sitting in Salem," said Mr. Saville, the elderly official whose back went up at Tammy's demeanor and the unmistakable smell of cow that attended her.

"I got a case," Tammy said, slamming her hand flat on the desk.

"Judge Philpot is sitting in Salem all week," Saville said in a tense monotone. "If you give me the particulars, I will put the matter before him."

Tammy launched into a long description of the wrongs that had been done to her by Oliver Younger. "My nephew's son, no less. My own flesh and blood that I raised up by hand, and he bites me like a mad dog. I want my rights. I want him locked up. And that whore, Judy Rhines, too. I blame her for this. He's too stupid to have thought it up. It was Judy Rhines."

Mr. Saville copied the names into his ledger. "The judge will determine whether there is a case. I will have word sent to you."

The moment Tammy realized that she would get no satisfaction then and there, she spit on the floor and hobbled out, with Allen shuffling after.

A few hours later, Oliver stood in the very same spot facing Mr. Saville. In his clean white shirt and neatly trimmed beard, he was the picture of a serious young man as he handed over the will with a polite bow. Mr. Saville took Oliver's testimony and said, "I must ask how you came by this document, Mr. Younger."

Polly had been standing a few steps behind Oliver, her eyes on the floor. But at that, she said, "Oh, Your Honor, Oliver just had to get that paper for us. Tammy never showed it to him and we were afraid she'd burn it. We're to be married, you see." She blushed. "And I'm afraid she means to make trouble for us."

"Don't worry yourself, my dear," said Saville, who liked being called "Your Honor" and thought her perfectly charming. "If Mr. Allen affirms his signature, the document will stand. And as for the special circumstances of its, uh, retrieval, I believe the parties can be made to come to an agreement."

Polly smiled and Judge Philpot never heard a word of the case. Mr. Saville despised the Honorable Matthew R. Philpot, who made no secret of his disdain for Gloucester, which he saw as a miserable backwater filled with criminals and fools. Rather than provide another excuse for him to dine out on the foibles of Cape Ann's "characters," the clerk dismissed the charge against Oliver, accepted the will in probate, and made his decision known with a posting on the town hall door.

The name of Oliver Younger was published again a few days later, when the banns announcing his marriage to Polly Wharf went up on the door of Second Parish.

Judy Rhines spent the days leading up to the wedding helping Polly sew her simple trousseau. She also brought gifts of fresh eggs and canned peaches and whatever else she could put her hands on, trying to make amends for what she hadn't done for Oliver in the past.

One evening, sitting with the couple after an early dinner, she cleared her breath and said, "I wish to talk to you both about something. It isn't my place, but I can't hold my tongue, so forgive an old maid's meddling."

She brushed off their protests and continued. "I think you should let Tammy stay in the house. It's yours to do with as you choose; no one disputes that. But if you take it, Tammy will live in one of those Dogtown cellars and she'll be dead by winter. I know you got no reason to show her any mercy, but I say let the devil take care of his own.

"Besides," Judy said, "it's an unhappy house and Tammy's not long for this world. And if you ask me, Dogtown is too far away from town for a confinement."

Oliver and Polly smiled at each other. "We'd more or less decided that for ourselves," Polly said.

"I want nothing to do with the place," Oliver added, softly. "I'll sell it the day she dies."

❖

The wedding took place on a sunny June morning. Judy stood beside Oliver as one of Polly's uncles walked her down the aisle. Easter Carter wore a loud green silk dress no one had ever seen before. Everett Mansfield attended, with his wife and daughters, who carried baskets of wildflowers and giggled at the new minister's unfortunate lisp. All of Polly's cousins attended, and although not one of them cracked a smile during the service, Aunt Hannah Goff turned out to be a brick, standing everyone to a respectable punch. She also moved them into a little cottage owned by Mr. Goff on the far upper reach of Washington Street on the edge of town; although it was hardly a fashionable neighborhood, at least it removed her niece from the shadowy associations of a Dogtown address.

Oliver took a job filleting mackerel, though the smell made Polly queasier as the weeks of her confinement passed. Otherwise she felt healthy enough to keep on sewing fancywork right up to the day the baby was born.

They named him Nathaniel, and he was a rosy, sweet-tempered boy. No new father ever doted on his son more than Oliver Younger, who spent every spare moment with the child, holding him, counting his fingers and toes, kissing his petal-soft cheeks, whispering endearments, and bestowing a thousand heartfelt promises and blessings that were fully and miraculously his to give.

Departure

AFTER THE baby was born, Judy Rhines moved in with Polly and Oliver for a month to help with the cooking and washing. Judy's presence made it a little easier for Oliver to tear himself away from his little family and go to work. After he left in the mornings, while Polly napped, Judy would take the boy in her arms, rock him and hum to him, and delight in his resolute yawns and sneezes. To her great surprise, Judy fell in love with him, and shared his besotted parents' belief that he was the best baby in creation. Oliver and Polly started calling her "Auntie Judy," a name that gave her more pleasure than they knew.

After Judy returned to her own house, the Youngers made a place for her in their home, leaving out her cot and the old rug for Greyling so she could stop over on her near-daily travels to and from Dogtown. By then, Judy had been retained by Judge Joshua Cook as a companion for his wife, Martha, who suffered from rashes, fever, and various other ailments and discomforts that kept her at home and in need of constant attention and distraction.

Judy was more than pleased about this new position. She had

never spent time with anyone as well read or as thoughtful as Martha Cook, who seemed a paragon of integrity and kindness. Martha, for her part, found a natural intelligence and curiosity in Judy that flattered the teacher in her. While Judy sewed, or tended to the flowers, or poured tea, Martha would read aloud from the Boston newspapers or from the books in the judge's leather-bound library. She tried to engage her attendant in conversation about the stories or style of her selections, but Judy was too aware of her deficiencies to do anything but defer to her mistress on every point.

When the days grew milder and the evenings longer, Martha declared it was the season for novels, and Judy was soon enchanted by the tales of English gentlewomen in straitened circumstances, most of whom were redeemed by noble friends and gallant lovers in the last chapter. Judy and Martha spent hours discussing the characters as though they were flesh-and-blood neighbors rather than figures in a book. After several months of encouragement, Martha managed to coax Judy into voicing an opinion of her own.

She also insisted on providing Judy with several well-made dresses that no longer fit her own dwindling frame and bought her a new pair of stylish shoes, which Judy wore indoors but left, wrapped in paper, in the Cooks' kitchen whenever she returned to Dogtown. Grateful as she was for the luxuries of her life in town, Judy would not agree to move into the Cooks' house. No matter how often Martha pressed, and regardless of the fact that the bedroom beside the kitchen was always warm, and the bed was far better than her own, she resisted "living in." Day work seemed more dignified and besides, Greyling didn't get along with the house cat, and the dog was never far from Judy's side, wherever she went.

As their first summer together ended, Martha began to read from a well-known series of books written by a distant kinswoman of hers, Sarah Maria Hastings. Mrs. Hastings's volumes contained all manner of writing: poems, letters, essays, and heartrending stories about the outrages and difficulties of women's lives. One particular tale of a wife in a loveless and childless marriage set Martha to such a fit of weeping that Judy began to cast a wondering eye at the judge. Martha never spoke ill of her husband and Judy had no other reason to think him anything but an exemplary man. He was mostly unknown to her since he traveled a good deal, and when he was in town he never took his midday meal at home. But now, these facts fed her growing suspicion that there was something amiss, and Martha's conjugal situation was often in her mind as she followed the roads in and out of Dogtown.

On the Saturdays when Judy remained up-country, she would take long walks to clear her mind. Following overgrown trails and shortcuts that she knew as well as the inside of her own house, she reveled in the solitude and peace of the woods. But in truth, nearly every path was strewn with memories, some trivial, some momentous. There was the fallen tree where she'd once seen a she-skunk leading a litter of seven tiny babies, their striped tails bobbing in a merry row. A hollow tree marked the spot where Sammy Stanley had stopped her once, to ask if she'd had a dollar to change for ten dimes. Such a strange child, she remembered. "How is your grandmother's health?" she'd asked, unable to think of any other question for a boy who lived in a brothel. He'd stared like she had grown an extra eye, and bolted from her.

There were changes in Dogtown's landscape from season to season, and from year to year: trees downed, mushrooms plentiful, or squirrels scarce. And yet, the forest was always the same. Perhaps that was why Judy could never fix the sequence of her out-of-doors memories: Had she met Sammy before or after the day she'd spotted the two poor doxies who lived at the Stanley house, too? She recalled that they were sitting on the big cracked grindstone beside one of the old abandoned houses. Easter had told her a few things about them she'd just as soon never have heard, so she'd pretended not to see Molly and Sally. But the picture of the tall dark head and the pale little blonde whispering together in the sunlight was still vivid in her mind's eye.

As was the day she came across Oliver and Polly kissing beside the natural edifice called Peter's Pulpit, among the tallest of the famous Dogtown boulders. When the young people saw her, they had let go of each other with a quick flutter, like a pair of birds flushed out of the brush.

"Hello, Judy," Oliver said, a little too loudly.

Polly put her hands behind her and dropped a silent curtsy.

Judy felt tongue-tied but managed to say, "Good afternoon, Oliver. Hello, Polly." She'd wanted to reassure Polly that her reputation was in no danger from her, but said only, "I'd best be going," and hurried away, confused by a sudden burst of anguish and longing. Why on earth should their happiness upset her?

Judy considered herself a reconciled old maid, but in her bed that night, she realized that she was still smarting from the image of the young lovers. Judy pulled the dog up from her usual place behind her knees and pressed her nose into the musty warmth. "Woe is me," she said, mocking her own moodiness. "Woe is me."

When Judy next saw Easter Carter, she said, "I think Oliver Younger may be keeping company with Polly."

Easter grinned. "Yes, dearie. John Wharf used to come up here to give them a chance at each other. He was counting on the boy taking care of her once he passed away. I used to tell him there wasn't a safer wager on land or sea."

"You knew that?" Judy said. "And you didn't tell me?"

"I figured you'd find out soon enough. Besides, I'm not that sort of a gossip."

"But Easter, it's me. It's Judy."

"I never told tales on you, neither," said Easter, softly but firmly.

The two women, usually so companionable, fell into an awkward silence that lasted until Judy suddenly remembered a pot left on the fire and departed, wasting a freshly poured cup of tea.

They had reconciled the very next day, as neither woman would permit anything to damage the bond between them, not even their secrets.

Wherever she walked, Judy was careful to steer her thoughts away from Cornelius. She never took the path where she'd first laid eyes on him, crouched over a squirrel trap. Their eyes had met just as he snapped the animal's neck. Judy smiled at him. She was no hypocrite: she ate squirrels and knew how they died. "Enjoy your dinner," she had said and walked off. When she arrived home, the animal was laying on her doorstep, gutted and skinned, the first of many gifts.

⁂

One night, alone in her Dogtown bed, Judy finally admitted to herself that she had been in love with Cornelius. "In love" precisely as it was described in the novels and poems she had read with Martha; love as a kind of sweet madness that colored everything. Judy had been shocked that strangers across the ocean could describe the workings of her Yankee heart: the preoccupation and yearning, the soaring happiness and keen appreciation of a man's hidden qualities, the sublime meeting of souls. And yet, there was never a mention of the sort of union she'd shared with Cornelius, the longing and fulfillment of the flesh that could transform two bodies into one.

In the books, love was expressed in sidelong glances and witty banter. Judy could recall only a few conversations with Cornelius. For them, love had been expressed in the interplay of tongues and fingers, the absolute conviction that their bodies belonged to each other, waking and sleeping. And if he never gave her testimonials, Judy remembered a thousand physical proofs of his tenderness and affection.

Judy wondered whether the literary silence about such matters might have had something to do with Cornelius's race, or with the British pedigree of the authoresses. Or perhaps there was something unnatural about her, to have welcomed him into her bed, and to have responded to his touch so freely.

With the years, her body had become drier and cooler and the memory of Cornelius's great legs astride her, his flesh pressed into hers, became strange and even repellent. Finally, Judy did not long for him anymore, and with the benefit of time came to believe that his disappearance had been for the best. He had proven himself untrustworthy and cruel, leaving her feeling cheapened and cheated. Since then, she had attached her heart to gentler and more constant subjects: Oliver and Polly, and their Natty. Easter. And poor Martha Cook.

❖

After nearly two years as Martha's companion, Judy had come to feel like a member of her family. Martha encouraged her to borrow freely from the library and to bring treats from the kitchen whenever she visited with Oliver, Polly, and Natty. Martha had not only told Judy to consider the house her own, she had made it so by dismissing a housemaid who'd muttered something about "that Dogtown witch and that cursed animal of hers." She even gave away the cat so that Greyling could come indoors freely, hoping to sway Judy to move into town.

"I don't like to think of you all alone in that wilderness," fretted Martha.

"I'm not alone," said Judy. "Easter's nearby, and Greyling watches over me. If I lived here, I fear you would discover just how simple I am and grow tired of me."

But the two of them became more and more like sisters, and when Martha's complaints took a turn for the worse, Judy nursed her as tenderly as any blood relation.

Chest pains kept Martha in bed for a week, and then what had been vague aches in her legs turned into hot daggers. Dr. Beech became a daily visitor, prescribing various potions, but to little effect. One sleeping draught gave Martha a headache that left her whimpering and begging for death.

After she recovered from that medicine, Dr. Beech said, "I have avoided this for as long as I dared, but there is no other course." He set out a vial of calomel. "We must treat the poisonous phlegm, which may be the cause of all your afflictions."

Judy knew about the dreadful effects of the purge, which was prescribed for all kinds of ailments. Martha would suffer mouth sores, loosened teeth, and racking heaves. Before the doctor left, she stopped him and said, "Mrs. Cook is already so weak, I fear this cure will be worse than the disease."

"Is that your medical opinion?" Dr. Beech said, his hand on the doorknob.

But Judy did not back down. "I will bring the matter up with Judge Cook. He should know of the danger, at least."

To her surprise, Dr. Beech removed his hat and said, "I want a word with you." He led her to the library and stood by the window, facing away from her as he spoke.

"I had no intention of mentioning this to you," he said. "But since you insist on pushing your way into the matter, and as you are to be Mrs. Cook's nurse, I am going to confide a terrible secret to you. Mrs. Cook is suffering from the French pox, for which only mercury has any effect.

"God protect all women against respectable husbands," Dr. Beech added, bitterly. He glanced at her and added, "I assume that you will do nothing to damage this unfortunate lady's reputation?"

"You have nothing to fear from me," Judy said, insulted at the suggestion.

"You may not tell Mrs. Cook the nature of her illness," said the doctor. "I have seen such news kill a woman of her sensibilities. I will measure the mercury in the smallest doses and pray that it will do her more good than harm. There is nothing else I can do for her, God help us."

Judy rarely left Martha's side after that, and spent most nights in a chair at her bedside. She fed her, washed her, and held the basin as her friend retched. She tidied the room and read aloud from the Gospels, which seemed to provide Martha with a little comfort.

After two miserable months, Martha recovered enough to keep down some toast and tea, and insisted that she be carried to the garden, to enjoy the flowers and the afternoon sun.

"The calomel has had a good effect, then," Judy said to Dr. Beech.

"Perhaps," he said. "But this malady is as unpredictable as the weather, and just as changeable. We may see a long spell of sunny days; there may be many good weeks or even months. But the storms are bound to return eventually, and it will be worse than ever."

His prediction gave Judy the shivers.

After the doctor left, Martha took Judy's hand and said, "You look terrible, my dear. It hurts me to see you so pale and so tired. Why don't you go up to your cottage for a few days and have a little holiday."

Judy's eyes watered at her friend's kindness. "You see, it is just as I warned. I have outstayed my welcome, and you are tired of me."

"Not at all," said Martha. "I am being selfish. I wish to have you smiling and blooming entirely for my own purposes. So take your Greyling and come back to me as soon as you can bear it. The judge has hired an extra girl, and he will be in residence for the rest of the month. I've even had the cook fill a basket for you."

Judy smiled. "You have thought of everything. I am banished."

On her way home, she stopped at the Youngers' and covered Natty with kisses. "Look how much he has grown behind my back! How dare he?" Since she'd last visited, Polly had taken in a puppy, too, a squat, white creature with a feathery tail that Natty had named Poppa. The pup wagged at Greyling and stretched his paws away from his body, inviting her to play. But the old dog took no notice at all, curling up on the cool hearthstone while Poppa sniffed for crumbs.

Refreshed by an hour of smiles, good news, and glowing health, Judy made her way back to her own Dogtown bed, where she slept soundly until midafternoon. When she finally woke up and looked around, she marveled at the perfect order and lack of dust. She would thank Polly for coming so far to do her this favor. Or perhaps it was Easter, who was not nearly such a good housekeeper in her own place.

In fact, it had been Cornelius. During Judy's long stay at the Cooks', he had taken it upon himself to wipe the table and sweep the floors, brush away the cobwebs, and even air the quilt. Long before that and for years on end, he'd been looking after Judy's house from the outside, making sure that the roof was sound, the windows tight.

He had watched over her person as well, finding safe vantages where he could see her cooking at her own hearth, sitting in quiet communion with Martha, dandling Natty Younger.

One cold winter night when he'd had a clear view into the Dogtown cottage, she stopped in the middle of the room and raised her nose up in the air, like a dog picking up a scent. If she had seen him, if she had caught his eye and called to him, he might have walked in and stayed. But she turned away, smiling, and said something to the dog. Wherever Judy slept, the dog was with her.

Cornelius had hated Greyling at first, jealous of the dog's constant presence. But he came to admire the animal's loyalty to Judy, and he realized that she showed him a kind of allegiance as well. Greyling would bark when anyone came within twenty feet of Judy Rhines's house, but she kept quiet when it was Cornelius, no matter how close he approached or how late he called. Perhaps she remembered him from the one night they'd both slept under Judy's roof, long ago. Or maybe she recognized his scent, knowing him to be harmless as a rabbit. Indeed, he'd even begun to worry about the dog, now white around the muzzle and so stiff in the joints that Judy had to slow her pace as they walked to and from the harbor.

⊰⟡⊱

Greyling died on a brilliant October morning. Judy had let her out and watched the dog stretch and shake before padding into the woods, her tail wagging. It wasn't until late in the day that Judy missed her.

She walked to Greyling's favorite spot, where the sun would heat a low granite outcrop so it warmed the dog's old bones from below as well as from above. When Judy saw red and golden leaves lying over the still, silver flank, she knew that her friend was gone.

She got a shovel and dug a grave beside her, rolling the not-quite-stiff body, suddenly so small, into the rocky hole. She laid a bouquet of autumn leaves and branches of orange bittersweet over her companion, and filled the grave, weeping.

That night in bed, Judy shivered, missing the shaggy heat and regular breathing of her closest friend. She was grateful that Greyling hadn't retreated far into the woods to die, like the wilder dogs. She would have worried for days if Greyling had simply disappeared.

Judy remembered the first time she'd seen Greyling, not much more than a puppy, skinny and skittish. It had been an autumn day as well. The dog was in the middle of the Commons Road chasing a leaf that was caught in a stiff breeze. It was a yellow maple leaf capering in the air like a butterfly. The dog had snapped at it and jumped until she'd caught it, then danced and wagged her tail and chewed it to bits.

A birdsong split the night silence and Judy Rhines held her breath, listening to the torrent of melody. She wanted to turn and ask, "It's too late for mockingbirds, isn't it?"

Had she ever said as much to the dog? Judy wondered. Had she imagined Greyling's reply in human speech, too? "Yes. But today was so warm, perhaps this one was fooled into thinking that summer's come back."

Was she that far gone?

"I will not take in another dog," she said, and let the tears begin again. "I will move into Martha's house. I will depend upon my friends, and if I'm fortunate I will die among them.

"I will not spend another winter here alone." She said that in a voice so loud, it seemed like an oath. Or at least, that's what it sounded like to Cornelius, who was keeping vigil by her window, mourning for Greyling, too, and for Judy's departure, and for his own lost hopes.

Cornelius

I<small>T WAS THE</small> middle of the night, but it might have been noon the way Cornelius was sweating. He'd woken out of a drowning dream into the sickening sense of being boiled alive. His shirt was drenched and the sour smell of his own bed made him queasy.

The window in his attic room faced away from the harbor, but Cornelius found no relief in the street either. The air was heavy and still: no halyard clanged, no wave lapped. The darkness seemed complete, too, without a moon or even a single candle flickering behind any window.

He set out to walk and decided to head to Dogtown for a change. Since Judy had left it two years ago, his old haunts provided little pleasure. Still, he went from time to time, just for the change of air and to have a look at her old house. He'd hammered over the broken windows, though he wasn't entirely sure why he bothered.

Walking past gloomy storefronts and dim houses, it seemed like the whole town had died in its sleep. Or that he was a ghost, haunting the town. Not that Cornelius held much with spirits. He had been ten years old when his mother died, and for years after that he had tried to believe that her soul lingered on to look after him. He'd poured pitchers of fresh water beside her bones every day and waited for a sign of her presence. But now he hadn't been to the grave in so long, he doubted he could even find the spot; the stones he'd piled there must have been scattered.

Cornelius followed Washington Street out of town, away from the harbor and its old reproaches. For years, he'd watched the black-skinned sailors wearing bright scarves and golden earrings, bold and relaxed even among their white shipmates. When they'd asked why a strong man like him didn't ship out, he had shrugged and said that the pitching of the waves made him sick as a dog.

It might have been true, too, but the fact was he'd never set foot on any vessel larger than a canoe. He could not beat back a suffocating fear of dying belowdecks, which he'd gotten from his mother on her deathbed. Her young body had survived the middle passage, and she had lived in the new world for twenty years: ten in Virginia and ten more on Cape Ann. But Cornelius knew that she died on the boat that had borne her over the sea.

When she grew ill, Mistress Finson brought fresh water and broth to her slave girl whenever she found a minute. The mistress changed her shift and bedding, but with her household to run and family to feed, it was Cornelius who sat beside the bed, holding his mother's hand and trying to understand her fevered gibberish. By the time he realized that "Senegambia" was a name, she was long past answering his questions.

In her mind, she was a child again, lying in chains in the dark hold of a slave ship. A storm rose up and turned the stifled, groaning misery of the journey into an even worse nightmare. As the belly of the ship pitched steeply from side to side, the suffering Africans believed themselves doomed not only to die but to capsize, which would have made it impossible for their spirits to find a way home.

"Don't cry, Senegambia," she wailed, trying to comfort some man or woman long dead. "It ain't your fault."

When she quieted down, Cornelius kept watch over the rise and fall of his mother's narrow chest, certain that his attention would somehow help keep her alive. He studied her face, so frightfully thin. He'd once heard Mistress say, "Our Maydee is good as gold, but homelier than dirt." What did she mean? he wondered. His mother's skin—a smooth, rich mahogany brown—made the whites look ugly as old cheese. Her smile was a crescent moon in a dark sky.

He stroked her bony hand as she whimpered in her sleep. Her face twisted in disgust. "The smell," she croaked. "Please, sir, some air."

He opened the windows and the door, and when that gave her no ease he washed the floor with vinegar-water. He brought pine boughs and broke the needles beneath her nose. Still, she wailed that the stench was choking her and Cornelius had to cover her mouth with a towel, lest Mistress Finson make good on her threat to fetch the doctor, who always brought death with him.

In her last hours, Maydee's skin burned to ash. She thrashed on the cot and would have tipped it over if Cornelius hadn't sat on it with her. "Maggots," she moaned, raking her fingers through her scalp and over her eyes. When Cornelius saw that she was drawing blood, he tied her hands down with soft rags. He was as gentle as he could be, but it set her to weeping, and he was ashamed.

When she finally fell asleep, Cornelius put his ear to her mouth to make sure that she was still breathing, and lay his head on his arms to rest beside her. He woke to see Maydee's head and shoulders lifted off the bed, straining every muscle upward, like she was trying to fly. She stared intently at the ceiling, her eyes hollow as teacups. Cornelius tried to push her down into the bed, but she was rigid and would not budge, until suddenly, she relented and fell back. Supple and light as a falling leaf, dead.

He rarely thought of his mother, but the memory of her death walked beside him on that sultry night, past the last few houses attached to the city, up to the spot where he turned back, out of habit, to make certain no one saw him step onto the old path into Dogtown.

Cornelius felt the familiar twinge in his left knee. He was sixty-one years old, and although his back was still straight and there were only a few strands of gray on his head, his legs were not what they used to be. He couldn't help but envy men of his years who spent their afternoons smoking pipes and recalling better times. Those were white men, of course. White men with generous daughters.

Cornelius was altogether alone. He touched no one and spoke to the people around him as little as possible. He had stopped butchering hogs mostly so he wouldn't have to talk to the likes of Silas Hutting and his vile neighbor, Eben Crowley. Both of them had taken to paying less than what they promised, daring him to dispute it, and calling him "Nigger Neal" into the bargain.

His one piece of luck was his job as bookkeeper for Jacob Somes, a fish wholesaler, who paid Cornelius a few dollars a week, plus room and board. Somes was pleased with Cornelius's steadiness and knew the man worked hard. But no one saw how much Cornelius cherished his position and labored over his rows of numbers, rechecking every calculation three times not only for accuracy but for appearance as well. He wanted every digit to be perfectly square and lined in exact rows, which required his total concentration. At the end of every day, he would set down the pen and run his weary eyes up and down the pages, savoring the order he'd created.

Numbers were forthright, definite, and reassuring, entirely unlike words, which were slippery and sharp. To Cornelius, language had come to seem untrustworthy, double-edged as a plow that could just as easily sever a foot as cut through sod.

He had quit reading some years back, dismayed by the half-truths and contradictions he found in print. One volume argued for the power of faith, another claimed that the works of man were ascendant. One newspaper article claimed the governor was a great man; another on the very next page called him a thief. The Bible was the worst of all, riddled with impossibilities, opposing accounts of the same story, and hideous acts of cruelty. If the Bible had been at all mathematical, he might have become a Christian.

Had Mrs. Somes known anything about Cornelius's theology, she would have had her excuse to throw him out of the attic. She had never wanted him there; he was too big, too black, too reticent, and she refused to believe her husband's reassurances that he was more civilized than half the fishermen in town. Somes withstood his wife's complaints in this matter as in little else because Cornelius was the only honest bookkeeper he'd ever hired. He thought him a good man, too, and at Christmas, shook his hand, presented him with a silver dollar, and insisted he take a cup of cider and a biscuit—when his wife's back was turned.

But Mrs. Somes never reconciled herself to having the African under her roof and festered at having to wash his meager linen and feed him. She would grumble and drop his plate on the table with a rude grunt. Cornelius ate what she served as quickly as he could, which ruined his digestion and confirmed his landlady's opinion that he was not entirely human.

Cornelius usually breathed better out from under her roof, but he found little ease on that hot, dark summer night. It was barely cooler under the trees, where the crickets shrilled, loud as crows. He stared at Judy's dark house for a moment and turned back, feeling as though he were still caught in the nightmare that had started him on this pointless ramble.

He hurried back to the main road and lengthened his stride, suddenly wanting nothing but his own bed. But Cornelius lost his footing and then he heard someone scream.

He had no way of knowing how long it was before he regained his senses and found himself lying on his side, clutching his knee, which felt like a harpoon had pierced the joint and was still lodged inside. Panting, he waited for the pain to subside before he tried to stand again, but the throbbing only grew stronger and faster. The longer he lay there, the more it seemed that the pounding in his leg was keeping time with the high-pitched thrum of the crickets.

Cornelius turned on his back and faced the sky and tried to slow his breathing and take stock. The numberless stars above him had the night to themselves. He thought he'd never seen anything so beautiful and wondered if there was a painter great enough to capture the wild riot of blue-white and blue-black above him. He'd watched the weekend painters of Cape Ann, dabbing at squares of canvas. But their efforts all seemed puny and washed out to him, as if they were seeking to hide rather than reveal the shining light before them.

He watched a star streak across the horizon. And another, and then another, until there were no more. Very well, Cornelius thought, it's time to go. He pushed himself to sitting, but when he tried to get his feet under him again, he saw a different kind of light. "Damn me," he bellowed. "Damn it all."

To be splayed out on the public road meant that someone would find him in the morning and there would be a fuss of getting him back to his room. The thought of Mrs. Somes's displeasure at seeing him in this condition pushed Cornelius to try to reach his feet again. But the pain felled him like a bullet, and he did not wake from that faint for a long while.

At first light, he heard a sound in the distance. Lifting his head, Cornelius thought he saw a brown skirt receding down the road. He lay back, wishing he'd fallen in the woods, where he might have died in peace, and closed his eyes again until a hoarse bark roused him. A wet nose grazed his cheek and a woman's voice called, "Poppa? Poppa, come here."

The white dog turned at the sound, trotted a few steps toward it, reconsidered, and returned to Cornelius's side, where he resumed his short, husky yapping. "Here, here, here," he barked.

"Poppa!" The voice was cross now and louder than before until Polly Younger was standing over him. "Cornelius?"

"It's my knee," he said.

"Oh, dear," she said. "I don't suppose you'd be lying there if you could walk, would you? I'll go fetch Oliver."

He watched her yellow gingham disappear, the dog waddling behind. Time passed and he began to wonder if he'd only dreamed that Polly had been there, or perhaps she had simply gone the way of the brown skirt. But then she was back with Oliver, dragging a rough plank sled.

"Sorry it took so long, old man," said Oliver. "I knew I'd never be able to carry you on my own, so I had to borrow this old thing. We can at least get you home on it."

Cornelius blinked at the barrage of cheerful words, and he did what he could to help get himself onto the plank. Oliver took up the rope and started dragging him, as slowly as he could, to ease his way in and out of the ruts, some as deep as a horse trough.

"Sorry, old man," he said at every bump. "I never forgot how you helped me out of that scrape at Peg Low's tavern. Course, that was before I was a married man. You don't find me in a tavern these days."

"There are plenty of married men in those places," said Polly.

The sled hit a big rock and Cornelius groaned.

"Sorry," said Oliver and Polly in unison.

"I think Easter might be best for looking after that leg," said Polly. "She's good with the rheumatiz, isn't she?"

"We could ask Judy, too," said Oliver.

"She's not much for bones, is she?"

"No need," Cornelius said.

The house wasn't much more than a hundred yards past the bend in the road where Cornelius had fallen. A baby wailed, and Polly ran toward the sound while Oliver settled him against a tree.

"I'll be right back," he said and followed his wife inside. Cornelius could hear their voices but not what they were saying. He tried to move his leg again, but the pain pinned him flat. He could not stand, couldn't even move away to relieve himself, a need that was becoming urgent. The baby's cries had ceased. Cornelius could not remember the last time he had felt so helpless or so afraid.

"It's far too hot inside the house for you," said Oliver, bringing him a cup of water. "You're better off out here where there's a chance of a breeze. I've got to get into work, but I'll stop and let Somes know about the accident. Polly will see to you until I can fetch Easter this evening, and then . . ."

"I'm afraid, I mean," Cornelius interrupted, "I don't, I mean I can't . . ."

"No need," Oliver said, rushing to reassure him that thanks were unnecessary. "What would have become of me if you hadn't dragged me home that day? What would have become of you if our foolish Poppa hadn't found you, eh?"

Cornelius shook his head.

Polly stood at the door with her new baby, David, on her shoulder. Three-year-old Natty peeked out from behind her dress. "Kindness is its own reward," she said.

"Not in my experience, Missus."

"I suppose not," she allowed.

Cornelius gestured for Oliver to bend down. "Mr. Younger, I must ask you to, I need to . . ."

"What is it, old man?" Oliver leaned in.

"Perhaps Mrs. Younger could go inside so I, with your help, if I could just . . ."

Oliver finally understood the problem. "Polly, my dear, if you'd excuse us, Mr. Cornelius and I will be just a moment."

As soon as she left, Oliver hoisted Cornelius up and supported him as he hopped a few feet toward the woods and left him leaning against a tree to do his business.

Cornelius cleared his throat to signal that he was done, and Oliver helped him back to where Polly had set a pallet out under a tree. After Oliver left for work, she brought him a piece of cold corn bread and a cup of cider.

"I'm afraid I haven't much more to offer till dinner," she said. "Oliver brings us fish for supper and whatever else he can pick up that's not too dear. My garden didn't do so well," she said, ducking her head. "I couldn't get to the watering in the last few weeks of my confinement and Judy was watching at Mrs. Cook's every day. Ollie was busy looking after Natty and me and, well, we lost the beans and squashes. I think we'll save the turnips and pumpkins."

"Thank you, Missus," said Cornelius, chewing the bread. "This is plenty. Thank you kindly."

Polly went indoors to nurse the baby and set some clothes on to boil. She returned after a while with a bowl of water and some cloths. "I don't have poultices or anything like that, but I could clean you up a little. It might make you feel better."

She spoke in tones she might use with a child and Cornelius bristled, wondering if she thought he was stupid. But her hands were so gentle as she draped a cool cloth over his ankle; a sigh of relief escaped him.

"Better?"

He nodded. "Thank you, Missus."

The knee was not so easy to get at. Polly's attempt to roll the trouser up hurt so much that she finally said, "I think you must remove your britches, Mr. Cornelius." She went inside and returned with a thin blue quilt, turning aside while Cornelius struggled to get free of his pants.

After an agony of twisting and pulling, he finally got them off and lay back, panting and bathed in sweat.

"Oh dear," said Polly, looking at his knee, which was twice the size it should have been. The compress helped a little, but as the day wore on, Cornelius felt the joint get stiffer and hotter. He pretended to sleep so Polly would leave him to his despair: a lame old African on his own might as well be dead.

Oliver returned bearing more than his usual number of bundles. After handing Polly a large fillet of mangled cod and a few carrots, he sat down beside Cornelius and fidgeted with a burlap sack. Finally, he said, "I'm sorry, old man. I went over to see Somes to warn him that you'd had a spill and might be a few days. But I saw his wife first and when I told her what happened, she said . . ." Oliver stopped. He would not repeat what she'd said. "She claims Mr. Somes had already decided to . . ."

Cornelius saved him the trouble of lying. "I won't be going back there."

"She gave me your things," Oliver said, handing him the bag. "Maybe you can talk to Jacob when you're up and about." The two men sat in silence until Natty toddled over and climbed onto his father's lap.

"How's my boy?" he whispered, nuzzling his fine blond hair.

After a while, Polly laid an old sheet on the ground and set their dinner on it. "It's so much cooler out here," she said, running in and out of the house with plates and forks, a platter of fried fish, a bowl of boiled carrots.

"Thanks, Missus," Cornelius whispered, whereupon Natty walked over to him, took a carrot from his plate, and patted his cheek. Oliver grinned and between bites said, "I'm going to fetch Easter."

"Could you look for a raspberry bush on the way?" Polly asked.

"'Sberry?" chirped Natty.

"If there's a berry to be had, you'll have it," Oliver promised as he set off.

"Don't you worry, Mr. Cornelius," said Polly, as she cleared the dishes. "Easter will know what to do. I expect you'll sleep better tonight."

Cornelius doubted that. Even if Easter had magic at her command and could get him dancing a jig by morning, his prospects would keep him awake. He'd lost both his job and his home.

He was so occupied by these unhappy considerations that Easter's face was a few inches from his own before he realized she'd arrived. "Cornelius Finson, as I live and breathe," she proclaimed. "I ain't seen you in a dog's age. Not that you were ever much of a visitor. Now let me have a look at what you've done to yourself."

She removed the cloth from his knee. "Ugly," she grimaced. "I'll wager it was paining you even before you took that fall. And what were you doing out on that road so early in the day, my good man?" she teased. "A city fellow like yourself, though Oliver here tells me that I might be seeing more of you up in Dogtown soon. I believe Charity Somes may be the worst-named woman I never did like."

Oliver gave Cornelius a sheepish look, embarrassed that he'd told Easter all of his business.

"I'll do what I can with what I brought," she said. "Polly, could you fetch me some boilt water for this roasted sorrel? We'll let it steep awhile. It makes a nice poultice when it's cooled; helps with lameness sometimes, not that it's going to fix this mess. Not by itself."

She got up and headed for the door, calling, "Polly! I need a cup of cider, too. I know you don't have any ale, though I keep telling you it's good for the milk. And how is your milk coming these days? Is that pretty baby fattening up?"

Oliver grinned. "She's a lot of noise, isn't she?"

Cornelius nodded.

"Then again," Oliver muttered to himself as he followed Easter inside, "between the two of you, it works out."

Easter applied the poultice, laying the soggy leaves so that none of them crossed. Then she wrapped the pile of it with a bandage made of stained and raveled muslin. "Does it hurt?" she asked. When Cornelius shook his head, she tightened the bandages until they were just about too snug for comfort.

"That's all for now," Easter said. "I'll be back with something else. Root of water lily might do for the swelling. I wager that fancy Dr. Beech in town would stick his little knives into it." She put her finger up beside her nose and said, "There's the real witchcraft, if you ask me. I don't care if he calls himself doctor or professor or His Majesty; only the devil asks for blood."

She dismissed Oliver's offer to walk her home with a wave. "I'm fine. You take care of each other and have a good night, my dears. Good night to you, too, Cornelius."

After she left and a comfortable silence settled on the house, Natty piped up, "'Sberry?"

"Oh, my sweet boy," said Oliver, lifting his son up. "I didn't forget, but all I found was still green and bitter. We'll go back in a week and gobble 'em right off the bush, just you and me. Will that do, my pet? My handsome fellow?"

Cornelius was exhausted. The avalanche of talk, the pain in his leg, the loss of his livelihood—he closed his eyes, hoping for sleep. But Oliver tapped him on the shoulder. "I can't let you stay out here, old man," he said. "The mosquitoes will chew you up."

Cornelius was too tired to disagree and let Oliver do with him as he wished, which was to settle him on the bed where he'd seen Judy Rhines lay her head many times. He slept badly in the heat and woke up sore and thirsty, determined to be as little bother as possible.

He ate when his hosts ate, slept when they slept, and spent the rest of the day sitting in the shade. And although he did nothing, Cornelius wore himself out traveling the distance from boredom to misery to resignation, and back again.

After three identical days, he finally noticed the ceaseless activity going on all around him. Polly washed the baby's bottom, carried the water, aired the linen, and all the while chattered to Natty, encouraging him to name his nose, his knees, the bucket, the dog. She cooked and served and washed dishes, washed the baby again, set more water on to boil, and sat down only to nurse.

Once Oliver returned in the evening, Polly had still more to do: cooking the fish and then clearing the dinner, handing Oliver the baby so she could hem the petticoats sent by ladies in town. Cornelius grew weary watching her go from one task to the next.

The next morning Polly had to lay down her bucket three times to attend to David, who kept wailing regardless of her every effort to soothe him. "He must be getting ready to cut a tooth," she said, wiping her brow.

"Sorry, Missus."

Polly considered his apology for a moment and held the red-faced baby out to him. "Would you hold him so I can get to the stream?"

"He's a good boy, honest," she said, arranging him upon Cornelius's chest. "Mostly what he wants is to be held so his belly is warm. I don't know why. Natty wasn't that way."

The baby settled the moment his stomach touched Cornelius, and Polly set off for the stream at a trot, glancing back three times before disappearing. Natty did not follow at his mother's heels as usual, but stayed and watched as the big man cradled his tiny brother. David smiled whenever Cornelius stroked his tiny bare feet, which provoked an unself-conscious smile in the big man as well. When Polly returned, David was fast asleep where she'd put him. "You sure you don't mind, now?" she asked from time to time, taking David up only to feed him or clean him.

That night in bed, Polly told Oliver about Cornelius's talent as a nursemaid. "I think he might enjoy it," she whispered. "I'm sure that I saw him kissing David's forehead. Can you imagine?"

The next morning, Cornelius reached out for the baby before Polly could ask. He was grateful for the distraction, and also fascinated by the feel and smell of the infant, and the way he responded to touch. When Polly disappeared into the house or down to the stream, he ran a light finger over David's hands and feet. He traced the bare outline of his eyebrows, the warm crooks of his elbows. He took the whole of David's hand on his thumb, in awe. But when he cupped a hand over the top of the baby's skull, Cornelius nearly jumped out of his skin.

The moment Polly returned from the stream he said, "Missus?"

"Yes, Cornelius," said Polly, eager for any word from him.

"I fear that David's head is not right."

Polly froze.

"There, on the top." He pointed. "Like a melon, Missus, with a soft place. It's not right. I'm so sorry. I didn't do anything . . ."

"Oh, no," said Polly, who felt her heart begin to beat again. "That's just how babies are made. The soft part there closes over soon enough. Natty's head was like that, but it's hard as a nut now. See?" She made him put his hand on the older boy's curls. "But I suppose it's not something you know till you have a baby of your own."

Cornelius nodded and Polly went silent, afraid she'd said something hurtful. Not that she had any hope of knowing the heart of this quiet shadow of a man. But she did know, and with complete certainty, that he treated her sons with the same affection and patience as Oliver or Judy. And she knew that he was grateful for every small kindness he was shown.

Cornelius's pain eased slowly, but his knee still throbbed and swelled whenever he put weight on it. "It's the dog days, that's what it is," Easter said, when she stopped to pack his bandage with a foul-smelling concoction of pickled burdock leaves. "This is the worst time of year for healing, and that's all there is to it. A few more weeks of rest will be the cure of you, and not even this heat can stop that. If you do as I say and keep off that peg of yours, you'll be on your way soon enough." Cornelius had little choice but to keep still and hope the old woman was right.

One day was much like the next, which made little events stand out: the late raspberries ripened and they all ate their fill. A few squashes added a tasteless but filling accompaniment to whatever leftover bits of cod or haddock Oliver brought home.

The weather cooled for a few days but then grew unspeakably hot again, and even sweet-tempered Natty turned sullen. One afternoon, when his mother was occupied with the baby and Cornelius was dozing, the usually tractable little boy started to wail. "Judy. Where is my Judy? I want my Judy!"

"Hush," said Polly. "Your Judy is tending Mrs. Cook, who must be very ill, indeed, else she'd be here. She's never been away from you so long, has she?"

Polly turned to Cornelius and explained, "Judy Rhines has been like a sister to me since Natty was born. He dotes on her but we haven't seen her in so long, have we, Natty? I'll go call at the Cooks' and have a good long chat with her, just as soon as I can get away from the house at last and from . . ." She stopped herself, and Cornelius realized that he was not the only one who dearly wished him fit enough to be on his way.

That night, Cornelius was unable to sleep. He was no longer disturbed by the dog's snoring, or the baby's night cries, or the murmured conversations and rustlings from Oliver and Polly's bed. He had to get out of the Youngers' house. Polly didn't need another man to take care of, and Oliver had to be paying extra for what they were feeding him.

He'd leave in the morning. He'd make do with a cane and move back to Dogtown. He'd take over Judy Rhines's place and be grateful for the peace and quiet of the woods. He would get by scavenging and doing odd jobs, just as he had in the past.

While Cornelius lay on his back and planned, a bird burst into song in the damp night air. At first he thought there might be more than one bird, cawing, warbling, whistling, trilling, grunting, and cooing. After a while he realized that a single mockingbird was responsible for the medley of faultless imitations: robin, gull, and dove, wild turkey and crow, and then (was it possible?) a frog's cheep, a cricket's chirp, and what sounded like the short, husky bark of the Youngers' ridiculous little dog.

Cornelius strained to find a pattern in the song until his head ached. I'm going mad, he thought. If I don't leave this place soon, I will be useless.

His leg did feel better the next day, a Sunday, which meant that Oliver was home. "I'm thinking about a cane," Cornelius said. "And leaving you in peace."

Polly heard the apology in his voice. "We'll be sorry to see you go," she said. Even though she had complained to Oliver about his lack of conversation, and even though having him there had meant an extra shirt to wash and an extra mouth to feed, he had been a great help with David and Natty. His attentions meant she'd had more time for sewing, which brought in the money they needed for shoes. She didn't remember how she'd managed both boys before Cornelius came; she fell asleep frowning.

Come morning, Polly had a new cause for concern: Cornelius was tossing on his bed, sweating, and moaning in his sleep. He woke up too dizzy to sit, much less stand.

"I don't like the look of him," Polly said to Oliver. "Easter isn't as handy with a fever as our Judy."

"I'll stop off there right now and see if I can't get her to walk back with me," he said, kissing her good-bye. "Don't fret. I'll bring her back and we'll all have a nice visit."

Judy Rhines was pouring water for Mrs. Cook's morning tea when Oliver's face appeared at the kitchen door. "Mistress Rhines," he said, in a mock-formal voice. "How good to see you. And how fares your patient?"

"She's not much worse today, but her spirits are very low."

"Even with you here as her nurse every day?"

"I wish I could do more than offer her compresses and company," Judy sighed, as Oliver entered the kitchen and threw his leg over a chair. "The doctor finally let off bleeding her, thank goodness. Between you and me, that man causes her more harm than good."

"I imagine Easter has told you all about our patient by now," Oliver said.

Judy busied herself with the tray. "You and Polly are saints for taking him in."

"Polly is doing all the real work. It's in her nature to look after strays. She took me in, didn't she?"

"Oh, it's in your nature, too," said Judy, fondly. "How many more puppies have you got up there now?"

He laughed. "Well, we would have a whole litter but Poppa is too jealous. But the reason I stopped by is on account of Cornelius. He woke with a terrible fever today; he's so bad, he can't even get out of the bed. I came to ask if you'd do him a good turn."

"Easter is as good a nurse as me any day," Judy said.

"Well, Polly thinks you're a better hand at fever. And the truth is, Natty was carrying on and crying for his aunt Judy. He misses you so much. Polly, too."

The mention of Nathaniel melted her reserve. "I miss them too," she said. "I suppose that if Martha is comfortable and since the Judge is here . . ."

"I'll stop by for you on my way home," Oliver said, and rushed out before Judy could make any excuses.

Judy knew that Martha would be fine without her for a few hours. Her misery eased in the evening and the Judge would be home and quite content to spend the evening reading in her room. The truth was that Judy had been staying away from the Youngers because Cornelius was there.

"Judy, dear?" Martha's voice returned her to the task at hand.

"I'm coming," she called, hurrying with the tray.

"Was that Oliver I heard?" said Martha as Judy entered the sick-room. "How is the baby?"

"I didn't even think to ask, can you imagine?"

"Dear, you must tell me the truth. Has there been a falling-out between you and the Youngers? You haven't been there in so long, and I don't recall the last time I heard you talk about Natty. Why is that?"

"There is no falling-out. It's just that I do not like to leave you." Judy noticed that the vases needed attention. No matter how often she freshened the flowers, trimmed the lamp wicks, and changed the linens, Martha's room looked forlorn.

"I'm not alone. That girl is here, day after day," Martha whined, in a good imitation of their new servant. "What a sullen chit she is, and her mother promised us a cheerful girl. But never mind that. The Judge is home tonight. Will Oliver return for you this after-noon?"

"Yes. They've taken in Cornelius Finson, who hurt his leg on the road." Judy fussed with the fading roses so that Martha could not see her face. "It seems he's low with a fever now."

"Well, if he has you as his nurse, he'll be healthy in no time. And I shall survive this one evening without you."

Judy read to Martha until she dozed off, and then tiptoed to the bureau and picked up the ivory hand mirror that lay facedown on the lace antimacassar. There were no surprises in the reflection: her hair had a white streak in it now, just beside her left cheek. Her whole face was thicker, the skin a bit mottled at the temples, and the jaw was no longer firm. She had become the complete spinster, she thought, bland and unremarkable. Martha could not bear to witness the way her once-pretty features decayed from month to month, but Judy was fascinated by the alterations in her appearance.

She examined herself dispassionately, without any thought to improving what she saw, glad to have avoided the perpetual frown that was nearly universal on unmarried ladies of her years. She widened her eyes and smiled brightly: at least her teeth were still sound. Martha stirred and Judy replaced the mirror precisely as it was before returning to her seat by the bed.

When Oliver arrived, she was ready with a satchel filled with fruit and a cake, as well as a small pouch of herbs: yarrow to bring on sweating and to draw out the heat of a fever, sorrel and licorice root for tea, slippery elm, in case there was a sore throat. And a packet of chamomile for Polly, who loved the smell.

As they set out, Judy asked Oliver for news about Natty and the baby, and he obliged in exquisite detail: David had a tooth already, and Natty was smart as a whip. "He can count to one hundred. Polly says Cornelius is teaching him the numbers."

"I'm bringing him some peaches," she said.

"He'll like that," Oliver said. "I cannot figure what on earth Cornelius might like, except for our boys. He smiles at them when he thinks no one is looking. But the man says so little . . ." Judy turned the conversation to Polly's health and welfare, which got them to the house before Oliver could say anything else about their patient.

Natty was hopping from one foot to the other by the side of the road waiting for them. When Judy came into sight, he squealed and ran for her, grabbing her tightly about the knees until she lifted him up for a hug. "If you get any bigger, I won't be able to do this anymore!"

Judy kissed Polly and declared her radiant. She exclaimed over David, who had become a different child since she'd seen him last, bigger and darker and reaching for everything, including her nose. She praised the tidiness of the yard and the house and exclaimed over the fine workmanship in the basket of mending on the bed. Only then did she glance at Cornelius, who was sleeping hard.

He was much thinner than the last time she'd seen him. His hair had grayed and his damp forehead seemed much longer than she remembered. The sight of him—lying still as a corpse—did not move her or upset her in any way, which was just what she'd hoped.

"He's resting easier at last," whispered Polly. "He was thrashing all day. Even David took fright."

"Let him sleep then," said Judy. "I'll tend to him after supper."

While Polly breaded the fish, Judy cradled the baby until Natty could not bear it for another moment and demanded that she put David down and give him the attention he expected from his auntie.

They dined amid familiar happy chatter. Natty babbled about the flowers he'd picked for his mamma, the slate she was going to get him, and the baby's bad smells. Neither Polly nor Oliver hushed him, and while Judy wondered if Natty would ever learn his manners, the fondness in the house worked upon her like wine, relaxing and warming her straight through. After dinner, Polly thought Judy looked a good ten years younger than when she had walked through the door.

A loud groan interrupted their party, and all heads turned— even the baby's. It took Cornelius a few moments to open his gummy eyelids. Judy turned away, resting her cheek against Natty's velvety forehead.

"Judy?" he croaked.

The sound of her name sent her to her feet and Natty tumbling to the floor. After a long, stunned, breathless moment the boy opened his mouth and howled.

"I'm sorry, my pet, my sweetkins, my lamb," Judy apologized breathlessly, and picked him up. "Your old auntie just took a start, is all." She carried him outside, kissing him all the while.

"Judy?" Cornelius said, naked longing in his voice. "Have you come to me? Judy? Is it my Judy, for true?"

Oliver and Polly stared.

"How does he know her?" she whispered.

He shrugged. "They both lived in Dogtown."

But Judy's distress and Cornelius's tone of voice signified something more than polite exchanges between neighbors. Polly wondered exactly what they had shared, how it might have started, why it had stopped, and how such a secret could have kept in such a small, gossipy place. "Poor things," she said.

Oliver frowned. He had tried to forget his boyish dreams of winning Judy for himself, and thought of her only as his auntie—his and Polly's, as well as Natty's and David's. It was unsettling to think of her in any man's arms, and for it to have been Cornelius seemed even more out of the natural order of things.

Judy walked Natty around the house a second time. He'd stopped crying after the first turn. "Put me down," he said.

"Put me down, please," she reminded, and let him go.

She circled the house once more to compose herself. The sound of her name in Cornelius's mouth had turned her upside down. If only she could walk away, back to Gloucester and her books. Even Martha's pain and suffering were preferable to this. But she had to show the Youngers that there was nothing between her and Cornelius. She had to prove it to herself. And to him, too, she supposed.

With shoulders squared and a crooked sort of smile fixed on her mouth, she returned to her friends and headed directly to the cot, where she had so often slept with Natty tucked under her arm.

"Polly," she said, briskly. "Put on the kettle, won't you, dear? I'll make a tea to draw out the heat further. And then we'll have some chamomile for compresses, with plenty of extra for your sachets, dear."

Cornelius listened to Judy's orders and Polly's replies, to the sound of the water being poured, to Natty's prattle and David's gurgles, to Oliver's footfalls on the uneven floor. He listened, waiting for Judy to speak his name.

When she gently laid the first cloth on his forehead, Cornelius released his breath and felt her startle. The next applications were more businesslike, with a quick pat, as though he were a dog.

"Cornelius," she said, briskly. "Cornelius, you must sit up and drink the infusion while it is still hot enough to do you some good."

He lifted his head to receive the scalding spoon. After a few mouthfuls, he felt the heat rise in him and kicked away the blanket.

"No," she said, tucking it tightly around his legs. "You must sweat more, not less. The tea is doing its work. Lie still."

Polly watched the two of them closely, but they had settled into their roles as nurse and patient and she doubted there would be any more clues forthcoming. Finally Polly's hunger for company overwhelmed her curiosity and she began a detailed comparison of the differences between Natty and David as babies, wondering why one boy was such a good sleeper and the other such an easy feeder, and how it was that Natty turned out to be blond but David's hair was darker than Oliver's.

Polly had a dozen questions for Judy, too. When should she approach Mrs. Stiles about sewing her second daughter's trousseau, and had everyone had a time with their beans that summer or had she done something wrong? Finally she dropped her voice and asked, "Is it true that Mrs. Cook is at death's door?"

"Heavens, no. She is sick, but Martha is not dying. Is that the gossip? How awful," Judy said. "She suffers terribly from the calomel, and I worry that the cure may be the death of her. But she is still very much with us.

"As for the rest of your questions, I am out of the house so little, I have no news to report about Mrs. Stiles or anyone else." Polly's disappointment prompted Judy to recount the tale of the Cooks' new young serving girl who was so inconsolable about being separated from her mother and sisters that she had run away twice. Judge Cook himself had gone to fetch her the second time.

Cornelius heard the bile in Judy's mouth whenever she mentioned the Judge, and wondered what he'd done to earn her enmity. Behind closed eyes, he waited for her to speak to him again, to say "Cornelius" as she used to. But now he would answer her. He would say, "Yes, Judy." He would do anything she wished.

He lay on his back, swaddled and sweating, and imagined himself telling her all the stories he knew that she would have liked to hear from him. He remembered the way he'd said nothing when she told him about her motherless childhood. He was still ashamed about that. He should have set aside his pride, or whatever it was that kept him from confiding in her, and admitted that he was fortunate by comparison; after all, Cornelius did remember his mother's love and care, and that was no small thing.

Their life had not been easy, but they had not lived so differently from their masters, with whom they had shared the same four rooms, eaten the same bland food at the same plank table, scratched at the same mosquitoes in the summer, and shivered in the same winter drafts.

Judy would have treated the stories about his mother like treasures. But Cornelius had not trusted Judy at first, and then he'd been afraid. Years of shame had followed, and now he was a poor, crippled, old black man. His boyhood stories would be burdens, not gifts.

Noticing his furrowed brow under the beading sweat, Judy applied one last compress.

"How fares the patient?" Oliver asked.

"I believe he will recover," she said, gathering her things. "This is a passing fever. I doubt that it had anything to do with the knee. I've done as much as I can do for tonight."

"Come back soon," Polly whispered so as not to wake Natty, who was asleep on her lap.

"I promise." Judy blew her a kiss.

Oliver and Judy walked out in the sunset.

"It's getting dark much earlier these days," she said. "There's a touch of fall tonight."

He took her bag and, on impulse, offered her his arm. "Allow me."

Judy took it and leaned against him, wrung out by the evening.

"You knew Cornelius in Dogtown, then?" Oliver asked, after they'd been walking for a while.

"Yes."

"Yes?"

"It was a long time ago," Judy said firmly, and Oliver heard the door close on any further conversation about the African.

Oliver patted her hand, and they continued for a long way without saying a word.

Judy had a headache, and she longed to lie down and sort out the anguish and anger and desire that had roiled up in her when she heard her name in Cornelius's mouth.

Oliver tried to reconcile his liking for Cornelius with queasy outrage over the way he had moaned for Judy. Her name in his mouth seemed obscene, and yet he was not sure why. Cornelius was a man, same as him, or Everett Mansfield, or every Wharf or Tarr, Tom or William, who ever walked Cape Ann.

The African question was too complicated for Oliver to fathom on his own. He would try to discuss it with Polly, he decided, and turned his attention back to Judy, who seemed to need cheering up.

He leaned toward his friend and, in a tone of lighthearted conspiracy, said, "I haven't told Polly yet, but I'm starting to look around for a new situation," and filled the rest of the journey with his plan for an escape from the stink of fish, which Polly could no longer wash out of his clothes.

Judy warmed to his plans and before they knew it, they had arrived. Judy clucked at the lights blazing from every window in the house. "That girl."

"I'll come by and tell you how he's faring," said Oliver, as he opened the garden gate for her.

"Thank you, my dear boy," she whispered. Before letting go of his arm, she reached up and kissed him lightly on the cheek, and wondered why she had never done that before.

⟡

By morning, Cornelius's fever was nearly gone and he was able to rise and limp outside. But overnight, something had changed in the household. Polly was as pleasant as ever, but she looked at him with obvious pity. Oliver did nothing out of the ordinary, but he would not meet his eye.

He left a few days later, his knee stiff but tolerable. "I'll be thanking you the rest of my days," he said.

Oliver shook his hand firmly.

"Will you come by and visit the boys?" Polly asked.

"I'll be seeing them," said Cornelius, running his hands over their silken heads.

He moved into Judy Rhines's cottage and returned to trapping and gathering whatever could be sold or bartered. And he resumed his nighttime rounds, using a cane and walking carefully when he went out for a glimpse of Judy through lace curtains in Gloucester.

He increased his circuit to include all the last of the Dogtown stragglers, down to Easter and Ruth, three creaky widows, and the sad crew at Mrs. Stanley's house.

He looked in on the Youngers almost every day, and even got himself a spyglass so he could follow David's progress as he learned to walk. Cornelius frowned and smiled to see how Natty teased his little brother and then helped, by turns. Wherever Cornelius went, he searched for little rustic oddities to scatter in the woods beside the Younger house. Sometimes, he'd hide nearby and wait for the excited shouts of the boys when they found the arrowhead or snakeskin, the outsize pinecone or tiny mouse skull. Natty brought the eggshells in to his mother, who exclaimed over the pretty colors. Polly collected a whole rainbow of them: pink, blue, gold, and tawny white, and arranged them in the perfect bird nest they'd also discovered. She set it out on a windowsill, so Cornelius could see that they remembered him, too.

His Own Man

I N THE EIGHT years since he'd left Dogtown, Sam had not been cold or hungry. Thanks to his well-earned reputation for politeness, sobriety, and diligence, a succession of widowed women gave him room and board in exchange for his assistance in caring for their homes and properties, and for his handsome companionship.

Over time, pretty little Sammy Stanley had become a striking man of twenty, blue-eyed and honey blond, with a fine, sharp nose and a chiseled jaw. He'd taken to calling himself Sam Maskey, which suited him. Years of hard work had thickened his neck and broadened his shoulders so that even a threadbare coat hung from him with military authority. The only shame, the ladies agreed, was that he'd not grown any taller than five feet. When he tried for a job at one of the new two-man quarries, he was turned away. "You're too damned short," said the foreman, not unkindly. "It'll be a backache for anyone to bend down to you. Come back when you grow." But he never did.

He might have married into a fortune or at least a good living. There were several willing maidens who would inherit farms or fishing vessels, but none of them tempted Sam enough to overcome his distaste for the grinding labor of the fields or the perils of the sea. The girls were impossibly boring, too, and the truth was that the idea of a bedmate repulsed him, a distaste that came of growing up among whores, he figured. Besides, he had no need of a housewife, as he preferred his own cooking and had yet to find anyone to iron a shirt as well as he did. And then there was the matter of being able to keep all his earnings, without any family obligations.

Sam managed to set aside a substantial pile of money over the years by "lending a hand," as he called it. He had done everything from unloading wagons and shucking clams, to painting rooms and harvesting turnips. He carried letters to Gloucester and fetched back newspapers, bolts of fabric, musical instruments, and some packages whose contents he could not guess. He traveled as far as Salem once, to deliver a little boy to his grandmother after his mother died. On that trip, he was offered a good price on half a case of Crown's Tonic, a favorite patent medicine among his elderly acquaintances. After selling all of those bottles for twice what he'd paid, Sam moved into the nostrum trade.

Every few months, he'd order a supply of the remedies advertised in the Boston newspapers, so that when a person in the northern reaches of Cape Ann wanted a dose of Fisher's Spirits, she need not suffer two weeks or more waiting for her cure to arrive. For his thirty percent, Sam could provide a bottle of Hamilton's Grand Restorative or Lee's Genuine Essence and Extract of Mustard on the spot. He accumulated an efficient inventory of elixirs, bilious pills, and worm-destroying lozenges, and even recommended one remedy or another to his neighbors, who came to trust his suggestions.

Sam's room at Widow Long's house was large enough to accommodate the crates and boxes. His landlady was more than happy to tolerate the clutter in exchange for a dependable reserve of Dr. Cotton's Soothing Syrup, a rather expensive potion imported from England.

"Without my syrup, I wouldn't get a wink of sleep," said Mrs. Long. Sam poured her a nightly dram of the honey-flavored brew, which contained more alcohol than anything else. She snored like a sailor after taking her medicine, and was never troubled by the knocking of the customers who visited him after dark.

Late one night in March, the door rattled with three short raps.

"Damn," Sam said. Three knocks meant it was Molly Jacobs, who came not to buy but to beg. "Hold your water," he barked. The old baggage had been coming at him with her hand out ever since he'd left Mrs. Stanley's place. She only came after midnight, announced by that *tap-tap-tapp*ing, like a timid woodpecker.

But when he opened the door, he found it was Alice Ives, who'd come looking for medicine to ease her father's cough. Sam sold her a bottle of Crown's Tonic, which would help the old man to sleep at the very least, ignoring Alice's blushes, cow eyes, and the way she touched his sleeve when she paid.

After she left, it occurred to Sam that Molly had not been begging for months. Had there been snow on the ground the last time she'd come? He couldn't remember.

Whenever Sam heard Molly's three taps, he swore an oath and got a few coins ready so he could press them into her hand quickly, before she could put a foot across the threshold. If it was raining hard or freezing cold, he'd let her in to warm herself for a moment, but he never offered her a seat or anything to eat or drink.

"Sally's thin as a rail these days, Sammy," said Molly, who never asked for herself. "She ain't had a cup of tea in a fortnight." It was always for Sally. "Her dress is in tatters," she sighed. "It's so awful for her, and it just about breaks my heart."

What he gave her was hardly worth the walk from Dogtown. Sam used to justify his stinginess by thinking some of it might find its way into John Stanwood's hands, but Sam didn't get any more generous after Stanwood's death, which was either the result of a barroom brawl or from drowning in a shallow ditch, depending on who told the story.

Molly would thank Sam for his pittance with a dignified curtsy and a set speech. "Me and Sally are real proud of you," she'd say. "Sally just about busts when I tell her how nice you're living, so respectable and clean. And so handsome! And I tell her that you're as good-hearted as you are good-looking. And she says she knows that's so."

It was the lying that kept him from giving her more money, or that's what Sam told himself. He owed them nothing. Molly and Sally were not kin, and although neither of them had ever smacked him or even scolded him, neither of them had ever made a move to help him in all those years of heavy chores. He'd never seen either woman show a lick of interest in anybody or anything but each other. They had no claim on him.

Still, Sam secretly hoped that his charity, which was regular if not openhanded, would serve as a kind of investment in his salvation. Sam wasn't sure he believed that God paid close attention to what he did with his money, but he noticed that the better sort of people at church let it be known that they gave to the support of orphans and widows. Sam had become a fixture at Sunday worship, sitting in the same pew every week. After the service, Reverend Jewett shook his hand firmly as he gripped his shoulder, which Sam took as a public signal of approval.

A sermon that touched upon Jesus' attention to the fallen Magdalene had made Sam feel so right with the world, he resolved to give Molly a silver dollar the next time she came tapping. Pondering why it had been such a long time between her visits, Sam reasoned that it had been an especially wet winter, with heavy snows that froze and left big, icy snowbanks everywhere, so walking would have been even more difficult than usual.

But that notion brought on a vision of Molly's body half-eaten by the awful yellow-eyed dogs in the woods. If they were dead—either of them or both—he would be expected to go up there and clean things up, one way or another. "Damn it to hell," he said.

He'd been back to Mrs. Stanley's house only three times in the years since Stanwood had chased him out. The first time was a few weeks after his escape, just to see if he might be able to sneak in and get his extra shirt and stockings. He had crept up to the window on a Tuesday afternoon, which was the only time that the house was ever deserted, and then only on the rare days when all three of them went into town, or for a visit with Easter. But both Sally and Molly were there, still in bed, wearing stained shifts he was sure had not been washed since he left.

He went a second time, on a whim, a few years later. Making his way into Gloucester on an errand, he stopped just to see if his childhood home was truly as awful as his memory of the place. The house was even more decrepit than he remembered it. The roof sagged and the path was overgrown with weeds right up to the door, which hung off its hinges so he could peek inside. The table was piled with dirty clothes and dishes, and the floor was littered with dry leaves. The mess gave Sam a kind of bitter pleasure, and when he got to town, he bought himself a new leather belt, not because he needed it but because he could have whatever he wanted.

His third visit had been just that past autumn. Molly had woken Sam early one morning. He'd leapt out of bed, furious that she'd come in daylight, fumbling for his money so she'd leave before anyone saw her. But, she had not come to beg.

"Mrs. Stanley died last night," said Molly. "We woke up this morning to the smell of it and you need to come get her for the funeral. Sally and me can't fetch her in. Besides, we figured you'd want to set it up with that minister chum of yours."

Sam was horrified that Molly knew of his friendship with Reverend Jewett and feared that if he didn't agree to take care of the matter, Molly would go to see him herself and provide the pastor with a pungent reminder of Sam's low connections.

"I'll do it," he said. "You go back to the house. I'll be there directly."

⊹

Reverend Jewett welcomed him into his study with a firm handshake and a smile. Sam studied the hat in his hand as he explained the reason for his visit. "Mrs. Stanley of Dogtown has died and her burial, well, it falls to me as I was, I mean, I am, that is . . ." he faltered. "There was no one else to call. There's no question of, well, a proper funeral. . . ."

"Master Maskey," Jewett interrupted. "It is only right that you should come to me on this occasion. It is most generous of you to take on such a commission. You of all people will understand that the work of the parish does not permit me to accompany you. In fact, there is a gravely ill lady who requires my attention today, and some other pressing matters.

"Your . . . that is to say, Mrs. Stanley was not churched, was she?" Sam shook his head.

"Why not just bury her out there, near her home. This is not uncommon in such cases," Jewett said. "Have you a Bible?"

"I could have the use of Mrs. Long's family Bible, I suppose," Sam said, mortified.

"No matter," said Jewett, who turned to his bookshelf and plucked out a volume with a broken spine and frayed cover. "I will make you a gift of this one. You can bring the Scripture to your, that is, to the departed, well, to the bereaved. Here, I will mark a reading for you."

He found the passage quickly, laid the ribbon on the page, and snapped the book closed with his right hand. "Jeremiah, Chapter Three.

"Godspeed," he said, but did not rise or extend his hand.

Sam felt the slight.

As he walked into Dogtown, his embarrassment gave way to clammy fear. He hadn't seen a corpse since the day he was pushed into the close, smoky room at Easter Carter's house. He made his way slowly, the Bible heavy in one hand, a shovel in the other.

Molly and Sally were waiting outside and led him in. The windows were open and the door was ajar, but no amount of fresh air could clear the stench of rot and rum. Mrs. Stanley was laid out on her bed, her hair neatly combed, her hands folded. He turned away as quickly as he could but not before catching sight of the bilious pallor on her ravaged face.

Sam walked out and said, "Where do you want me to dig?"

"Ain't we taking her to that nice little cemetery on the hill?" asked Sally.

Sam had forgotten the high-pitched, nasal voice. Sally seemed a faded version of herself, the blonde gone to white, the porcelain skin flaked and ashy. Even the yellow of her dress had bleached to an ivory whisper of gingham. Sam fancied that if she stood in bright sunlight, he'd be able to see clear through her. Her distracted glance was the same, though, as was the painfully sweet smile.

"Now, Sally," Molly said, catching on to Sam's plan. "You know we ain't got time for that sort of funeral. But that pastor must be on his way, isn't he?"

"He won't be coming," Sam said. "He gave me this Bible to read over her. We'll do it private."

Once the smile faded from Molly's face, Sam could see the permanent squint etched around her nearsighted eyes.

"Wrap her in the sheets," he said.

"No coffin, eh?" asked Sally.

"A winding sheet is plenty good," said Molly, trying to make the best of it. "We'll tuck her in."

"Help me find some place I can plant her," Sam said.

Molly winced at his language, but pointed to a grassy field that still showed the effects of a bygone plow. Sam picked a likely, treeless spot but hit a boulder with the first jab of the shovel: it took him five attempts before he found a place thawed enough to dig even a shallow grave.

By the time the hole was deep enough to serve, the afternoon was dimming and a biting wind had kicked up. They hurried with the body, wrapped in a sling of yellowed bedding. The old whore weighed more than Sam had expected, and the stiffness of the body made his skin crawl. But when they got her to the grave, they stopped, not knowing how to get the corpse into it.

"You go in and we'll hand her down to you," said Molly.

"Not me," he said.

"Well, I can't do it," Molly said. "My knees . . ."

"Oh for goodness sake, just drop her," Sally said. "She wouldn't do half as much for us."

The plain truth of her statement struck Sam as funny, and he couldn't keep from smiling when Mrs. Stanley landed with a soft thud. He shoveled the dirt in as fast as he could, and then he picked up the Bible. Sally and Molly bowed their heads as he opened the book and read, "'Hast thou seen that which backsliding Israel hath done? She is gone up upon every high mountain and under every green tree, and there hath played the harlot.'"

Sally's head snapped up and Molly gasped, but Sam continued.

"'And I said after she had done all these things, Turn thou unto me. But she returned not. And her treacherous sister Judah saw it.

"'And I saw, when for all the causes whereby backsliding Israel committed adultery I had put her away, and given her a bill of divorce; yet her treacherous sister Judah feared not, but went and played the harlot also.'"

Molly cleared her throat with obvious meaning, but Sam only

raised his voice. "'And it came to pass through the lightness of her whoredom, that she defiled the land, and committed adultery with stones and with stocks.'"

He stopped there, short of the end of the stinging passage. Sally walked over to him and slapped his face as hard as she could. Molly followed her into the house without a glance back and slammed the crooked door, which immediately creaked open.

He started back for his lodgings thinking, Good riddance. It had been cruel of him to read what Reverend Jewett had marked for him; it had been unkind of the Reverend to choose those harsh words. It had been like delivering lashes to Sally and Molly, who were nothing but pitiful and spent sinners anymore. And yet, the prophet's merciless condemnation of harlots and whoring had pleased him in ways he could barely name. Jeremiah's anger seemed hot enough to burn away the awful disgrace of his childhood, which haunted him still.

He would have given any amount to forget about his Dogtown beginnings. During the day, Sam rarely thought of his past, but sunset brought back the endless evenings he spent buried under his blanket and coat, his eyes clenched tight, his fingers in his ears. He had pretended not to understand what was going on around him for as long as he could. But by the time he was eight years old, he knew what a whore was, how she made her living, and that his grandmother sold not only herself, but Molly and Sally, too.

He tried to separate himself from the family business as best he could by going to school and spending time with respectable people, but the night belonged to Dogtown. He could smell the men around him, and he heard the bass rumble of their laughter, their oaths, their uncensored cries. He was terrified by the involuntary stirrings of his own member and tried to ignore what was happening to him. He wrapped his hands in the blanket, left his feet out of the covers to freeze in the cold, and whispered the words of Jeremiah. He tried to run wherever he needed to go and to work to exhaustion so that he'd sleep as soon as his head touched the bed.

But his body would not be forsworn. Night after night, he wrestled with self-loathing and a terror of being caught, but need and pleasure always triumphed. Weeping for shame, Sam would loosen his trousers, relieve himself quickly, and swear not to do it ever again. He dreaded nightfall even as he looked forward to it, guilt and anticipation contending.

Unleashing the scripture's thunder over Mrs. Stanley's grave had felt like cautery on an unhealed wound. If those words were hard enough to crack an old whore's heart, then surely they were strong enough to cleanse his heart and soul, Sam thought. He was done with the place and its taint forever. He was free.

As he neared his lodgings, Sam decided that his first act as a free man would be to bathe in the hottest water he could stand. When he opened the door, however, Widow Long was waiting for him with a toddy in her hand. "Dear boy," she said. "Here's something to warm you after your sad day."

"Thank you, ma'am," Sam said, as she sat down with him. Smiling and looking more alert than she had in weeks, she said, "Well, then?"

"Well, then, what, Mistress Long?"

"What did you find up there in Dogtown? What did Mrs. Stanley look like?"

He stared at her eager face and said, "She looked dead."

"Did she die of a blow or was it the pox? Did you see a wound? And what of the others?" she pressed. "Will they stay up there, those two horrid creatures? Will that Molly woman keep pestering at you for money?"

Sam startled at the question.

"Oh, I know about her visits. I'm not so addled that I don't know what's going on under my own roof!" she said. "I remember the first time I laid eyes on those appalling women. Mr. Long used to call 'em city rats."

The more his landlady pestered him with questions, the lower Sam's spirits sank. His name would be linked to those two dolly-mops until they were dead and gone. Which is why he could not permit them to starve: as much as he wished for their speedy demise, it would reflect poorly on him if they died of neglect.

❖

Alice Ives's unnerving taps had reminded him of this burdensome responsibility. He would have to find out whether something was seriously amiss in Dogtown, but the idea of returning to that house was so noxious, Sam was up the whole night, brooding. By dawn, he had a plan for doing Molly and Sally a good turn without going anywhere near them, and get the credit for it among his neighbors.

Later that morning, Sam stopped at Alice's door to inquire after her father. "I've brought a special lozenge for Mr. Ives that might be helpful," he said. "My gift, of course."

After a second cup of tea, Sam lowered his voice and asked Alice, in the most solicitous if not flirtatious voice, if she might consider doing the mercy of taking some food to two of Dogtown's last lost souls. "No one has seen so much as a hair of the women for months now," said Sam. "I could certainly pay them a visit myself, but I am given to understand that the poor unfortunate suffer less shame when help arrives on the arm of a lovely maiden, like yourself." Alice immediately agreed to take on Sam's commission.

"I'll bring the basket later today," he said.

When Sam asked Mrs. Long if she would fill a basket for Molly and Sally, she would not hear of his paying for the food, so she could advertise her own good deed while trumpeting Sam's. He would be hailed as a redeemer of the old ladies of Dogtown, a consideration that might just eclipse the fact that they were not, nor ever had been, "ladies."

Alice delivered the food and hurried back to Sam, wearing a new bonnet and shade of powder that did her no favors. "Oh, Mr. Maskey," her eyes shining with the tale, "it was awful. The smell," she said. "Like an outhouse."

Sam put on a grave face while Alice delivered her report. She had discovered Molly and Sally huddled on their mattress on the floor. It took her a moment to find them under the stack of blankets and clothes, which was nearly all that was left inside the place. They had burned all the furniture for heat, and a dusting of fresh snow had blown in through the chinks in the wall.

"A terrible thing," he said. "We Christians cannot permit such misery, can we, Mistress Ives." He kissed her hand and left immediately, borrowing a horse to ride into Gloucester. Sam directed the town clerk to have Molly and Sally taken to the workhouse and laid five silver dollars on the desk. "This should cover the cost of bringing them in, and the rest is to be applied to their care." The fellow didn't have time to open his ledger before Sam was gone.

Molly and Sally spent the rest of March and April in the workhouse, knitting or mending as required by the matron, who found them polite and tractable, nothing like what she'd expected of prostitutes. At night, they held hands across the gap between their narrow cots and whispered to each other.

When Molly caught the fever that had killed off the three last residents, Sally tended to her night and day, and for a while it seemed that Molly would pull through. When she died, the matron thought her friend would turn her face to the wall and be dead within a fortnight as well. But Sally disappeared two nights after Molly passed away, taking every scrap of bedding and clothing with her, including the matron's wool shawl. She pinched a heavy pewter tankard, too, which was the only item of any value in the whole miserable place.

When Sam heard that both of them were gone, he bowed his head and covered his eyes with his hands. Widow Long told everyone about how he had been overcome with grief, and what a good-hearted fellow he was to have bothered with such awful trash. In fact, Sam had hidden his face so no one could see the relief and satisfaction he feared would be all too evident there.

It might take a year or even five, but eventually his name would be uncoupled from the Dogtown doxies. Newcomers might never even hear the name "Sammy Stanley." And even if a few stories lingered about that unlucky boy, no one would ever think to connect him to Samuel S. Maskey, a deacon in his church, the captain of the fire volunteers, part-owner of the town's first cotton mill. A different man altogether.

Easter and Ruth

EASTER CARTER knew her days in Dogtown were numbered. With the widows long dead and Judy Rhines living in Gloucester, the news that Molly and Sally had been taken to the workhouse turned out to be the last straw. Tammy was still around, though not even Easter would have welcomed a visit—however unlikely—from that bitter pill. Cornelius flitted around like a bat, but he never stopped in. Of course, Ruth was right there under her own roof, but Easter might just as well wait for one of the wild dogs to inquire about her aching knees as expect her boarder to sit down for a chat. Ruth was the only reason she'd been able to stay in her house for as long as she had. The meat, pelts, and feathers from Ruth's traps brought in enough to trade for sugar, needles, and the few other things they could not grow, scavenge, or mend. But the fact was, Ruth gave her the mopes. Easter needed company.

So when Judy Rhines made a special trip to talk to her about the possibility of a situation in town, Easter heard her out. It seemed that Louisa Tuttle, newly widowed, needed help at the tavern she'd inherited from her husband. She did not want a man around telling her what to do anymore, and she was wary of younger women who might get themselves into trouble or just up and leave if a husband happened by. Easter posed no threats and had no prospects but still enjoyed some reputation as a friendly and honest publican. "You'd get two rooms above the tavern at the green," Judy said. "I saw them, Easter, and they're more cheerful than you might expect. And you know that I'd be pleased if you were closer by."

Judy had told Louise that Easter would never leave her own house, but she had agreed to tender the offer because she was concerned about Easter's health: her dress hung off her like a scarecrow.

Easter looked around and considered. She certainly did love her house and liked having her way. It would be hard leaving the roomy parlor and setting things exactly where she wanted them. Starting over at sixty seemed an awfully steep mountain to climb. But after a year without a single paying visitor, she had to admit that her business was dead.

"I'll do it," she said.

Judy gasped. Easter was herself surprised as well; not only about how easily she'd decided, but also at the way the words had immediately lifted a weight off her shoulders. She was sick of eating squirrel, and the walk into Gloucester seemed to get longer and steeper from one month to the next. But the main reason for her relief was that Easter was starved for conversation.

At supper—the only meal Ruth was ever there for—the African usually took her plate upstairs. On the rare occasion Easter insisted she stay at the table, Ruth never answered a question with anything more than a shrug or a nod. After a thousand nights of cheerful attempts, Easter had admitted defeat: Ruth's silence was as much a part of her as her nose. Easter didn't like eating alone, so she ate too little and sighed too much.

Once Easter said yes, it wasn't more than two weeks before she was ready to move. The night before she left, Easter made an especially big pot of stew and enough bread for a week. She motioned for Ruth to sit down at the table and then held her by the arm until she'd had her say.

"I'll be going tomorrow, Ruth, but I'm counting on you to stay right here." Easter spoke slowly, wanting to be sure the African heard every word, even if she made no reply. "I ain't selling the place, 'cause I ain't sure that I won't be back. I know you'll take good care of things for me. You keep the town boys from taking any of my timber, or the windows. They steal the windows first. And you mind that the roof stays tight."

Easter waited until Ruth nodded.

"I'm going to leave you the table and my good chair, and a few other things. You get out of that attic and hunker down by the fire, too. You've been a good boarder," Easter said, her voice quivering at the thought of Ruth alone in the house. "I got no complaints, there, and I hope you . . ." But she didn't really have any hopes for Ruth, who had retreated inside herself, more every year.

Ruth's head hung below her shoulders, like a dog getting a scolding. They finished eating in silence. Finally, Easter released her for the last time. "Good night, dearie," she said and went back to the last of her sorting and packing. Ruth scraped the chair getting to her feet and Easter startled, thinking maybe she heard a good-bye. But when she turned, Ruth was on her way up the stairs.

Judy Rhines arrived early with Oliver driving the Cooks' wagon. It was April, but rainy and raw, a miserable day for moving the piles of clothes, bedding, pots, dishes, and everything else Easter had collected. There wasn't much she'd discarded over the years, or much she wanted to leave behind. When a paper box of rusty keys broke and spilled into a muddy puddle, Judy Rhines actually showed a little irritation. "A whole heap of useless," she muttered, loud enough for Oliver to overhear. He spent the rest of the day teasing his famously patient friend about her "evil temper," which helped him shrug off the discomfort of getting soaked to the skin when he ought to be cozy at home with Polly and the boys.

When the last bundle was tied and secure, Easter said, "Hold up a minute," and started rummaging through sacks already lashed tight, loosening the ropes, and making a mess of Oliver's careful work.

"I know it's a bother, my dears," Easter said, scurrying back inside with a large pot, a ladle, a blanket, a plate, cups, forks, one more knife, and a few other housekeeping oddments. "I'm sorry to hold you up, but she's got nothing in there, and, well, I was thinking how I don't need more than one ladle, do I? And she might as well have this pan as well."

Ruth heard the sadness in Easter's voice. She'd lain upstairs in the attic all morning, listening to the comings and goings, the orders and laughter, the unspoken regret. She told herself that she should get up and help. She should have offered her hand to Easter, too. She should have found some way to say good-bye and thank you.

Mimba's words had bubbled back to her all that day. She could hear the island cadence that sounded like singing to her. Mimba would have said, "You are a good old soul, you, Easter, you. I was born lucky to share a roof with you. Go you now in peace."

But it had been too many years for Ruth to say such a thing out loud, so she lay still on her pallet, her stomach aching, her breath shallow, and hoped that Easter knew that she would care for her house with thankful hands for as long as she was able. Easter had been a better friend than she deserved.

The horse snorted and shook off the rain as it pulled away from the house. A few minutes later, the storm gained force and pounded the roof like a thousand hammers. They would have a rough time on the road, Ruth thought. She went out and stood in the gray downpour, letting the rain serve as her tears.

The next morning, she woke shivering in the damp house. Bundled in her blanket, she checked the position of her four protecting stones and found all of them off-kilter. She carried her bedding downstairs, where the parlor seemed empty as a church, echoing her steps. All but one of the rag rugs were gone. A big pile of castoffs cluttered one end of the table: a few dishrags, a coverlet, a ragged shawl, jumbled cutlery and dishes enough for a family of four, a pitcher. Easter had left her best cauldron, too, a great black pot with a solid handle and feet. Ruth saw it for the generous gift it was meant to be.

She sank into the armchair and listened to the rain, which filled her head with a relentless drumming that relaxed her nearly to dozing. Until she heard a change, a small shift, a different pitch of the splash near the window. Someone was outside. Her eyes glittered in the dimness. She rushed to see who or what it might be, but there was nothing and no one. Just sheets of rain washing new grooves into the gullies, pounding the grasses flat.

It could have been Cornelius, she thought. Or even one of the dogs. Ruth remembered how she had been taken by surprise on her first day in Dogtown by a brown cur on the road. The raw girl who had walked hundreds of miles in search of her mother's grave seemed like a complete stranger to her now, which made yesterday's vivid memory of Mimba even more of a puzzle. Ruth lived day to day, without thoughts of the future or of her past. Her dreams were timeless, too: in one, she was a bird with wings so big, it took only three strong thrusts to send her soaring from Folly Cove all the way to Good Harbor.

She had another dream about being a large black dog, very much like the shaggy cur named Bear, who had been the pack's leader when she first arrived. Had there been a successor anything like him, Ruth would never have been able to get as close to his descendants as she had.

Ruth had begun visiting the dogs in their high meadow two

years after Henry Brimfield's appearance on Cape Ann, which was also the last time Bear was seen. Ruth had kept her distance at first, no closer than fifty feet. She crept to within forty feet the next summer, twenty the following year, until she was close enough to stretch out her hand and touch them. Not that she ever did any such thing, nor did she make any sudden moves or speak a single word, thus proving herself trustworthy. Or at least tolerable.

Studying the dogs, she had learned how to live within herself entirely: to sit without expectation, to rest, eyes half-closed, and panting through the stifling heat, sniffing subtle changes in the air, succumbing to sleep when it came.

The dogs were neither noisy nor silent, neither idle nor busy. They snored and sighed, coughed, scratched, and snapped at buzzing passersby. They stood and stretched, ambled to the bushes to lift a leg or crouch, returned to shade or tall grass to circle and settle again. They smelled one another lazily, chewed on the grass, lifted their chins to follow the motion of a bird or a scent on the wind. Ruth passed whole days among them, floating through time like it was warm water.

In the days after Easter's departure, Ruth took note of the greening trees and began to look forward to the coming summer afternoons. But her anticipation was undercut with dread, too, for the pack was dwindling fast. When Ruth first arrived in Dogtown, there were nearly twenty-five dogs in the hills, living like a nearby but separate neighborhood, at peace with the people next door—a little standoffish, perhaps, but friendly enough. By the time Easter moved to Gloucester, there were no more than eight of them left, and those few were bony and mangy.

That spring, Ruth caught sight of the last breeding-age female, waddling and swollen with puppies, and hoped there might yet be a future for the pack. But the litter was stillborn and the mother lost too much blood in her labors and died as well. Ruth found little

Brindle's body in the woods a few weeks later, his ribs showing beneath his dull, dusty fur: she buried him where he lay.

In August she counted the last six dogs, sprawled in their sun-baked pasture overlooking the sea. Ruth turned at the sound of a rasping sigh, and watched as Brownie sank gently into death, as if the earth were welcoming his body home.

Tan got to her feet immediately and padded to Brownie's side, where she lay down with her head on her paws. Ruth knew that she was mourning her companion, though not in the manner of men and women, who make much of themselves when death takes a loved one. Her sorrow seemed purely selfless by comparison. The other dogs made a show of shaking their coats and sneezing before they walked into the forest, leaving Tan to absorb her loss alone.

Ruth fetched a shovel so that she would not have to watch the crows pick Brownie's body clean. Tan was still there when she returned but walked away when she started to dig a small oval hole, which hugged the curled-up corpse in a neat embrace.

The blue of the sea caught Ruth's eye as she wiped the dirt from her hands, and she felt an involuntary shiver of pleasure at being alive. She was not quite one of the dogs, she thought, kneeling to arrange a cairn of stones on top of the freshly turned earth. It felt good to finish something properly, even if it was something as inconsequential as piling rocks over the bones of a wild dog.

As she bedded down that night, Ruth felt the dirt of the grave under her nails, and listened to the silence left by Easter's absence, regretting again that she had not said a proper thank-you. She closed her eyes and summoned up her landlady's impish face and wondered, though it had only been a few months, whether Easter still walked the earth. Ruth hated to think of that pleasant spirit trapped forever in a narrow wooden box.

❖

Had Ruth tried to find out, she would have discovered that there was no cause to worry about Easter: she had flourished from her first day at the tavern. Her fond smile could still melt the ice off a pump, and she knew how to make the dullest fellow feel so clever, he'd order another draught just to remain close to the glow of her attention.

Easter had a talent for making out a person's mood, knowing when to comfort a lonesome traveler and when to back away from a black mood. She understood that most people needed only a semblance of interest, and that some men got downright testy if she paid too much attention, suspecting her of trying to catch them in a lie.

There were times that Easter missed being the mistress—especially when Louisa Tuttle gave her the evil eye for pocketing a little bonus from some grateful fellow. But all in all, she was as happy as she'd been in twenty years.

Easter was a favorite with the regulars, who loved her stories and jokes. And she had many pets among the sailors and merchants and farmers, with a soft spot for handsome faces. When the greenest eyes she'd ever seen stopped at her counter, she fluttered right over to see what he'd drink. His name was Robert Newell, and a fetching lock of brown hair curled over his wide forehead. He had nice manners, matched her smile for smile, and made Easter giggle like a girl.

Newell told her that he was a chandler from Ipswich with business in the harbor and an elderly relative on Cape Ann. After he finished his ale, he announced, "I'd better be going. My auntie is waiting supper for me."

"Too bad," said Easter, who had forgotten herself completely and laid her weathered hand on top of his.

"Well, I wouldn't say no to a cup of tea before facing that wind."

"Will you be wanting me to tell you your fortune?" she purred.

Newell leaned forward and teased, "You got the vision?"

"Dearie, I used to be so good at this, some of that stiff-necked lot accused me of being a witch."

"A sweet thing like you?"

Easter saw a fellow across the table roll his eyes and realized that she was making a fool of herself. She rushed off to get his tea, red-faced and flustered.

"I think I'll take my chances on the witchcraft. Go ahead and tell me my fortune, won't you, Mistress?" Newell said.

"Just call me Easter."

"Well then, Easter. Will you?"

"You got to drink it first."

Newell gulped his tea and handed her the cup while a few men gathered to watch. Easter picked it up, eyed her audience with a mysterious twinkle, and swirled the dregs. Covering the cup with a saucer, she flipped it over in a quick motion and set it on the counter.

"We got to let it settle," Easter said, prolonging the drama. "Someone bring a lamp so I can get a good look."

Lifting it off the saucer with a great flourish, she leaned forward to study what was left in the cup. "Hmmmm."

Newell crossed his arms and smiled.

"I see you on a journey," she said.

"That's no mystery, Easter," mocked a voice from the crowd. "He's up here from Ipswich. He'll be going home."

"Let the woman talk," Newell said.

Her nose was an inch above the rim. "You're heading somewhere else soon. Someplace real steep. Up a mountain. You are in a great hurry."

"That couldn't be this trip then, since the fellow's been in here all afternoon." It was Henry Riley, cutting up.

"Shhhh."

"You're climbing this steep hill, and there's a . . . well, I'm not sure what it is. What is it you call them critters with the humps on the back?"

"A hunchback?" Riley said.

"Naw," Easter shot back. "Like a horse but with bumps on 'em."

"A camel?" said Newell.

"That's it."

"What's that supposed to mean? Is that a good sign or a bad one?"

Easter shrugged. "Couldn't say. I'm just telling you what I see."

"Camels come from Africa," said a smooth-faced young sailor. "You headed to Africa, mister?"

Newell smiled and shook his head. "No, but I do have to head up to my auntie's house, or my supper will be burned. Thank you for a most diverting afternoon, Mistress Easter," he said and pressed a coin into her hands as he rose. "I'll keep a good eye out for camels, though."

Everyone laughed at that, including Easter. But Riley wouldn't leave it alone. "Now, Easter," he wheedled. "If you see an elephant in my tea leaves, does it mean I'm going to India? Or that I'm going to need the outhouse in a big way." Easter smiled into his face and silently wished him a painful bout of constipation.

When Newell returned six months later with the unlikely report that he'd seen a camel during an unexpected trip to Quebec City, the story brought a fresh crop of men and even a few women to the tavern, seeking clues to the future. Easter brewed a great deal of tea, laid out cards, and hung straight pins on strings over big bellies, too. No one seemed to mind how rarely she was right in her predictions about business deals, or luck in love, or whether the baby turned out to be a he or she. Easter tried to tell people what they wanted to hear and never hurt a soul with any of her prophecies. With the extra income, she ordered three dresses in bright colors from Polly Younger, and a new cap of fine green batiste, which topped off her smiling face with a rakish flourish that would have looked foolish on anyone but Easter.

Judy Rhines took great satisfaction in seeing the apples return to her friend's cheeks and the dimples to her hands. She would stop in at Easter's rooms in the mornings for tea and conversation, though there were times she grew impatient with Easter's endless reminiscence about the old days in Dogtown. After Easter spent a solid hour chewing over Cornelius Finson's fate and fortunes, Judy let a good week pass before visiting again. But when Tammy Younger died, which happened almost a year to the day after Easter moved to Gloucester, they attended her funeral arm in arm.

It was Mrs. Pulcifer who had discovered the body. That bony busybody had been making her way home after a long, gossipy tea with Betsy Hodgkins down the road from the Younger place. She heard the lowing of a cow in desperate need of milking and followed the pitiful sound to Tammy's place. Peeking through the open window, she'd gotten what she called "the shockingest sight of my life."

Tammy was seated at her table, facedown in a bowl of moldering stew. She must have been lying there for a few days at least. Mice had been in and out, nibbling what was left on the plate and chewing the old woman's hair. From the look of the round, bloody bites out of her hands and on the back of her neck, some crows must have hopped through the window, too.

"If I didn't have my grandmother's constitution," said Mrs. Pulcifer, taking a third glass of cordial from Oliver, "I would have fainted right on the spot. The smell was the worst part of it. Any other lady would have fallen into a faint."

Polly Younger argued against having any sort of funeral for Tammy. But Oliver gave in to Mrs. Pulcifer's fuss about laying her to rest with some dignity after the "shameful" way she'd been "abandoned" to die.

Oliver agreed to pay for the coffin and bought a better class of spirits than any of them were used to. The day he learned of

Tammy's death, Oliver sold the house and lands to Nathaniel Babson for enough money to buy a share in Everett Mansfield's store, add two rooms to his house, and buy Polly an extravagant bolt of blue cotton he knew she was pining for.

Pouring the liquor made it easier for him to be in that house. He liked people thinking of him as a spendthrift if only to prove that he was an entirely different sort of Younger than his awful aunt. A dozen people were gathered around Tammy's wooden table for the funeral tea: Oliver and Polly were there with their three boys—baby Isaac having only recently joined the family; Easter Carter and Judy Rhines helped to serve and clear. Mrs. Pulcifer wouldn't have missed it for the world, of course. Finally, there were John and Betsy Hodgkins, who brought their balky nine-year-old twins.

There wasn't much conversation beyond small talk about the weather and the newspaper that had begun publishing in Gloucester. Even those paltry exchanges ebbed into silence quickly and Judy noticed that everyone, even the children, was staring into their cups or mugs, wondering how long before they would be released.

"The service was just awful," Mrs. Pulcifer said, as she had several times that afternoon. At the cemetery, the pastor had read a single psalm over the casket, remanded dust to dust, and left it at that. "It was an insult to the dead. I've a mind to say something to that Reverend Lionel."

"For goodness sake, Hester," Easter said. "It was Tammy Younger, after all. Did you expect the man to lie about her with a Bible in his hands?"

Judy Rhines decided it was time to leave. She'd felt poorly all day, somehow overwrought and sleepy at the same time. She was there only because Oliver had come right out and begged her to help him "muddle through the day."

She hadn't seen Tammy since the day she helped Oliver retrieve his birthright; she counted back and discovered that it had been eight years. Judy probably hated Tammy Younger as much as Polly or anyone else on Cape Ann, not that she could explain what riled her so deeply. Not even her dreadful treatment of Oliver explained the way that Judy had wanted to beat her with a hot poker. Attending her funeral seemed a way to make amends for those unspeakable feelings, but it also made her feel like the worst sort of hypocrite.

Judy wanted only to be back in her room, where she could drink tea and finish her book; an American novel this time, about a colonial maid who loses her British fiancé to the sea and finds herself in love with a noble-minded savage.

"We're all pegging out, eh, Judy Rhines?" asked Easter, taking her friend's bitten lip as a sign of sadness. "There's so few of us left from Dogtown days."

"I'm ready to go home," Judy said.

Easter had wanted to ask Judy to accompany her into Dogtown; she'd wanted to take a look at her house—and Ruth. But she could see that Judy was determined, and she didn't want to go by herself. "I'll walk back with you, then."

Overhearing them, the wine-fuddled Pulcifer trilled, "But no one's so much as raised a glass to Tammy Younger. Someone should say something. Wooon't be proper."

Hodgkins, who had drunk the most, raised his glass. "I'll do it. Here's to the sorry end of that old bitch and baggage. The last witch of Dogtown."

"Now, John," Betsy sniffed. "No need to speak ill of the dead."

"You were whistling a different tune last night," he shot back.

Betsy Hodgkins was a sharp-elbowed woman, greatly relieved to be rid of her notorious neighbor, whose proximity had always seemed an insult. Her whole life, she'd dismissed all talk of witchcraft as so much stuff and nonsense. But the night before the funeral, when Hodgkins had brought her coffin into the kitchen for a quick coat of wax, Betsy had gotten a strange chill up her back. Such skittishness wasn't like her; her husband had brought many coffins indoors without any effect on her.

But then, both of the twins had startled up in bed with nightmares, screaming and sweating so that she'd had to slap them before they recognized their own mother. After that, she dropped her favorite china teacup with the hand-painted yellow rose on the bottom. What finally unnerved her was the heavy thud of a bird flinging itself against the kitchen window, again and again. She made John go outside with a broom to chase it off and when he returned, ordered, "Get that thing of evil out of my house."

"Don't be a fool," he snapped. "I need to wax the top and I'll be done."

Betsy folded her arms and clamped her mouth so that her lips disappeared—a portent of a long sulk—so he put his coat back on and took the coffin back to the barn, where he consoled himself with a long pull from a hidden bottle.

Hodgkins's rough toast put an end to the gathering. Judy and Easter rushed away, refusing Oliver's offer to drive them in his new wagon. "We're not as old as all that," said Judy, squeezing his hand. "Besides, it's turned into a lovely day."

Oliver was the last one out and loaded the wagon with the few barrels of plates and pots that Polly decided she could use. When he climbed up into the rig, he handed Polly the reins and took the baby out of her arms. Within a month, Babson sent a crew to strip the house, leaving nothing but a cellar hole and some piles of trash, which burned before the first snow.

❖

Cornelius Finson heard of Tammy's death from the Widow Fletcher in Sandy Bay, where he'd stopped with a bucket of clams. She gave him a cup of weak tea, making it clear that he was to drink it standing in the kitchen while she got her change purse and talked about her aches and pains. As he was ready to go, she said, "With that Younger woman dead, you're the last one left in Dogtown."

Cornelius did not bother to contradict the old woman, who had forgotten about Ruth, who was still rattling around in Easter's house. He seemed to be the only one who remembered that Ruth was still there.

She must be content with her solitude, he decided. As far as he knew, Ruth had not gone into Gloucester or Sandy Bay even once in the year since Easter left. But he'd noticed that the light-colored dog was living with her now. Seeing Tan tag after Ruth reminded Cornelius of Judy Rhines and her Greyling, though he'd never heard Ruth say a word to the dog, and the animal kept much more distance between them.

Cornelius had seen them from afar, and close up, too. In fact, he had walked near enough to Easter's house, morning, midday, and evening, to give Ruth the opportunity to speak to him. Once, he even saw her drawing back from the window as he passed. In the end, he thought it just as well. The last two Africans on Cape Ann had been in the same room on occasion over the years. They had nodded silent greetings on the road, but they had never spoken. What would they say to each other after so many years? he wondered. He did not wish to be questioned by a virtual stranger, even if she was, in some way, a sister in the skin. He imagined that she probably felt even less need to talk than he did.

Cornelius was not nearly as cut off from the world as Ruth. He continued to make his rounds, secretly watching over the Younger family and Judy Rhines. He sold meat, fish, and berries to some of the up-country farmers' wives and widows and he stopped in at Oliver's store at least once every month to buy oil, cornmeal, and candles. He did his marketing late in the day, when the streets were nearly empty, since the morning he overheard a woman telling her little boy, "If you don't do as you're told, Black Neal over there is going to come to steal you from your bed and sell you to the devil."

Cornelius was ready for winter when it hit, hard and cold. The house was snug, and his larder was stocked. He passed the days taking care of his own small needs and whittling. Every night before bed he stepped outside and sniffed for the smoke rising from Ruth's chimney.

On the cold December evening when he smelled nothing but winter, Cornelius hurried over to find her a few steps from the open door, with four dogs huddled against her shivering body. She might have been lying there the whole day or even since the night before, for all he knew. The fire was long dead. The dogs had kept her from freezing.

When Cornelius arrived, three of the hounds sprinted out, but Tan stayed where she was, growling softly as he crouched. He moved slowly and met the dog's steady gaze to reassure her that he meant no harm.

"Ruth," said Cornelius, gently.

Tan's ears flattened back against her head.

"Ruth," he repeated.

She opened her eyes and recognized the face, but not the expression on it. Nor could she summon a name.

She tried to open her mouth. She tried to lift her hand.

"Can you hear me?" he said, louder.

She managed a strangled squeak.

Tan whined.

"Ruth?" shouted the man with the heavy eyes. She blinked at him. He got to his feet. From where she lay, it seemed that he'd retreated all the way to the sky, more like a tree than a man.

He looked down at her, soaked and soiled, her face puddled into a mess of features that once belonged to Ruth. She was trembling.

"I've got to get you into town," he said, doubting that she understood. She blinked, and he wondered if maybe she did.

Cornelius lit a fire and dragged Ruth near the warmth, dismayed by the heaviness of her limp body: he would not be able to carry her on his back. He warmed some water and found a cloth and some extra clothes.

"I'm sorry," he whispered, as he took down her trousers and wiped away at the mess, trying not to soil his hands any more than he had to, trying not to retch, trying to keep his eyes averted. Tan watched, panting lightly.

Cornelius found the tea and made a cup, but he couldn't figure out how to get any of it into Ruth's flaccid mouth. "I'm sorry," he said, and tried to reassure her. "We'll go at first light. Easter'll take care of you, I figure."

Ruth blinked. Easter was the little woman who should have been sitting by the fire. Not this tall, sad man. She fell back into sleep, or something like it.

"You're not dead, are you?" said Cornelius, alarmed.

Her eyes flew open and the man jumped. He got to his feet and poked at the fire and then put his coat on top of the blankets he had already piled on top of her. "I'm going to find that sledge of yours," he said and walked outside, glad for the freshness of the icy air.

Tan moved closer and lay down, pressing the length of herself against Ruth, whose eyes brimmed over.

As soon as the sky began to lighten, Cornelius hoisted her onto the sled and bound her with ropes. "I'm sorry," he said, again and again, worried that he was hurting her.

Ruth blinked. "Thank you," she blinked. "Thank you."

The trip into Gloucester was torturous for them both. If only there had been more snow, thought Cornelius; then he could have glided her part of the way, at least. As it was, he had to drag her over rocks and deep ruts so that nearly every step tossed her head from side to side and rattled her teeth. Ruth tasted blood on her tongue. Her bladder loosed itself again, and she squeezed her eyes tight, ashamed. Tan followed, step for step, ten feet behind.

The tavern was still dark and shuttered when Cornelius pounded on the door. Louisa Tuttle opened an upstairs window with a pitcher of water to dump over the rowdy who dared disturb them at such an hour. When she saw the African and what she took to be a corpse, she pulled back. A moment later, Easter flung open the door.

"Oh, dear me," she wailed. "Oh, the poor creature."

"She's not dead," Cornelius said.

"Bring her right inside."

Louisa frowned mightily at the prospect of such a scene and smell in her public room. By midmorning, they had taken her to the workhouse, which is where she woke up. Someone removed her shirt and she felt warm water, then cold water and a thin garment that was almost an insult in the chill of the room. She was rolled from side to side onto a hard bed, and covered with a rough blanket that provided no warmth or comfort. Voices echoed around her, near and far.

Ruth wondered how she was a part of this tumult and then remembered the way that beach roses fold in upon themselves at night, and slept. She woke up in darkness, unsure if she was dreaming or thinking. A hand touched her forehead, as warm as sunlight, as light as paper. Or maybe that was part of a dream.

After a day, or two, or perhaps even three, Ruth's eyes opened again. It was dark but there was a candle somewhere behind her and she realized where she was. She had finally been relegated to the bottommost rung of life on Cape Ann, a final holding pen for the old and infirm who had neither money nor children. The windows rattled and sent a draft strong enough to ruffle the sheet on Ruth's chest. She closed her eyes until morning when she found Easter sitting beside her, rummaging in her basket.

"How are you today, dearie?" she asked, without the slightest expectation of any response. When she glanced over and saw that Ruth's eyes were open, she jumped to her feet. "Oh my goodness gracious," she exclaimed. "Look at you. And they said there wasn't a prayer. Well! Didn't I just know better? Didn't I just? I'll get you up to snuff in quick order. I'll get some of this broth in you, and then we'll see who's doomed and who's not, eh? Eh?"

The beaming pleasure on Easter's face was almost too much for Ruth to bear, and she closed her eyes again as Easter lifted the covers and set to cleaning her up again.

"You ain't near as bad off as them others," she said. "You've got me." Within the hour, Easter had gotten her to swallow some of the soup she'd brought, and recounted the story of her rescue by the dogs and Cornelius. Then she leaned in and told what she knew about the two other residents of the place. "Mistress Woe over there, her daughter just died without leaving her a grandchild or anything else to speak of. They found her on the floor of her room, too," Easter whispered. "Town clerk sold her two sticks of furniture and whatnots, and that's paying for a little extra food and a woman to wash her bottom. She's been here a month." Easter bit her tongue before finishing the thought that it don't look like she was going to die before the money ran out.

"Down there," Easter pointed to a screen near the far wall, "is a young feller they found under the docks, robbed of everything and bleeding from a bad cut on his head. No one knows his name, or which ship he came in on." The doctor predicted his death within the week, which was fine with the matron: with only the pittance from the town for his support, she had to swab the sailor down herself.

Compared to those poor souls, Ruth got treated like royalty. Easter came to spoon-feed her broth and tea and gossip every morning, slipping the matron a few coins for an extra blanket and the promise to call her if Ruth took a bad turn. And she'd pressed Judy Rhines into an hour of service during the evening, when Easter could not leave the tavern.

Judy arrived at dusk to wash Ruth's hands and face, and feed her some milk toast and egg. Then she'd sit beside her and read softly from the newspaper.

Ruth wondered if she knew this woman with the spectacles and the sweet voice, but she could not get her thoughts to rest on any one thing for more than a moment at a time. Her attention flitted from the ragged breath of the man behind the screen to the nasal whine of the elderly lady across the room, to a memory of a stone well placed, a meal once eaten, the dog. She trolled her mind for words to thank the little woman (Easter, whose name returned to her from time to time) who wiped her chin, washed her bottom, and fed her, all with such good cheer.

Ruth was not too alarmed by her inability to find words to express her ideas or urges. Last summer, lying among the dogs, she had been unable to summon the word for "cloud" or "itch." It had not mattered to her then: her voice had always seemed out-of-tune to her own ear. It had been a relief to become more and more mute. But she did want to thank Easter, and the other woman. And the man who brought her, the tall one. And what of the tan dog? Where was she?

⚜

Tan was outside. Easter caught sight of her lurking in the alley beside the workhouse and called, "Here, girl." But the dog ran down the lane and disappeared. Judy Rhines brought a meaty bone and hid it under a rotten barrel, but a city mongrel took it. After a week of watching, Tan was starved and listless. But when she caught Cornelius's scent, her ears pricked up and she crept out of her hole.

He arrived after midnight and went in to stare at what was left of Ruth. She was wasted, diminished to what looked like half the size of her healthy self. It seemed impossible that this frail woman—for there was no mistaking this fine-boned creature for a man anymore—had once been as strong as him. Knotted mats of white hair escaped from the too-small cap on her head. She was so still, he wondered if she was dead.

Just then, her eyes flew open and searched the ceiling, as though she was expecting a visitor from on high. She looked frantic and afraid until she saw him and moaned.

"What is it?" he whispered.

She flailed her head from side to side and he saw tears glitter at the corners of her eyes. Her suffering overwhelmed him. She was alone and terrified, in pain, despairing.

He could deliver her from this misery with the blanket or even with his bare hands, he thought. It would be a mercy, like putting down a horse with a broken leg. But he had never killed a horse, much less a woman. It was not in him. "I'm sorry," he said.

Ruth closed her eyes and grew still again. Perhaps she had understood his apology. Perhaps she had just been dreaming. Whatever her thoughts, Cornelius felt that he'd been dismissed. He set down the pile of kindling he'd brought and fled.

When he reached the Dogtown cottage that he would always think of as Judy's house, he held the door open for Tan, who had followed him. She hesitated for a moment but then ran to a corner, watching him. He lit the fire and stared at the flames, haunted by the image of Ruth alone and forgotten in a cold room on a hard bed. Cornelius looked at Ruth's dog, who had made her way to the hearth and was curled at his feet. He wished her mistress an easy death. Then he wished the same for himself.

❖

Sometimes, when Easter was there, Ruth tried to speak. But all she could muster was a croak.

"Does it hurt?" Easter asked, alarmed. "Would you like a dram?"

Ruth closed her eyes wishing she could say, "I need nothing." She would have taken Easter's hand and finally said her thank-yous.

Though speech was lost to her, Ruth's hearing seemed sharper than ever. In the night, she heard the halyards clang in the harbor and thought about how different winter sounded in Dogtown—a dark hum in the pines, a slow hiss in the leaves.

Through the thin panes of glass, she heard the splash of waves and remembered how the ocean had made itself heard all the way up in the hills; the surf on distant boulders like a muffled knock on an enormous door.

Ruth heard snow against the workhouse window, and recalled a storm that had coated the bare trees with salt spray, which disappeared in the morning sunlight with a brittle clatter of falling ice.

During the day, Ruth listened to the sounds from the street: horses clopping, wagons rumbling, the mismatched chorus of voices: greeting, laughing, swearing, selling, urging. There were gulls, too, barking and shrieking, like gulls everywhere.

Days passed over, around, and through Ruth. One morning during Easter's visit, the doomed sailor woke up, shouting and cursing. Easter ran over to see what had happened and rushed back to give Ruth the full report. "No one can talk French, but he was pointing to his mouth and to his stomach clear enough," she said. "Poor feller was half-starved, of course. When Matron brought him the thin stuff she passes off as gruel, he threw it at her. They sold everything he had, down to the boots, don't you know," Easter confided, as though she and Ruth had always shared these kinds of stories. "They counted on him dying, so now they got to scramble up some clothes and shoes for him. You should have seen the fellow's face! Mad as a wet hen."

The sailor's departure seemed like a good omen to Easter, who'd always thought the workhouse a stepping-stone to the grave. But within the day, the angel of death did take up residence, as the old lady's cough grew deeper and louder, wearing her out so that every breath became a gasp. It was Judy Rhines who noticed the solid silence under her blanket.

After the brief, hushed commotion of removing the body, Ruth listened to the steady *tap-tap* of Judy's knitting needles and the sound settled her to sleep.

In the morning, Ruth's eyes were gummy and unfocused. She did not blink or glance about, and by midday her face was hot to the touch. She slept all afternoon and Judy could not rouse her for supper. She'd brought a camphor rub, and applied it to her chest thinking that Ruth was sleeping just like Polly's babies: as though she was working at it. As though it was her calling.

In Ruth's dream, she was in the high meadow with Tan and Bear and others from the old pack. It was summer, and mice skittered in the brush. There was a swarming of bees, screaming cicadas, and a great symphony of birdcalls: robin, jay, mockingbird, pigeon, pheasant, woodpecker, duck, and goose. She sank into the thicket of wild music, to the beat of her own heart.

Suddenly, a racket of gulls drowned out all the other sounds. Ruth was amazed by the variety of their calls: one was just like a crow's *caw-caw,* another sounded like the creaking of a broken tree limb. There was wild laughter, braying, screaming, keening. One of the birds sounded exactly like a weeping woman. "Oh, oh, oh," it sobbed, nearly human.

"There, there," Ruth said in her dream. She opened her lips and nearly summoned the words, but not quite. No matter, she thought. It's only a gull.

❖

Easter decided she wanted a proper burial for the African and got a couple of gravediggers, two of her loyal customers, to help her buy a spot inside the cemetery, not outside the wall, where vagrants and paupers were usually buried. Easter was ready to pay for a coffin, too, but Judy told her that Africans had a horror of being buried in a box. Instead, she volunteered a winding sheet: a fine damask table-cloth from Martha Cook's trousseau, which had never been used and would never be missed.

"She looks like a lily before it opens up," Judy whispered as they wrapped her neat and tight.

"I hope this is what she'd have wanted," said Easter, sadly, for she had no idea.

The day of the burial was sunny and windless and the sea was brilliant in tribute. But only Easter was there to bear witness.

Judy Rhines was sick with the grippe. Oliver would have been there to provide Easter an arm to lean on, but Everett was in Boston that day, which meant he was needed in the store. Polly had a wedding dress to finish and the baby to nurse. No one remembered to send for Cornelius.

Easter met the gravediggers at the workhouse, where they rolled the mummylike corpse onto a plank.

"Wasn't much left to her, was there," said one of the men.

"She wasted away that last month," Easter said.

They carried Ruth, slow and solemn, to the graveside and laid her gently in the hole. Easter watched them fill it in, her nose red as a hothouse poppy. When they finished, the men stood on either side of her, shovels in hand, waiting.

"I don't know what to say," Easter said.

"Rest in peace?"

"I hope so," she sighed. "I should have brought a Bible or a stone, or something."

"Come on, old gal," said one of the men, replacing his cap and pulling her arm through his. "We're going to stand you for a toddy."

Easter recounted all of this to Judy Rhines, who'd never seen her friend so downcast. "We went back to the tavern and I said, 'Everyone raise a glass to the memory of—' and damn me if I didn't know what to say. I didn't know if I should call her John Woodman or Black Ruth. I just couldn't stand for anyone to laugh at her." Easter's eyes brimmed over and she shook her head. "It wasn't good, Judy Rhines. I tell you, it was the saddest send-off ever."

"You were good to her," Judy insisted.

"I didn't do much."

"She wasn't alone at the end. You were a good friend and Ruth knew it, too. I'm certain of that."

"Maybe," said Easter, softly. "I suppose."

A Last Wish

THE MONTHS following Ruth's death were dry and gray, a perpetual twilight unbroken by snow or sun, and a great sadness settled in Cornelius. His head ached. He found it difficult to wake and slept the morning away, passing what was left of the short, cold days making brooms and then whittling scraps of wood into blocks like the ones he'd once seen the Younger boys play with. He did not go into town.

His only company was the tan dog. Though she spent most of her day outdoors and out of sight, she returned in the evening to eat what he fed her, and curl up near his feet. Cornelius never spoke to the dog, mortified by the depth of his gratitude for her presence.

After three months without seeing him, Oliver decided he had to find out if Cornelius was dead or alive, and he left the shop early one afternoon to walk into Dogtown.

"I wondered how you were getting on without your tea," Oliver said, only partly cheered to discover his worst fears unmet. The smell of wet dog and unwashed clothes hung in the air. Wood shavings littered the floor of Judy's once spotless floor, scattered plates with dried bits of food lay about, and a mound of peat crumbled by the hearth.

Cornelius shrugged and poked at the fire. He was thinner and grayer than the last time Oliver had seen him. There was a decided stoop to his shoulders and something else was amiss, too, though he couldn't quite put his hand on it. "I worry about you, old man," he said, gently.

"No need," Cornelius said, feeling that he'd been scolded.

"Polly sends her good wishes," he lied, for she had no idea that he'd come. "And the boys, too. Nathaniel is the best student at mathematics. Mrs. Hammond says it's a wonder the way he adds and figures. I put that to your teaching him. Remember?"

Cornelius said nothing.

"Maybe you don't recall. While you were laid up, you said the numbers to him, and it seems like he picked 'em up. David has started at the school, too. And I don't know if you've seen Isaac yet, the baby. He's a redhead, of all things, but Polly says her granddad had that coloring."

Cornelius did not turn to face Oliver, who chatted on in the manner of an old friend. He carried on for as long as he could but finally stopped. Getting no response or acknowledgment, he gave up. "Well, I'll be going. You will come down to the shop with some mallows, won't you? I've got ladies clamoring for mallows already," he said, and picking up one of the blocks piled on the table, added, "I might be able to sell these for you, too." He ran a finger over the carved images of dogs and birds. "Would it be all right if I take one for Isaac?"

Cornelius nodded.

"I'll be going then," said Oliver and put his hand out, but Cornelius was already holding the door for him.

Oliver put his collar up and decided not to tell Polly that he'd been there. She would be hurt if he told her about Cornelius's rudeness, and indeed, he had to admit to feeling the sting of it, himself.

After walking all the way up that miserable road just to pay a call, Cornelius hadn't even asked him to sit down.

Everett and Polly often teased Oliver of being an easy mark for anyone with a hard-luck story, and where Cornelius was concerned, he knew it was true. The African was a touchstone for Oliver's Dogtown days, and Oliver had longed to step in and help Cornelius, as no one had helped him. He'd given Cornelius more than a fair bargain in the store, but since those few weeks when he and Polly had cared for him after he'd hurt his leg, Oliver had found no way to do the man a good turn.

As he made his way home, Oliver pulled the wooden block out of his pocket and decided it was as handsome as any he'd ever seen. He'd go back the following week, he decided, and buy the rest of them, certain he could sell them to the summer trade.

And he'd bring a spring tonic, too. What Cornelius needed was a good strong purge. This plan made Oliver feel better about the whole visit. For a moment, he thought of telling Judy Rhines about Cornelius's sad state, and of his plan to help. But of course he would not speak of it to her. It would embarrass both of them, especially now that she had become such a lady.

❖

Since Martha Cook's death, Judy had become "Mistress Rhines" in town, greeted with deference by the shopkeepers and with polite smiles by the neighboring matrons. She wore soft leather slippers outdoors as well as inside and favored lace collars when she attended the Sunday service at First Parish, where Reverend Hildreth's sermons now extolled the importance of good works. She had Cape Ann's best library at her disposal, and she savored its riches under a satin coverlet in what had once been the best guest room, but was now her bedchamber.

She bought herself oranges whenever she wished. She felt like a princess.

Martha Cook used to assure her that, after her death, the Judge would turn her gratitude into a material reward, but Judy had harbored few expectations of a man she so thoroughly detested. As Martha weakened, Judy had tried to resign herself to a life of service as a nurse or companion in some lesser home where she would be treated like a servant rather than a sister. These thoughts shamed her terribly during Martha's gruesome last weeks, but they would not abate and added extra pangs to her grief.

The day of the funeral was long and bitter. A somber multitude of Gloucester's most prominent citizens walked through the house, whispering, sipping, and shaking their heads. Most of them looked straight through Judy, as invisible as the housemaid.

After the last guest had murmured her condolences to the Judge, he asked Judy to join him in the parlor. But as she began to clear the clutter of teacups and wineglasses, he took them from her hands and said, "Please, Mistress Rhines. I wonder if I could impose upon you to sit with me for a few moments." He drew two chairs together, forcing her to sit knee to knee and face him squarely.

Joshua Cook was a well-made man, admired for his aristocratic nose, strong chin, and deep-set eyes fringed with the kind of lashes that were the envy of every girl and woman who ever met him. "I wish to speak frankly," he said. "I hope that you will forgive me for my candor, but it is necessary to make things clear as glass between us so that I can discuss your future in a forthright manner."

The Judge's demeanor was formal as befits a member of the bench, though it had been several years since he'd resigned his court duties. Judy had always found it difficult to decipher his mood, but she could see the agitation beneath his polished manner. She folded her hands and stared at her shoes, afraid that she would not be able to mask her disgust for the man who had caused the death of her friend.

"Did you ever wonder how it was that I was never taken ill? Especially given the nature of Mrs. Cook's distress."

Judy was so startled that she let down her guard and glared at him with undisguised anger.

"I beg your pardon," he said. "But Dr. Beech has informed me that he had shared his diagnosis of Martha with you, so I assume that you, like he, consider me the worst sort of man, a degenerate. A monster who, well . . ." He sighed. "It explains your coolness toward me these past years. But now that I understand the source of your enmity, it speaks even more highly of your devotion to Martha and of your perfect discretion.

"Which brings me, again, to the question of whether you ever puzzled over the mystery of my good health. Especially given your belief that I was the reason for, that is to say, given your assumption about the cause of my wife's illness." The Judge was not only stammering but sweating.

"I mean no disrespect to my wife's memory, I swear. But, you see, long before you were part of this household, Mrs. Cook accompanied me on many visits to my mother's home in Maryland. I have a large family there, and Martha was a favorite with my sisters and my cousins." He took a breath. "With one cousin, in particular. A cousin by marriage: James Ridell."

Judy prayed for the kitchen maid to call for her, or for lightning to strike the house. Martha had often spoken of James Ridell and of the gracious hospitality he had provided when she and the Judge had stayed in Baltimore. She had referred to him as Captain Ridell and described him warmly as a true gentleman of the South, dashing, intelligent, and kind; a man who had married beneath him in the odious and shrewish Constance, who was the very least of her husband's otherwise refined relatives.

"Martha and Ridell were thrown together a good deal, as Connie was so often ill in her confinements." The Judge stared at Judy until she met his gaze. "Do I make myself clear?" he asked. She nodded, miserable.

"I tell you this not to poison your memory of Martha. She was not at fault here, not really." His voice dropped again. "You see, I was not much of a husband to her in certain ways. I mean to say, well, that I was not able to . . . That is, she needed . . ." He stopped, unable to find the words to express his meaning politely. But Judy understood.

"I can see that I have shocked you," he said. "You must think me a brute to speak of her in this manner, and today of all days."

Judy was shocked, though not in the way that the Judge imagined. His words had conjured the vivid sensation of Cornelius's hand on her breast, his mouth on her neck. He had been the other secret she had kept from Martha. Her physical connection to Cornelius, the longing and the pleasure, had been something for which she barely had words. And yet, it seemed this was something she and Martha had both known and lost.

The Judge handed Judy a glass of sherry. "Please, let me explain why I have spoken about things that should never be discussed, and which I will never mention again.

"Martha always spoke of you as a sister, and I am more than happy to honor the requests she made on your behalf. You will be remembered in my will, and I will make you a generous gift in parting should you choose to leave. However, I have another proposal that would have pleased Martha a great deal. One, I believe, that might serve you well given your, again I beg pardon, your circumstances. Am I correct in assuming that you do not wish to return to your life in, er, up-island?"

Judy winced at Judge Cook's reticence, as though mentioning Dogtown by name would be an insult. "You are correct."

"In that case, I would like you to stay on here, to take full charge of the house. It is my intention to winter with my sister, who now resides in Washington. I will return here for the summer and expect that some of my nieces and nephews and their children will join me for the season. But this plan depends, in part, upon placing my home in capable hands. Mistress Rhines, I would certainly understand your wish to leave a place filled with such sad and difficult memories; however, if you choose to go, I am doubtful of finding a suitable person, or one in whom I have such great confidence. I have received a reasonable offer for the house and grounds, but my inclination is not to act hurriedly."

Judy turned her gaze to the view of the harbor from the long parlor windows and nearly wept with relief. Until that moment, she had not permitted herself to face the pinched life that awaited her in a room above a shop or behind a kitchen.

"There will be an income for you, of course," he continued. "Full charge of the housekeeping monies as well. In the summer, when there is need of additional help, a cook and maids and such, they would be under your stewardship. Please understand, whatever you decide, I have already altered my will to reflect the great service you rendered to Mrs. Cook these many years. Not merely service, of course, but devotion and tenderness."

Judy finally met his eyes. With her smile, she all but sealed the agreement, but the Judge bowed and gave her the last word. "May I expect your decision by the end of the week?"

"Yes," she agreed. "By the end of the week."

Judge Cook was as good as his word. Before he left for the winter, Judy Rhines was given the keys, the ledger, a large allowance, and a free hand to make any changes or improvements she thought necessary. She stayed busy in the empty house, cleaning, canning, meeting with the gardener, and preparing the linens to serve a house filled with guests. She gave a detailed account of her efforts and outlays in a fortnightly letter to Judge Cook, which he answered promptly with a bank draft, thanks, and eventually with particulars about his arrival and his family's. He would be back in Gloucester by June, he wrote, with several guests in July and August, including four children and their nurse.

As summer approached, Judy hired two girls to serve as parlor maids, and Easter helped her locate a footman who would also help in the garden. But there simply was no local woman accomplished enough for the formal meals required by the Judge's sister, so Judy took the bold step of placing an advertisement in a Boston newspaper.

She received only one response, from a Mrs. Harriet Plant, who wrote that a temporary situation would suit her especially, and included a list of what she described as her "highly praised specialties." She also enclosed a letter from her employer, a dean at Harvard College, explaining that he would be in England for the summer and recommending "his Harriet" as an honest woman and a gastronomical treasure.

When the lilacs began to bloom, Judy moved out of the upstairs bedroom, with its harbor view and lace curtains, back into her old room off the kitchen, where she would be in very close quarters with the cook until the end of August. It was not a happy prospect, until the day that Mrs. Plant stepped off the coach.

Harriet turned out to be cut of the same cloth as Easter Carter: bluff, talkative, and unabashedly affectionate. Like Easter, she was a short woman, though she was nearly as wide as she was tall, with auburn hair and freckles down to her fingertips. She was born in Liverpool, England, and at a tender age was sent out to service in the kitchen of a grand country house where she was apprenticed to an accomplished French chef. Below stairs, the staff ate snails and garlic and things that sounded like swill but tasted like heaven, while the gentry consumed roasted joints and creamed soups of surpassing blandness sneered at by the Frenchman.

Judy learned all this and a good deal more within an hour of

Harriet's arrival. Her stories were funny and the tea she'd brought with her was first-rate, but Judy was alarmed at the prospect of her boisterous presence for three months. Despite all the changes life in town had made in her, she still favored great helpings of solitude. And yet, before she knew it, Judy was entirely accustomed to Harriet Plant's expansive ways and captivated by her cooking. Indeed, within a few weeks, she was finding it difficult to fasten her dress at the waist.

On her first full day in Gloucester, Harriet went to market, demanding that the shopkeepers let her taste everything before she bought. Then, with little more than butter, sugar, and flour, she tested the oven by baking a series of cakes and biscuits that brought tears to Judy's eyes. Harriet turned a basket of eggs into an airy construction spiced with some green herbal concoction she'd brought with her, and she made a cold potato soup that was the most refreshing thing Judy had ever tasted. Harriet was delighted by her new friend's keen appreciation and responded to her praises with precise and reverent descriptions of her methods.

"No recipes?" Judy asked, amazed that Harriet arrived without books or cards.

"No need," she said and pointed to her head. "We'll see what these Washington folks will ask for. I can cook mush, squeak, and dowdy as dull as anyone else this side of the pond. My professor has been to Italy and France so I can cook as I please when it's just him for dinner, and thank God for that. When he entertains, it's nothing but charred beef and custard."

Judge Cook arrived several weeks before the rest of his family and spent his days at his desk, reading mail and receiving local acquaintances in the library. He met with Judy to review the books and noted, "Mrs. Plant seems quite a treasure. Well done."

After Judy returned from her interview with their employer, Harriet plied her with questions. "Now there's a likely looking man. Is he good to you? Is he still in law? Will he remarry, do you think?"

"I'm sure I don't know what Joshua Cook has in mind," said Judy. "I think it unlikely that he'll marry again, though."

"Why's that? He's young enough, and easy on the eyes. Is he pining for his wife, then?"

"Really, Harriet, I haven't any idea. And I'm not entirely sure I approve of gossiping about the master of the house."

"Well then, what about you?" she said, brightly.

"Me?"

"I can ask if you've ever been married, can't I?"

Judy smiled in spite of herself. "No. I have not been married."

"Why not?" Harriet asked.

"No dowry, no family, no prospects."

"Oh, tosh. You've a fine head on your shoulders, and a face that don't curdle milk."

"Flatterer!" said Judy.

"I got me a husband, for a while at least. And you can see I'm no beauty!" Harriet said. "Maybe we should go see the fortune-teller at the tavern that I heard tell of; maybe she can see clear to finding you a husband."

Judy laughed at the idea. "If you're talking about Easter Carter, she can't see into the future any more than you or me."

"That's not what I heard."

"Well, you heard a pack of nonsense," Judy said, and told her about Easter's real gifts, of their days together in Dogtown, and the odd assortment of neighbors they'd known and buried. "Now that we're both in town, I can't fathom why we stayed there as long as we did."

"It's never easy to make a big change," Harriet said. "Anyone left up there anymore?"

"Just one, I believe."

"Which one?"

"Cornelius Finson."

"You didn't mention him."

"Didn't I?" Judy said. "There's not too much to tell, though he is the last African in these parts. He lives by his wits, trapping and hunting. Quite the hermit by now. He took over my old cottage, not that it was ever really mine. I just moved in when Ivy Perkins went to live with her sister in Lanesville, and no one ever told me to leave. I guess there's still no claim on it if Cornelius is there."

Harriet smiled. "Sounds like a good story to me. Did he have a wife?"

"No," said Judy, firmly.

Harriet perked up at the certainty in that answer. "You seem awful sure about that."

"Well, I suppose I don't know for certain," said Judy, giving away nothing. "Is there anything you wish me to order for dinner tonight?"

⋄⋄⋄

Harriet's good-natured but persistent questioning about everything on Cape Ann ended with the arrival of the summer guests. The responsibility of running the house consumed Judy's waking hours. She could hardly finish a sentence without interruption, as a hundred small details demanded her immediate attention.

The children arose early, needing breakfast. Card games and conversation lasted late into the night, with calls for savories and cider. All day, the sea air sharpened city appetites so that the kitchen never stopped and Judy was pressed into service, helping organize seaside picnics, elaborate teas, and formal dinners.

The young ones tracked sand everywhere, trampled flowers, spilled food, and filled the place with shrill shouts and giddy laughter. A nursemaid followed them from one adventure to the next, but Judy had to oversee the unending cleanup in their busy wake, while anticipating the needs of adults used to a much larger staff.

She felt a great sense of satisfaction in keeping the linens fresh, the larder filled, and the guests fed. She basked in the Judge's pride in his well-run house. In bed, she relived the day's failings (not enough milk for the children's supper) and triumphs (praise for the gardens). But on the August morning she found herself cutting late roses for the dinner table, she realized that she'd been cheated out of a whole summer's pleasures. She could not recall smelling the lilacs that year. She had not said much more than hello to Easter since June, nor visited with the Youngers. She had brought Polly in to do some mending, which at least got her up to date on the news about her little boys.

Harriet found a fresh source for Dogtown stories in Polly, who obliged with old tales of witches, a detailed recitation about the terrible Tammy Younger, and the notorious Mrs. Stanley.

"Doxies in Dogtown!" Harriet exclaimed. "Whatever happened to the boy?"

"He goes by the name of Maskey now, and he built himself a fine house in the center of Sandy Bay," Polly said. "He's quite the model citizen, a church deacon. Have you seen him in his whiskers, Judy? And that ebony cane? He wears boots that give him an extra two inches, and they make him strut like a little rooster. He's a bit of a laughingstock, I'm afraid.

"He hasn't married, though he might have his pick. He's an odd one," said Polly. She glanced at Judy and said, "Some folks say he's as strange as Cornelius Finson."

"What about that Cornelius fellow?" Harriet asked. "I'm simply fascinated by the Africans."

"He keeps to himself more than ever," said Polly. "My Oliver worries about the poor man. We got to know him quite well a while back." She told Harriet about how their dog found Cornelius lying on the road, and how Oliver had brought him to stay with them till he was well enough to go.

"How extraordinary," Harriet said, "taking a stranger into your home like that. My goodness."

"Cornelius wasn't a stranger, really," Polly said. "Though he's become one now. He hasn't come into town for months and months. It's become a kind of dare among the boys in town, to go hunting for a glimpse of the last man left in Dogtown.

"I've always felt sorry for him," said Polly. "I'm not sure I ever met anyone so lonesome." She peeked at Judy's face as she bit off a thread. "Don't you feel sorry for him?"

"Well, of course I do," said Judy, and she got up to see that the table was laid out properly for dinner.

❖❖❖

August ended, the guests departed, and the house itself seemed to sigh with relief. The evening before the Judge left, he called Judy to the study and handed her an envelope. "A token of my appreciation for a wonderful summer." He rose and took her hand. "I hope that you will stay with us for years to come. For now, however, I want you to take your ease. We quite wore you out these past months. I order you to have a good rest, Mistress Rhines. It's well deserved."

Harriet Plant departed in a shower of tearful kisses, having exacted a promise of regular correspondence from Judy. On the way to the coach, she pouted, "I don't see why you won't spend Christmas with me in Cambridge."

"Perhaps I will," said Judy.

When Judy returned to the empty house, she clapped her hands at the pleasure of having it all to herself again. She moved her clothes back upstairs to the high ceilings and windows she'd missed all summer, and then strolled through the quiet rooms, stopping in the library, where she emptied the dregs of the Judge's sherry into a crystal glass, put up her feet, and watched the sunset turn the harbor into a pink punch bowl. The great clock ticked while the gulls became black apostrophes against the line of one endless lavender cloud that stretched to the horizon.

After a few more busy weeks—washing and mending, airing and folding—Judy paid off the maids and became a lady of leisure, just as the Judge had suggested. She lounged in bed until nine in the morning, drinking tea and reading novels. After lunch, she set to work, draping the furniture and closing up the drawing room, the dining room, and all the bedrooms save hers. As September ended, she had the gardener shutter the windows for winter. The darkened house saddened her a little, but it would save on dusting and preserve the carpets, she told herself. And as the days grew shorter and cooler, every week provided extra hours to read and rest and to imagine that this was the life she was meant for. As she drew a satin coverlet over her shoulders at night, her years in the rustic Dogtown cottage seemed like a detour or a bad dream.

⟡

That same house had become Cornelius's paramount blessing. His sorrowful mood had lifted with the lengthening days, and he spent the summer cleaning and mending until the place was back in good order. He lived more quietly than ever, eating the small game he caught and harvesting the volunteer beans and squash that grew in the abandoned kitchen gardens of Dogtown.

Oliver had brought him a good price for the pile of wooden blocks that had kept him from cutting his own wrists. Cornelius had welcomed him back that day with a cup of rose hip tea, and he agreed to Oliver's suggestion that he try carving whales on the next ones.

When his visitor made to leave, Cornelius offered his hand, looked him in the eye, and said, "You're a good man."

Oliver was flustered by the unexpected praise, shook his hand, and promised, "I'll be back."

When he told Polly what Cornelius had said to him, she smiled and said, "He's right."

Oliver tried to get back to Dogtown every fortnight if he could, trading oil, tea, and meal for pelts or mallows or whatever Cornelius had on hand. After they did their business, the two men said little, but Cornelius would not let Oliver leave without taking a cup of the broth or stew he seemed always to have on the fire. The concoction warmed Oliver like nothing he'd ever tasted, and he looked forward to it as he walked up the Dogtown road, especially as the days grew colder again.

That December, an early snow fell steadily for three solid days and three nights. In Gloucester, wagons could not pass and almost no one ventured outdoors. The scene outside of Judy's windows was peaceful and beautiful, but by the end of the third day, she was starting to feel trapped and lonely in a way she never had in Dogtown. The knock on the kitchen door felt like a gift and she threw it wide, hoping for Oliver, who sometimes dropped by at that hour on his way home.

But the expression that greeted her was so pinched and grim, Judy cried, "Has something happened to one of the boys?"

"No, no," Oliver hurried to reassure her. "They are well. Polly is fine, too."

"Come in," Judy said. Before he could take a step, Tan darted into the room, startling them both.

"That's his dog," Oliver said. "She followed us all the way down. It's Cornelius. I found him outside in the snow, wandering without a coat. He didn't know me at first. But then he started weeping and I couldn't leave him there."

"Of course not," said Judy. "It's good of you to take him in again."

"No," Oliver interrupted. "I couldn't take him home. There's barely room for all of us anymore, and he's in a real bad way. He would have scared the boys and so, well, I'm sorry to tell you, but I took him to the workhouse."

Judy understood. Cornelius was dying.

"The reason I came here," said Oliver, "is that by the time we got to town, he was raving. First he called for his mother, and then he started calling for you. He was wailing, and, well, he was saying other things, too." Oliver lowered his voice. "Of a personal nature. I figured you ought to know right away."

She touched his arm. "I'll get my cloak."

⊰⊱

In the year since Judy had visited Ruth in the workhouse, it had grown even more desolate. The floor was slack and no one had bothered to sweep it for some time. As her eyes adjusted to the chilly dimness, a loud voice announced, "This must be Judy come for her nigger." A large, blowsy woman smirked from a bed in the center of the room.

Cornelius was huddled on a cot in the back corner, farthest from the scant warmth thrown off by the stove. She threw off the dirty blanket covering him, laid her wool cloak over him, and folded her scarf for a pillow.

"Is there no water?" Judy asked.

The woman tried to hide the jug beside her bed. "We got nothing here till morning. And they don't want us moving nothing," she warned as Judy picked up a stool and placed it beside Cornelius, sitting with her back to the room.

His eyes glittered in the dark. She took his hand and whispered,

"Sleep now, my dear. I'll be here when you wake up. Take your rest. Judy's here."

In the morning, the matron gasped at the sight of them lying in each other's arms and rushed out to find Easter, whom she knew to be Judy Rhines's friend. Judy and Cornelius were still asleep when they returned, her pale hand resting upon his dark cheek. Easter sighed and shook her head. She'd been right then, all those years ago.

"Let's get him out of here," Easter said, tapping Judy's shoulder.

"He's coming home with me," she said, instantly awake.

"You sure that's wise?" Easter whispered, as though they could keep anything secret in that place.

"I don't care. He's coming with me."

Oliver arrived soon after, and the three of them got Cornelius on his feet and out into the blinding sunlight and melting snow. Passersby stared as the haggard African staggered down the street, with Oliver supporting him on one side and Judy on the other. Easter brought up the rear and watched as heads turned and the whispering began: she knew the story would be all over town before noon.

Judy threw an extravagant number of logs on the fire and sent Oliver to find her a fresh-killed chicken. After she got Cornelius out of his filthy clothes and settled in bed, Easter took her aside and asked, "What's the Judge going to say when he finds out about all this?"

"I don't care," Judy announced, in a voice that was new for her. "I do not give a tinker's damn what he says, or anyone else."

"You may yet," Easter said. "I've got to get back to the tavern." She would have a lot of explaining to do if she was going to save anything of her friend's reputation. "I'll be back quick as I can. Tomorrow morning at the latest."

Judy placed a cool cloth on Cornelius's brow, which was nearly as hot as the kettle. The stubble on his chin was white. He had grown so old, and yet she thought she'd never seen a more noble face.

Oliver brought back a piece of ham wrapped in paper, and he stood over the sleeping man.

"He looks better," Judy said.

Oliver had been thinking how much worse he appeared. "I'll stop back later. I may even have a chicken by then."

That evening, Easter sent over a boy carrying a pail of beer, a slice of pie, and a scrawled slip of paper that read, *"Keep up yr own strenth."*

Judy was grateful for her friends' attentions, but the truth was that she wished only to be left alone with Cornelius so that she could care for him without having to feign distance or disinterest. She wondered how she could feel so much happiness at such a terrible time. Cornelius had not opened his eyes all day. Her good name was lost, and with it her sinecure from Judge Cook. She would be destitute. And yet, as she climbed into the bed beside him and inhaled his still-familiar musk, she felt like singing.

He woke up near midnight, still feverish but clearheaded, and returned the pressure of her fingers. They stared at each other by the candle's light. The whites of his eyes were a frightening shade of orange, but Judy smiled into them with such tenderness, the stabbing pains in Cornelius's back eased a little. Perhaps there was a God, he thought, returning Judy's steady gaze. How else could he explain the miracle of her presence beside him?

"I must tell you," he began, but a coughing fit seized him, wreaking new agonies.

"Hush, dear," Judy urged him. "Don't tire yourself. There is no need to say anything now."

"I have something I have to say to you before I can die. . . ."

She shuddered, but met his eyes and nodded.

Cornelius took a shallow sip of air and began. "Abraham Wharf was mostly dead when I first saw him. But the old man still had some life in him. I came upon him in the evening, and he was still warm. When I tapped him on the back, he didn't wake up. And I left him there."

"I don't care," she said. "Save your strength."

"I could have shaken him," Cornelius continued, taking breaths between every few words. "I could have carried him inside somewhere. I could have saved him. But I walked away, and I let him lie there, under those stones. Next morning, he was stiff."

"Oh, Cornelius," Judy said, stroking his cheek. "It was so long ago."

"I went back to make sure he was dead. And then I cut his throat. I did it to keep him quiet in death." Cornelius spoke this part with his eyes closed, so that he would not have to see Judy's reaction. "It was a kind of magic I heard from my mother. Wharf was a devil. Blackhearted. Mean. He knew about you and me. He said he'd turn me over to a bounty hunter. Tell Stanwood. Paint them a picture, he said. Like a bear covering a doe, he said. And worse."

He groaned. "But that's not the worst I did, Judy. I am a sorry man. I am a coward," he said, ignoring her attempts at hushing him. "I used to tell myself I stayed away from you to protect you from the gossip. If Wharf knew about us, I figured it was only a matter of time before others knew. And you would be ruined.

"But that wasn't the half of it," he said. "The truth is, I was afraid on my own account. They kill us like dogs, like nothing. They need no excuse. And you were a fine excuse."

Tears leaked through his lashes. "But worst is how I treated you. How I never said your name. I knew what you wanted of me, to tell you things. To say your name. I did not even give you that. You were so fine to me, and I was too afraid to tell you. To love you."

Breathless and worn out by his confession, Cornelius fell into a deep and peaceful sleep that gave Judy a few hours of hope. But the fever returned in the morning, worse than before. With it came waves of pain that he could not beat back without screaming. Easter stopped in but did not stay long.

By the time the afternoon light started to fade, Cornelius was at his weakest. Judy sat beside him, her head in her hands, until she felt his touch on her knee.

"Talk to me," he whispered.

She wiped her eyes and rallied. "I was glad to see that you took in the dog, the tan. Oliver says she's been with you for some time now. She's still here, you know. Over there by the fire, watching. She's a nice one, I can tell. Reminds me of my Grey, a little. Did you think of that?"

Cornelius smiled behind his closed eyes.

Judy took his hand and told him about her friendship with Martha Cook, the secret of her illness, and of the Judge's decency. She recounted Easter's camel story and described Harriet's cooking in detail. All through that short winter sunset and deep into the night, she talked. She confessed, to herself as well as to Cornelius, that last summer's work had been too much for her. Her neck and legs still ached from the long days. She was too old for it.

Judy paused for a moment and stared into the candle. The silence in the room startled her and she cried, "Cornelius?"

His eyes fluttered open and met hers.

"Should I go on?"

He nodded.

"I don't know what else I can tell you," Judy said. But then she began, "When I was a little girl, I used to think that my sister, Priscilla, could do anything." She was surprised at what her memory washed up, especially since she had never spoken about her childhood. "Priscilla was ten years older than me. She was the pretty one, and the only mother I knew since ours died giving birth to me.

"I don't remember much from those days," Judy said. "I had a doll with a red dress. Priss taught me how to read. She hogged the blankets at night. And then she left.

"I think she ran off with a man and I can't imagine that it ended well or she would have come for me. Or that's what I told myself. Pa never spoke of her again.

"He broke his leg when I was eight, which is when he bound me out to service, so I'd learn housekeeping. I went to Mrs. Clarkson first. She was a widow with twin sons, thick-waisted boys, walleyed and shy as a couple of rabbits.

"She wasn't a bad sort," Judy remembered. "She was, well, disappointed, I suppose is what you'd call her. She took to her bed every evening right after dinner, and stayed there till I made the breakfast. She was a watery sort of person. She made tea so weak, and soupy stew, and sometimes her biscuits came to the table as gruel.

"After she passed away, I stayed on and cared for the boys till I was eighteen and I got a place with a family in Gloucester, where I met a boy named Arthur. We used to go walking on Sundays when we should have been in church. I thought we'd get married, but he got into some kind of trouble and shipped out without a good-bye. That decided me against marriage.

"Not that he ever asked," she said.

Cornelius raised a finger to signal that he was still listening. "I worked for some other families after that. None of them were cruel to me. None were all that kind, either. But wherever I lived, I never felt at home. I never had a sound sleep. Even my dreams were full of being told to clean a mess, or haul some more water, or stir a pot.

"But that seems like a hundred years ago," she said. "Like I'm talking about a girl in a book someone else wrote.

"Then the day I wandered into Dogtown and stopped at Easter Carter's house, it was, well, like some revelation. There she was, living on her own—that was long before Ruth moved in. Tiny Easter Carter in that big house, all by herself. Bold as brass, and didn't care

who said what about her. I asked her wasn't she afraid to sleep up there all alone. She said she liked being where no one else was breathing up the fresh air.

"That planted the seed," Judy said. "Knowing that Easter would be near helped me get up the gumption. So even if I never stopped being a scullery girl, and even if I was poor, I could be my own mistress in Dogtown. I suppose it was the same for you, too, wasn't it, Cornelius, dear? You could be your own master there. As much as anywhere." Judy put his hand to her lips. He squeezed her fingers.

"You changed that, Cornelius. When you came to my house, to my bed, I was not the mistress of my own heart any longer. And when you did not return to me, I was more alone than ever, even more than when my sister left. I used to think about going to sleep out in the cold like Abraham Wharf.

"I suppose Easter kept me from it. And Greyling. Isn't it odd how much comfort a dog can be." Judy stopped, hoarse and exhausted from three days of weeping and whispering. She watched Cornelius's chest rise and sink, the breaths shallow and more uneven than before. His skin was clammy, and he was quiet for so long, she wondered if he was past hearing her.

His eyes flew open. "No coffin," he rasped.

"Oh, my dear," she said. "I know. I won't let them put you in a box. Is there something else I can do, anything else?"

"Shepherd," he croaked.

"Shepherd?"

"Lord. Shepherd."

Judy ran to the library and took the large Bible from its stand, riffling through its gilt-edged pages until she found it.

"'The Lord is my shepherd,'" she read, slowly. "'I shall not want.'" "By 'forever,'" he was sleeping soundly.

"Shall I read another?" she asked, not expecting an answer. Judy read the Twenty-fourth Psalm, the Twenty-fifth, and the

rest of them, to the last "Praise ye the Lord." Only then did she set
the book on the floor and lie down beside him.

When she woke up, he was gone.

✧

There was no funeral gathering for Cornelius, no spirits or biscuits
after his cold burial. Even so, Judy was not alone at the cemetery.
Oliver and Polly brought their boys, and Natty and David carried
giant pinecones to place on the grave. Easter was there with Louisa
Tuttle from the tavern. Four well-dressed Gloucester ladies arrived
in a group, old acquaintances of Martha Cook's, curious to discover
if Judy Rhines was really as brazen as the gossip painted her. Reverend Hildreth's appearance caused a ripple of surprise among their
ranks.

Judy Rhines had called upon the clergyman to ask for his service
at the burial, and discovered that despite his Universalist leanings
and abolitionist sermons, he had no desire to be seen anywhere near
a real African, not even a dead one. There were certain members of
his flock who barely tolerated his politics, and given the strong smell
of scandal that now clung to Mistress Rhines, the minister had been
less than gentle in declining her request.

"It is not my practice to provide the sacraments to those who are
not of my congregation," he had said, expecting her to wilt and
scurry away. But she had done no such thing.

"Sir, if you do not bring your Bible and lay Cornelius to rest
properly," she said, "I stand ready to call upon your wife and ask if
she is aware of your visits to a particular mansion on High Street and
of your ministry to the lady of that house. Or perhaps it would be
easier if I simply tell certain people that they need not keep this secret
close anymore."

As he began the service, the pastor raised his chin and put his

famously resonant voice to good use, so that even the deafest of the ladies heard every word. "'As for man, his days are as grass; as a flower of the field so he flourisheth. For the wind passeth over it, and it is gone; and the place thereof shall know it no more.'"

He paused, turned the page, and began, "'The Lord is my shepherd, I shall not want.'"

At that, Judy Rhines doubled over and sobbed with such inconsolable sorrow, Natty and David burst into tears as well. Oliver reached out to comfort his friend and found he had to hold fast to keep her from flinging herself into the grave.

"'Forever and ever. Amen,'" said Reverend Hildreth crisply, snapped his Bible shut, and began shaking hands with everyone in the little circle. Judy turned away from his outstretched hand and walked off, by herself. When she returned to the house, the tan was gone.

As the winter deepened, Judy found it harder and harder to fall asleep. She'd lie in bed at night, listening to the wind at the windows. Easter was alarmed by her friend's lethargy and pallor, and visited every morning with a pail of beer and funny stories from the tavern.

"And what are they saying about randy Judy Rhines?" she asked.

"They'll stop talking about it," said Easter. "You'll see. Soon enough, they won't give it a second thought."

But Judy knew better. She would always be a lighthouse of gossip, a beacon signal reminding people of the shocking tale of Black Neal and his Dogtown mistress. They might stop snickering into her face. They might forget to curl their lips when they told her they had no green thread in stock when the spool was in clear view. But as soon as she turned the corner or left the shop, an eyebrow would arch and someone would recount the particulars of their shocking liaison, with all kinds of indecent details invented out of whole cloth.

Judy considered moving back to the quiet of Dogtown, fixing up her old house, and living far from the wagging tongues. But that

idea made her feel even more like walking off a long pier in the cold of the night.

Six weeks after Cornelius died, Judy went to the study, lit a fire, lifted the covers from the desk, and wrote two letters. The first one was addressed to Judge Cook and covered many pages. She explained the reason for her departure from Gloucester and included a long list of instructions about the care of the house. She concluded with heartfelt thanks, an apology for once having misjudged him, and her best wishes.

The second letter took only a few minutes, and was addressed to Mrs. Harriet Plant.

A month later, Judy Rhines vanished.

When Easter Carter learned that her friend had left Cape Ann without so much as a word to her, she was frantic, angry, and bereft. It was the first time that anyone had ever seen her weep. Louisa sent for Oliver and Polly, who visited at her bedside, where she spent a week eating nothing and drinking only a little beer.

Oliver accosted everyone who came to the store for word of Judy Rhines, and he discovered that she'd hired a buggy to take her to the Ipswich coach stop, where she'd boarded the carriage for Boston.

Her letter arrived in May.

Dearest Easter:

Forgive me. It was wrong of me to leave as I did, but I could not face your reproaches or your sadness. I could not bear the weight of my memories or the hatefulness of my neighbors. I am not as strong as you.

I am living in Cambridge, where our friend Harriet gave me refuge and found me a position as housekeeper for another dean at the college. I have a room to myself with a door that leads out to a small cottage garden that is to be mine.

My situation is only a few streets away from Harriet's, which

---

is a great comfort. She has some acquaintances who have welcomed me into their little circle. They are very patient with me. I find it restful to live without a past. Now that the spring has arrived, we spinsters stroll along the river, where there is rowing. It makes a pretty sight.

The Harvard boys are merry and gallant for the most part. One of the lads is to give me his dog when he leaves at the end of term. It is a tiny little creature named Pip, and as different from our Dogtown crew as a berry from a pumpkin. Already I am quite the fool for him.

Please do not worry about me. Except for missing you, Oliver, Polly, and their precious boys, I am rarely unhappy. There is one thing that remains heavy on my heart and makes me dare to ask a great favor of you. By now, you have discovered the banknote. If you can forgive my leaving without a farewell, you will use this money to place a headstone upon his grave. Have them carve his name so there is at least that much of a token that he lived. Knowing your goodness as I do, I don't doubt that you will do this thing for me. Just writing these words gives me a little peace.

I do miss you, my dear Easter. I think of your smile every day. Please show this letter to Oliver and Polly. I promise to write to them soon. Deliver kisses to Nathaniel, David, and little Isaac. (Is his hair still carrot-colored?) Tell them not to forget their

Aunt Judy.
I will never forget any of you.

ACKNOWLEDGMENTS

Amy Hoffman and Steve McCauley are my writing-group partners, and this book would not have happened without their insight, patience, and support. The same goes for Jim Ball, my sweet, indispensable husband.

For expert advice, reading drafts, and loving encouragement, I am indebted to Wayne Baker, D.M.D.; Ellen Grabiner; Valerie Monroe; Judith Paley, M.D.; Barbara Penzner; Sondra Stein; Liza Stern; Joan Thompson; Tom Wolfe; Bob Wyatt; and Andé Zellman. Thanks to Ben Loeterman for the old books, to Lesly Hershman and Maria Campo for their research assistance, to Scott Elledge and Jonathan Strong for many wonderful tramps through the woods of Cape Ann. The librarians at the Cape Ann Historical Society and the Newton Free Library were gracious and helpful. The Diamant family cheerleading squad—daughter Emilia, brother Harry, and mother Hélène—was as terrific as ever. Thanks again to Amanda Urban of ICM and to the Scribner team: Nan Graham, Sarah McGrath, and Susan Moldow.